A Patriot's Price

BARB BALTRINIC

Dedicated with great love to
Michael Baltrinic

Table of Contents

Part One
Innocence to Tortured Soul

Chapter 1
Andrew Clark Comes of Age

Now
April, 1780

Andrew tried to recall his mother's face. A faint image came to mind and he struggled to hold onto it. His mother, Sarah Clark, was standing near the fireplace, stoking the fire. Andrew watched her as she held back her skirting to avoid the sparks which flew into the room. The soft glow of the fire illuminated her face, outlining her strong features against the darkening room. Andrew had only known his mother's face to move between one of concern in her day to day activities, and one of undivided attention when talking with her children or grandson. Sarah Clark, mother of ten, had already buried two of her children, yet remained strong and resilient to the ever changing life she faced during these turbulent years. Andrew could not remember the last time his mother allowed her hair to flow freely, or the last time he truly heard her laugh. The silvery, honeyed voice Andrew remembered from childhood was replaced by a voice filled with uncertainty when she spoke of her husband or her two sons who were training to be officers. Andrew strained to listen to what she was saying. He concentrated and watched her face as she talked. She was telling him the barn needed a new stall for the new calf. Andrew laughed to himself, thinking the calf would be sold soon so building a new stall was rather unnecessary. Resources were scarce on the Clark farm with his father being away in Congress and his mother trying to keep the farm going while taking care of the younger children, her daughter-in-law, and grandson. She never complained about the work. She always found ways to surprise her brood with fresh berries which were mixed into their morning cornmeal mush. Occasionally fresh shellfish served as a pleasant change to their ordinary diet. His mother never let her children see her fears for their safety; although Andrew was old enough now to realize that fear had replaced his father as his mother's constant companion.

Andrew and his siblings grew up knowing his father's occupation of land surveyor often took him away from the Clark farm. It was not a huge adjustment for them when Abraham Clark was called to serve in the Continental Congress. The Clark children were sworn to secrecy as to their father's new occupation. To talk openly about Abraham having willfully performed the ultimate treasonous act against King George would put the entire family in jeopardy. Neighbors knew Abraham Clark was a land surveyor and often represented the poor in land suits. They were accustomed to his being away dealing with his work, and those who suspected his new allegiance never said anything aloud to disturb the safety of the Clark family.

Andrew tried to listen again to his mother's conversation. It wasn't anything of huge importance, just the normal small talk they shared every day. It was such an ordinary conversation. It was one like thousands of others he had with his mother. He concentrated again on her voice. He could see her lips moving, but he could not understand what she was saying. Suddenly the sound of her soft voice slowly morphed into a retching sound. The violent rocking of the ship pulled Andrew into an alert state again and his mother's face immediately disappeared from his grasp. The retching sound was coming from the man next to him heaving bile from his empty belly. The sound filled Andrew's ears and he fought to drown it out. The momentary lapse into memory was broken and this retching sound became exaggerated in Andrew's head. He fought to keep from imitation. Andrew once again became painfully aware of his own empty stomach and the pounding in his head. The darkness in the belly of this ship, and the stifling and putrid air around him further pushed Andrew into a fit of despair. Uncontrollably the gnawing feeling in his stomach overcame him and he realized a low bellowing wail was escaping his lips. He clutched tightly to his coat and blanket, his only comfort, praying it would not be pulled from him by the invisible companions also interred in this hell ship.

Then
June, 1775

For several years now there was heated talk of the various taxes placed on the colonists. Men would meet at the Clark farm, or at the local tavern, and discuss the changes and the effect these changes had on the inhabitants of Elizabethtown. At first, many of the new taxes did not directly affect them, but it appeared that with each new tax, another was soon to follow. When asked if the colonists could send representatives to discuss the impact of these taxes on the colonies, they were refused. Already there were skirmishes in protest to the British demands on the colonists. Most recently the British soldiers began setting up camp on Staten Island, which was about six miles from the New Jersey shore. Armed soldiers frequented the streets, and the colonists were treated less like fellow British citizens than underlings who were to remain subservient to those in Great Britain. While some of the colonists quickly set up positive relations with the British, guaranteeing that they were completely in support of all the changes which were being inflicted on the Americans, others began grave talk of revolution. Such talk was treason, so meetings were secretive. The seriousness of this greatly impacted Andrew who had been an outgoing boy, but was now a cautious and quiet young man who continually scanned a suspicious eye on everyone he met.

A Patriot's Price

Abraham Clark, or Abra as he was called by family and friends, was quick to embrace the politics of change. Abra was drawn into meetings at the Terrill Tavern on King's Highway, which was near the Clark farm. These meetings provided Abra and the other local men an opportunity to talk about the political changes in New Jersey and identification of who could be trusted in the area and who could not. Such information was vital in these changing times as conversations and off-hand comments could easily be the fodder for repercussions from the British soldiers stationed throughout the area. There certainly were many Loyalists in the area. Other local taverns also became meeting places for the newly formed Patriots.

Abra had often held informal, yet secretive meetings at the Clark farm, or met with men at the local taverns, always careful as to who was in attendance, and careful to meet at various locations as to not draw the suspicions of Loyalist neighbors. Andrew sometimes attended the meetings, but he would be stationed at the door to watch for specifically named neighbors or townspeople who were anxious to maintain the status quo, keeping the colonists and the British forever connected. Many of these townsmen would meet with the British soldiers and pledge their allegiance; often times giving the names of those they suspected were seeking separation from Britain. To vocalize treasonous opinions which could be overheard by the British soldiers, or even those who declared themselves to be loyal to Britain, meant you were filled with fear of retaliation and arrest. Thus the meetings remained quiet and secretive. Only recently Andrew was allowed to sit with the men to discuss the politics of change happening in their once quiet Elizabethtown.

Sarah was not initially pleased that a third son was already being drawn into the conflict, but she respected her husband's belief that British control needed to end. Sarah's pride in her husband and her two oldest sons, Aaron and Thomas, was always evident, although when alone her prayer was to find a peaceful settlement between Brittan and the colonies. She prayed daily for the safety of Aaron and Thomas who had trained as officers and were already out with the troops. War was never a part of her life, but times were changing, and Sarah, like many other women could only support the changes which would eventually provide a better life for her children. The Clarks and the Hetfields, Sarah's family, had immigrated to the colonies many generations ago. Stories had been passed down through both families emphasizing the need for the freedoms promised to those who immigrated to the colonies. It saddened Sarah that these freedoms were gradually disappearing.

The meetings among the Patriots focused upon how Elizabethtown would protect itself from the British invasion which was already occurring. New Jersey had about 175,000 citizens, and of those only 50,000 were men between the ages 16-50. A large percentage of the residents were Quakers who would not fight. When the men talked about a militia, it became obvious that many New Jersey men had already signed on as privateers who were privately attacking British boats and stealing the stolen supplies. This left New Jersey with a very small population able to fight the British should they be pushed into such violent action.

Andrew recalled how his brothers decided to join the militia and train as officers when the New Jersey Provincial Congress passed the militia act in June, 1775. Aaron had read a copy of the act to Thomas and Andrew.

The Congress taking Into consideration the cruel and arbitrary measures adopted and pursued by the British Parliament and present Ministry for the purpose of subjugating the American Colonies to the most abject servitude, and being apprehensive that all pacific measures for the redress of our grievances will prove Ineffectual, do think it highly necessary that the inhabitants of this Province be forthwith properly armed and disciplined for defense of the cause of American freedom. And further considering that, to answer this desirable end, it is requisite that such persons be entrusted with the command of the Militia as can be confided in by the people, and are truly zealous in support of our just rights and privileges, do recommend and advise that the good people of this Province hence forward strictly observe the following rules and regulations, until this Congress shall make further order therein:

1st. That one or more companies, as the case may require, be Immediately formed in each Township or Corporation, and, to this end, that the several Committees in this Province do, as soon as may be, acquaint themselves with the number of male inhabitants in their respective districts, from the age of sixteen to fifty, who are capable of bearing arms; and thereupon form them into companies, consisting as near as may be of eighty men each; which companies so formed shall, each by itself, assemble and choose, by plurality of voices, four persons among themselves, of sufficient substance and capacity for its officers, namely, one captain, two lieutenants, and an ensign.

Thomas looked at Aaron. "This act does not require militia service."

Aaron responded, "It appears it is not required, however it is recommended. The age spread is 16-50. If both you and I muster up, we would need to guarantee that someone remain behind to watch over the farm. Father is just old enough to fall into the end of the age requirement."

"What about me," asked Andrew? "The act says sixteen years."

Aaron paused for a moment. "Andrew, we would need someone to keep watch over our mother and the farm. Father is always away on business either surveying or representing someone in the courts. If the stories are true, the British will be in the harbor area which means our farms here in Elizabethtown stand to be raided."

A Patriot's Price

Andrew was at first put out by being excluded, but he knew that there was no one to keep watch over the Clark women and children. Aaron and Thomas went on to talk about training for officer roles. Andrew listened and felt pride that his two older brothers were actively taking leadership. Thomas was already married, so he knew Thomas would need to make arrangements for his wife and child before he would be able to leave for training. With both Aaron and Thomas mustering, Andrew would be left in charge. Being the head of the household in his father's absence was a huge responsibility, but Andrew was certain he could do the job.

Two months passed and it did not take long for New Jersey men to answer the requirements of the act. They had formed twenty six regiments from the various counties: Bergen 1 regiment, Essex 2 regiments or four battalions, Middlesex 2 regiments, Monmouth 3 regiments, Morris 2 regiments and one battalion, Sussex 2 regiments and one battalion, Burlington 2 regiments and one company of rangers, Gloucester 3 battalions, Salem 1 regiment, Cumberland 2 battalions, Cape May one battalion, Somerset 2 regiments, and Hunterdon 4 regiments. Each regiment had ten companies of 60-80 men. Additionally, the Continental Congress appointed four thousand men to be Minutemen. Andrew listened to the many reports that came in about the forming of a militia in New Jersey. He had enough book learning to be able to read reports and to write down the information so he could share it with his father and brothers when they were not able to attend the local meetings. Andrew felt a sense of importance in his role of protector of the house, yet he also longed for the days where potential war was not a constant topic of discussion.

For as long as he could remember his father was frequently away from home surveying properties or surveying highways. He was also called to represent the small landowners who felt they were being cheated out of property when the larger landowners claimed streams or pieces of their land actually belonged to them. Abraham stressed to his sons about how unfair the legal system was for the poor. "All too often the small property owner cannot fight on equal footing with those who can afford fancy lawyers who will tie up the cases in court to a point where the poor cannot gain equal footing."

"But, Father, you wanted to be a lawyer. You told us this was your dream when you were young," said Andrew.

"It continues to be my dream," replied Abraham, "but my dreams are now to protect those who have the least chance to protect themselves. Our ancestors came to the colonies to be rid of the aristocracy and bureaucracy of Great Britain. What we have here is the same thing happening among the colonies. There are those who have secured large tracts of land and have made a favorable income. In turn, too often, their avarice has made them forget that others are struggling to just get by. We built this land on the backs of the savages. We are now extending that to those less favored by those of wealth and power. My working as legal counsel to those who can ill afford the more traditional routes is a way to even the playing field. I say we need to beware of those who put their greed before the needs of their fellow man. 'Behold the man that made not God his strength, but put confidence in the abundance of his riches, and strengthened himself in his avarice.'"

Andrew always marveled at his father's ability to support his rationale with Bible passages. He admired his father for his principles and determination to do what was right, although he felt he did not have the advantage his older brothers had in having him at home with them more of the time. Andrew shook off the memory as he dealt with the current problem of his brothers leaving the farm to train for war. There would be much to do in preparation for Andrew to take over running the household and farm.

Once Aaron had left for training, Thomas moved his wife, Elizabeth, to his parents' home knowing he, too, would soon leave. Before he left he wanted to be certain the farm was in good repair. He and Andrew were building a shelter for the animals beyond the woods surrounding the house in order to protect the livestock from anyone coming onto the Clark farm looking for food. The farm was too close to the British headquarters, so such provisions would be sought. The Clarks feared not only the British soldiers, but also fellow New Jersey men who were hungry and would not wince at invading a fellow countryman's farm for food. The reality of war was something Andrew was not prepared to understand. His thinking was permanently changed to that of someone needing skills to survive.

While the brothers worked side by side, Andrew took the opportunity to talk with his brother about the formation of a militia as he didn't completely understand the protocols being designed for their state. "What's the difference between the militia men and the minute men?" asked Andrew as he and Thomas worked to build stalls within the barn.

Thomas stopped and leaned on the side of the stall. "The Continental Congress wants to appoint 4,000 men in New Jersey for the Committee of Safety. They are to be ready at a moment's notice, ready to march where they would be needed in this or any neighboring colony. They would have sixty four privates in each company, and there is to be ten battalions for the entire Province. They would serve four months then go on inactive duty unless they would be needed for a longer period of time."

Andrew asked, "How are they to be paid?"

"The act which passed requires taxes which will provide the funds for equipping and supplying the Militia," answered Thomas. "Father has signed on to work on the Committee of Safety."

"What? Father is too old to be marching off with the minute men," exclaimed Andrew.

"No, he is to serve as secretary of the Safety Committee for New Jersey's militia. He figures this would be good use of

his networks. He knows so many people through his surveying work and his representing men in their land disputes. He
figures this will help get people to muster and protect New
Jersey's shore and farmlands," said Thomas as he picked up a
nail to reinforce the railing. Andrew became lost in thought as
he considered how their peaceful Elizabethtown was already
changing in appearance. Men now carried their muskets
and flintlocks wherever they went, including church. Their
eyes constantly searched for the hateful red of the British
uniforms. The men carried tension in their faces and their
stature. Friendly greetings were often met with suspicion as
the men of Elizabethtown studied each person to determine if
they were for or against the Crown.

By October, 1775, Thomas had left for training. On the
rare occasions when Abra was home, he was often pulled
away for his work on the New Jersey Committee of Safety.
When he was home the local men would come to the Clark
farm and they would talk about the impending war. It was
not unusual for the Clark farm to host informal gatherings
of men who called themselves "Patriots." Abra was quick to
admonish them. "Be fairly confident as to whom you vocalize that title. You might find your prideful designation to be
a designation for your own death sentence. There are many
among our neighbors who do not find this current political
trend to be favored." The men nodded in agreement, and
quietly named off neighbors who were for the cause, and

those against. It became clear to Andrew that this was serious business and he must never identify his father or his brothers as Patriots. If asked he would just say his father was off doing surveying work, and his brothers were older and living away from Elizabethtown. The risk was far too high a price for casually sharing the truth of their loyalties, or disloyalties.

One evening Andrew returned home to find several neighborhood men and his father huddled over a copy of "An Ordinance for Regulating the Militia of New Jersey." "What does it say, Father," asked Andrew.

Abra read,

Whereas, The ordinances of the late Provincial Congress for regulating the Militia of this Colony have been found insufficient to answer the good purposes intended, and it appearing to be essentially necessary that some further regulations be adopted at this time of imminent danger.

Abner Collins said, "Insufficient? What new regulations are they proposing?"

Abra said, "They are proposing that men from 16-50 enroll in the militia unless their religion forbids them to do so. If men do not enroll they will be penalized. The militia will be on duty for a month at a time and fines will be given if he does not turn out."

Collins responded, "It sounds like the act they originally passed; only now they are adding penalties for non-compliance.

If we didn't think this was getting serious, this latest regulation certainly shows Congress has grave concerns."

"There is also an outline of equipment needed by the militia," continued Abra. "Each man should have a musket or firelock and bayonet, sword or tomahawk, a steel ramrod, priming wire and brush fitted to his equipment, a cartridge box with twenty-three rounds of cartridges, twelve flints, and a knapsack. He would also need one pound of powder and three pounds of bullets of size agreeable to his equipment. Those without can pay two shillings for a musket or firelock and one shilling for other equipment."

"That is certainly a thorough listing of supplies needed," said Andrew.

"Equipment is only part of what they outline. They are also to choose officers for their companies. Officers are to be certain their men are exercised twice a week and be prepared for active duty. The militia will then be paid one shilling and sixpence for every part of a day they are employed in the militia. Officers will be paid in proportion to the number of men they command."

"Father, aren't those good wages?" asked Andrew. The other men also nodded in agreement.

"It is comparable to a skilled tradesman's wage. I just hope that New Jersey can afford these wages, said Abra. "The act states that the money is to be raised by tax on inhabitants of the townships and collected in the same manner as Provincial taxes are paid."

Robert Ross scratched his head and said, "Well, if men and their grown sons of sixteen and older are called to duty, who will work the farms to raise the taxes?"

"That's right," said Elnathan Cory. "Who will be left on the farm to earn the tax money? Our women folk and the children?" Abner Cory, who had been quiet throughout this discussion, turned his head to see how Abra would respond.

Abra sighed. "There are certainly a lot of questions to be answered. I think we realize that this is brewing up for a full forced retaliation by the British and New Jersey is just trying to prepare ourselves for protecting what is ours."

Andrew thought about what he heard that night. Already two brothers were out for officer training, his father was out working on the Committee of Safety, and he was fast approaching age sixteen. It was not hard to see that life was no longer going to be the same on the Clark farm, or in New Jersey, or in the colonies.

Andrew continued to manage the Clark farm; however he was becoming anxious to join up. More and more of his friends were joining the militia or the Continental Army. 1776 was a year of change for the Clarks. Aaron was already a lieutenant in Captain Daniel Neil's Company of Artillery for the New Jersey State Troops. His brother Thomas was commissioned as first Lieutenant on March 1st.

The biggest change for the Clark family was when Abraham Clark was persuaded to serve in the Congress. The delegates in Congress who had been serving were told that a Declaration of Independence was to be drafted which would officially announce a break the colonies from Britain's control. Many left either because of their opposition to the plan, or because they feared retaliation for the traitorous act of supporting it. New Jersey was left scrambling to find replacements. Both John Hart and Dr. Witherspoon suggested Abra's name as a delegate because of his support of the cause, and because of the respect he had with the local citizens of Elizabethtown and beyond. When asked, Abra first sought Sarah's blessing. Once given, he agreed and left immediately for Philadelphia.

This, too, further changed life on the Clark farm. Abra was now a traitor and this knowledge in the hands of British could mean retaliation. His father would be hung if identified and caught, and the Clark farm could be surrendered to the British, leaving the Clark family to flee for their lives and existence. Andrew's new responsibilities in protecting the family and the farm seemed to be overwhelming.

The three youngest Clark children had to play their part. Elizabeth was only ten, Abraham was eight, and Abigail was only four, yet they, too, had to be trained. Andrew practiced with his younger siblings in how to answer if anyone questioned what their father did for a living. They were only to respond that Father was a surveyor and that he represented men in land disputes. There was to be no mention of his being part of the Patriot cause. To do so put all of them in jeopardy.

Andrew felt difficulty in this as he was so proud of his father's conviction to the Patriot cause. His father was not like the other delegates. He did not wear the ruffled shirts or the powdered wigs like the other delegates. He vowed to remain true to who he was: a common man. Perhaps this would in essence save the Clark family from retaliation, thought Andrew. The British would be looking for someone with a larger estate. There were many Clarks in New Jersey. In the meantime, Andrew felt it was best to prepare his younger siblings to camouflage the truth of their identities to better protect them from British retaliation. Andrew also knew the local Loyalists could easily turn against the Clarks by identifying to the British Abra's role in the traitorous act. Many of the Loyalists in Elizabethtown respected Abra Clark, however it was now war and all former alliances were no longer to be trusted. It was best to keep a low profile.

Andrew knew that his father and mother had both prayed over the decision for Abra to leave for Philadelphia. Abra's faith was strong. Andrew hoped that God would have the same faith in Abra and protect his family during his absence. In the evenings Andrew would sit in Abra's chair near the fire missing his father and his brothers. He pulled the family Bible to his lap and opened it, hoping to find something that would give him guidance in these troubled times. The pages opened to Ephesians 6:11-17. Andrew read the words and comfortable warmth crept over his body.

"Put on the full armor of God, that you may be able to stand firm against the schemes of the devil. For our struggle is not against flesh and blood, but against the rulers, against the powers, against the world forces of this darkness, against the spiritual forces of wickedness in the heavenly places. Therefore, take up the full armor of God, that you may be able to resist in the evil day, and having done everything, to stand firm. Stand firm therefore, having girded your loins with truth, and having put on the breastplate of righteousness, and having shod your feet with the preparation of the gospel of peace; in addition to all, taking up the shield of faith with which you will be able to extinguish all the flaming missiles of the evil one. And take the helmet of salvation, and the sword of the Spirit, which is the word of God."

Isn't this what he was looking for? Was God talking to him? Wasn't King George, much like the devil, filling their world with wickedness through taxes and treatment of the colonists, their fellow citizens, in a manner that was both unfair and unjust? Was God showing Andrew that he, too, should be prepared to fight for this cause? Besides, he was now sixteen and would be penalized for not serving.

The weight of a major decision had rested on Andrew's shoulders for months. Andrew had difficulty sleeping and was constantly restless. His farm duties were systematically done as his mind focused on making a plan. Finally, he made peace after having made his decision. That night he fell into a deep sleep. The warmth of the morning sun awakened Andrew. He could hear his mother humming in the kitchen and the sound of the younger children arguing about whose turn it was to gather the eggs from the chicken coop. Andrew slowly rose out of bed and pulled on his britches, ran his fingers through his hair, then sat on the edge of his narrow bed to pull on his boots. He looked around the small bedroom which he had shared with his two older brothers. Andrew now shared the room with Abraham, who was eight years younger than him. Andrew was surprised he had overslept, especially since young Abraham was anything but quiet when he rose. Andrew arose refreshed and determined.

Andrew went into the kitchen area and kissed his mother, picked up the water pail and went outdoors to fill it at the well. He stood looking toward the long path leading to the road. So much had changed on the Clark farm. He knew that both Aaron and Thomas had already seen a lot of action in the war. The few communications they received shared just enough information to let them know that although they had been in harm's way, God had protected them. His father had remained in Philadelphia, unlike many of the other signers. Because so many of the signers were well known and had vast property, they had quickly left Philadelphia after signing the Declaration to make arrangements to protect their families and property. Abra had neither huge amounts of money or property. His dedication to the cause meant he rarely made it home from Philadelphia. That same year his ten year old daughter, Elizabeth, had died of smallpox. His wife was left to quietly mourn her daughter and have her buried without her husband or older sons there to comfort the rest of the family.

Andrew thought about the huge responsibility that was put upon his shoulders. There were only his mother, his brother, Abraham, and his three sisters, Hannah, Sarah, and Abigail left on the farm; as well as Thomas' wife, Elizabeth, and their infant son, Jonathan. Andrew longed to join and join his brothers in battle. He looked back at the clapboard house and he mused about what he would need to do before he left. He made a mental list of the chores he needed to do and provisions to be made so he could ensure his mother, younger siblings and Thomas' wife and child would be safe. The sooner he mustered, the sooner this war would come to an end.

Andrew wanted to make certain he made a choice that would cause the least disruption for his mother and siblings. On March 23, 1776, the Continental Congress had passed an act which outlined the use of commissioned ships as privateers. Owners of ships would post bonds and follow the regulations outlined in the Letters of Marque. When British vessels were captured, the privateers would pull into port and sell the cargo as well as the ship and split the profits between the government and the privateer, crew, and investors of the privateer. For the Americans, it was like having a private navy.

For the colonists it allowed involvement in the cause and a chance to recoup losses incurred from the war.

Stories were heard of many of the militia men using the whaleboats to raid the British shipments in the New York Harbor. Originally the boats were tethered to large ships as a means of transporting cargo or men from the ship to shore, and even to hunt whale in the open waters near the ship. The whaleboats were double-ended boats typically 24-48 feet long. Each had one or two masts and militia men would handle the newly mounted weapons on the boats. Because of the shape the boats could carry many men. The boats were oared in pairs and the militia were able to row the boats quickly which worked to their advantage. While they were not built to be military transportation, they were adopted by the Revolutionaries as a convenient and useful vehicle.

Andrew heard the stories of privateers who looked to profit from the raids on the British ships. They would capture goods from the British ships then sell their war prizes on the open market. Money from these sales was shared with officers and the crews of the whaleboats. At a time when the Continental Army was struggling to get men to muster into the army, a number of men enticed by the promise of profits was quick to serve as privateers.

Andrew had heard stories of Captain William Marriner and Captain John Schenck who were the leaders of the local whaleboat militia. They had lived in the area and knew the area well. It worked to their advantage as their whaleboats would hug the shore line at night and hide within the bay areas during the day in order to escape being spotted by the British. Schenck would hide the whaleboats in the tall grasses along the shore and he and his men would go into town on their raids. Homes of wealthy and prominent Loyalists were the targets of the raids. Confiscating possessions as well as taking the Loyalist leaders prisoners was the ultimate goal of the raids. Each group of men was armed with a large piece of wood to be used as a battering ram and each squad would time their attack at the same time. The raids were swift, well planned, and met little opposition. Because those who were captured were valuable to the British army, the Patriots used this as a great bargaining chip. The prisoners were taken back to Matawan and used for prisoner exchange with the British to free captured patriots or officers of the Continental Army. Both Marriner and Schenck prided themselves in being able to outwit the British navy, which was considered the greatest force in the world.

Marriner became very bold in his raids. On one occasion when the water was treacherous, several British sloops where anchored in a cove seeking protection against the weather. Marriner's whaleboat fleet captured the three sloops and an armed schooner. They forced the sloops ashore and took all the cargo, then set the boats on fire. The schooner was confiscated to be used by the Patriots. It was a profitable night for his men as each man earned hundreds of dollars in one night's work.

The thought of being part of the whaleboat privateers appealed to Andrew. He felt that he could raise extra money to send home to his mother which would help her to finance the needs of the family, or even have bribe money should they be confronted by the British. The additional money could help her in keeping the family safe and secure food should their farm perish. He liked the idea that there was little, if any, gunfire, and the freeing of prisoners through exchange seemed like a step in a good direction for ending the war.

Of course, his other choice could be with the New Jersey militia. Andrew knew that the New Jersey militia had several thousand men who guarded against the British coming from Staten Island. Half of the men could serve for a month, and then the other half would take over. This, too, appealed to Andrew as he would be able to serve yet be home during alternative months to help out on the farm. The militia set terms of service by the month, while those in the Continental Army of 1776 were to serve for three years.

A third choice was with the Continental Army. There were problems in joining the Continental Army. A three year commitment was problematic. Punishment was severe for those in the Continental Army who deserted. Often they were flogged. Andrew knew of a local man who had deserted to return home to check on his family. Guards arrived and hauled him back to camp and he was flogged so severely the skin off his back was left hanging in strips. The guards felt this was a way to keep men from deserting. When Andrew heard of this he determined he could not join the Army.

Perhaps the militia would be a better choice. It seemed many of the local men would show up in great numbers for the militia when British troops were arriving on the New Jersey shore, only to withdraw to their farms once immediate danger passed. Andrew respected his brothers' opinions, but both Aaron and Thomas told Andrew that Washington was not pleased with the militia as he felt they were unreliable and he preferred that men join the Continental Army.

Andrew had to make up his mind where he could best serve and still provide help to his mother and family. Remaining non-committed was not an option.

Chapter 2
Choices

Now
May 1780

The air was thick with sickness and death below decks
on the prison ship, The Jersey. The air never stirred until the
heavy grate which stood between the upper decks and the
prison hold below was removed, and even then there was not
much relief to those held captive. With the dawning light there
was a subtle opaqueness of light which entered through the
heavy grates that separated the hated rebels from the ship's
crew. The ship rocked and Andrew listened to the sounds of the
men around him. Hacking noises were a constant annoyance.
Andrew shivered in the morning cold. Many of the men were
lying nearly naked in the bowels of this hell hole. "Keeping
vermin from crawling in your clothing" was the excuse they
were given for having much of their clothing taken. Andrew
suspected it was more likely to keep some of the rebels from

tearing off strips of clothing to use as weapons against the British and other captors on the ship. Andrew was frightened to think that thoughts of making a noose to use on his captors was something he actually entertained. The nakedness kept the men humbled and fearful to escape. Clothing often indicated when one was incarcerated. Some men were pushed below decks with clothing and carry items intact, while others were subjected to inspections by the hated Lobsterbacks who took great joy in demeaning the Americans and submitting them the both physical and mental anguish. Andrew tried to see around him in the faint light. All around him lay the filth covered bodies of fellow prisoners. The man beside him had not made a sound for hours. For this, Andrew was relieved. He hated this ship, and he hated even more the British who held them captive in conditions that were not fit for humans.

The Jersey was not the first prison ship. In March, 1776, General Howe appointed a Boston Tory, Joshua Loring, to be Commissioner General of Military Prisoners. Many claimed he got this post because General Howe had taken a fancy to Loring's wife. The position kept Loring too busy to pay attention to the actions of his wife. Loring soon realized he had nowhere to imprison rebels as the war escalated. He quickly ran out of available barns, houses, and even churches. Once Washington moved his troops from Brooklyn Heights, the British quickly took control of the area and it was at this time Howe and Loring decided to move rebel captives to the various vessels in the Gravesend Bay. On August 29, 400 Americans were moved to the H.M.S. Pacific. The British menaced the Americans by striking them, or striking whips in the air, warning that if they became troublesome they could expect more severe treatment. The prisoners were also told they were being shipped to England to be executed for treason. The dismayed and emotionally abused prisoners were eventually moved to the H.M.S. Lord Rutherford which was a smaller ship, making conditions much more crowded and the prisoners' morale even lower. Soon other British ships in the harbor, the Mentor, Whitby and Argo, filled with prisoners who also received horrific treatment from the British. It did not matter to the British the status of the prisoners. They were equally abused.

One such case was General Nathan Woodhull who was the President of the New York Provincial Congress. He was taken to the Mentor after having already been abused by his captors. Upon arrival on the Mentor, the crew cut and hacked at him and left him to lie on the bare boards of the ship. Fellow prisoners feared what was in store for them if the British treated Woodhull, an esteemed and respected American, in such a vile manner.

At one time *The HMS Jersey* was a war ship for the British, manufactured in 1736. She served the British well until 1759. In her glory days she had a crew of 400 and was a 60 gun fourth rate ship of the Royal Navy. In 1771 the British had moored her in Wallabout Bay off Long Island in New York. Her masts had been removed and she served as a hospital ship. Once the war began with the colonies, the British used the sixteen abandoned ships in the New York harbor as prison ships. Of all the ships, *The Jersey* was notorious for its mistreatment of prisoners. It was called *Hell* by both the British and the prisoners who landed there. Andrew was now among these men.

Andrew tried to remain focused and follow a ritual which he hoped would sustain him. Once day dawned the British would go about their rituals to having the dead removed from below decks, and the excrement tubs removed. Once this task was completed the men would be granted permission to go topside for their food rations. Andrew knew it would be at least an hour or two before he would be permitted to move from his prison. He knew that if he followed a set protocol each day he stood a better chance of survival as his mind would remain engaged and he would be able to think clearly. So many below decks had given up and Andrew watched their lives slip away. Every morning upon awakening, Andrew would recite the prayers he had said throughout his life.

O Lord our heavenly Father, Almighty and everlasting God, who hast safely brought us to the beginning of this day; Defend us in the same with thy mighty power; and grant that this day we fall into no sin, neither run into any kind of danger; but that all our doings may be ordered by thy governance, to do always that is righteous in thy sight, through Jesus Christ our Lord. Amen.

At first his prayers were dedicated to the safety of his mother and younger siblings he had left behind. He was filled with self-loathing and guilt for having left them on the un- protected farm and perhaps left to the hands of the British, or even worse, the Hessians and savages which the British had employed for their cause. He prayed for his brothers' safety knowing that as officers they would be the first targets of the British when fighting. He had heard all the stories of short supplies and food for the army and he prayed that his brothers were not succumbing to such conditions. He prayed for his father who was now targeted as a traitor of the King. Andrew had been proud of his father's rebellious act of signing the document which had propelled this war into its present state. Andrew had grown up watching his father protect those who needed the most help, and in signing the Declaration and supporting this rebellion he knew he was protecting all of the colonists from King George's greed. Andrew knew what his father had done was for a greater good, even though it put his own family in jeopardy. Andrew focused and concentrated on prayers to keep his father safe. Finally, Andrew prayed for divine intervention from this hell he was in. The smell, the constant rocking of the ship, the non-ending retching, cough- ing and vomiting of the men below decks all sickened Andrew. He had only recently recovered from his own near-death experience from the infectious wound which his mother, brother Abraham, and the Negro woman, Rose, had worked so hard to heal. He prayed that he would not again fall victim to the weakness he felt as surely in this setting it would be a death sentence. Andrew prayed that he would not succumb to the pain of hunger which all of the prisoners faced daily. Andrew strained to recall the words of Reverend Caldwell, their church pastor, who had inspired his congregation that God was on their side and that with God's help, they would be victorious. Andrew prayed until exhaustion from the mere act of thinking finally overtook him and his mind drifted to better days.

Then
December 1776

Andrew was now seventeen. He had pondered his decision for months. It was Washington's intention to protect New York from the British. The New Jersey militia was to man a "Flying Camp" to defend against any movement of the British. The flying camp was to move quickly to defend an area in jeopardy. In 1776 the militia only had to serve one month from spring until late fall, so the New Jersey men were eager to serve in this capacity. However, when Washington lost New York City, Fort Washington, and Fort Lee, the New Jersey men began to refuse to report for duty. It was reported that the troops were angry at the loss of ground through Washington's leadership. Reports came in that Washington's troops were being followed by the British and the Hessians. Chaos was happening. Although the British commander, General Howe, ordered no looting, confusion still reined. Howe then offered any New Jersey man who sided with the British protection papers. There was no loyalty among many of the New Jersey men. Many signed on. As a result, homes and the towns were looted and destroyed by the Hessians, the British, and even the New Jersey citizens. Reports of rape were becoming a regular issue. Safety was an impossible dream.

Andrew heard many of the local men arguing about how all of this dystopian life started because of the British. When stories of rape happening to the local girls and women, many of the New Jersey men stated they had had enough. This madness had to stop. There was a resurrection of support for the militia to fight against the British and force them off New Jersey ground. The New Jersey men banded together and began attacking the British soldiers who were easily identified by the red uniforms. It was obvious that the attacks against the British were being done not by Continental Army soldiers, but by New Jersey residents who had not mustered for the militia in protest against the cruel behavior against their womenfolk.

When the British began to count increased casualties, General Howe issued an order against anyone who fought against soldiers or residents.

A Patriot's Price

Head Quarters Trenton

12th of December 1776

Small straggling parties, not dressed like Soldiers and without Officers, not being admissible in War, who presume to Molest or fire upon Soldiers, or peaceable Inhabitants of the Country, will be immediately hanged without Tryal as Assassins.

The order was meant to protect the British, the Hessians, and the Loyalists. Needless to say, this further enraged the New Jersey men. Many began to officially join the militia to push the British and their General Howe out of New Jersey. When the British commander sent twenty four year old Cornet Geary and a squad of British Dragoons to raid and destroy colonial supplies in Flemington, they met an ambush. Geary was to seek out a rumored store of salt pork meant to be sent to the Continental Army. On the way back from the raid, Geary and his men were ambushed. Led by Captain John Schenck and a group of Amwell militia men a battle ensued leaving Geary shot in the forehead. The British fled and Geary was buried along the side of the road. It was soon realized that Geary was the oldest son of British Admiral Sir Francis Geary Baronet. For the New Jersey militia it was a victory and they sent a message to the British war leaders that they were serious in their efforts to protect their land. While news of the successful ambush was good, General Washington knew he had to rein in the New Jersey men from fighting on their own with a vigilante mentality. He needed them to join forces with the Continental Army so they would have a more powerful and organized army to fight the British.

By the end of 1776 Washington and the Continental Army were facing poor support from the colonists. The British in turn felt increased confidence in their ability to quell the rebellion. It was the retaliation of the New Jersey militia, especially in the Geary ambush that sparked a renewed belief among the colonists that they could beat the British. General Washington realized he needed the strength of the New Jersey militia to keep the momentum. A message was sent out from Washington, asking them to join the Continental Army.

To the Friends of America in the State of New Jersey

The Army of the American States under my Command being lately greatly reinforced, and having again entered the State of New Jersey, I most warmly request the Militia of Said State at this Important Crisis to Evince their Love of their Country, by boldly Stepping forth and defending the Cause of Freedom. The Inhabitants may be Assured that by a manly or spirited Conduct they may now relieve their Distinguished State from the depredations of our Enemies-I have therefore dispatched Coll. Neilson, Majors Taylor, Van Emburgh, and Frelinghuysen together with some other Gentlemen of your State to call together and Embody your Militia, not doubting but Success will attend their Endeavors-

A Patriot's Price

The overwhelming feeling of patriotism and Washington's plea moved many New Jersey men to again muster with the Continental Army. Meanwhile, the British planned retaliation against the New Jersey men for having ambushed Geary. The British moved their men from Bulls Island. Spies for Washington divulged the plan and Washington used this opportunity to hide the Durham boats which would be used in a well-planned attack on the Hessians. It was Christmas night when Washington and his troops crossed the Delaware in the Durham boats and led a surprise attack on the Hessian and British troops. Finally, momentum for the colonists had shifted their way. Andrew knew that his brother, Thomas, was among those who were with Washington in the crossing of the Delaware River that Christmas night. Andrew was filled with pride knowing that Thomas was among those who led the first grand victory of the rebellion.

Despite General Washington's request for New Jersey men to join the Continental Army, Andrew made his own decision. He would join those privateers in the whaleboats. Andrew's brothers, Aaron and Thomas had told Andrew that Washington did not feel that the local militias or even the whaleboats could get the job done. Andrew reasoned that he would be closer to home, and that he could make some money which would help offset costs at home which would keep food on the table for his mother and younger siblings and sister-in-law and nephew. Besides, he had promised his father he would remain home, however he was already nearly seventeen and by rights he should be with others his age defending the cause. Serving on the whaleboats would help him fight for the cause, while at the same time allow him to protect his family.

Andrew first learned about the privateers and the danger of their mission at the tavern where Clark and other Elizabethtown farmers and business owners often met. The Terrill Tavern was owned by Abraham Terrill who early on had begun to fight against the British. Terrill proved his patriotism when General Hugh Mercer needed a schooner to attack the British on Staten Island. The schooner was owned by both Terrill and Charles Tooker. Mercer, a Scotsman who immigrated to America in 1747, had been appointed Brigadier General of the Army in June, 1776. In July, Mercer attacked the British, however the schooner was sunk. Mercer turned over the cost of Terrill and Tooker's schooner to the New Jersey legislature. Abra Clark had handled the monetary compensation for the loss.

It was during this time that Abra was called upon to become a delegate in Congress where he would sign the Declaration of Independence, thereby placing himself in mortal danger of retaliation for his treasonous act against the Crown. The other New Jersey delegates in Congress had resigned either for fear of their safety or the loss of their farms, or because they wanted to remain loyal to the Crown. Clark was respected for his work, his support of all men, and his dedication to the cause. Once his wife and family gave their blessing, Abra left for Philadelphia. Andrew was left to watch over the family. For Andrew, the work of the privateers, although dangerous, offered him the best opportunity to protect his mother and family and help the cause.

Andrew signed on with Captain William Marriner. He had heard Marriner speaking at a local tavern about his own decision to become a whaleboat captain. He was a big and strong man with a wry sense of humor. Although Marriner had begun his service with Lord William Alexander Stirling in a New Jersey regiment, he left it to keep his tavern running. "Yes, I had done some service with the local militia, but I would return home to protect my business. I didn't want to be gone and come home to find some Redcoat tending my inn. It was right after I came home from serving with Stirling that various men came into the tavern and shared stories of the whaleboat men. Yes, we began holding meetings at the tavern and I became more and more intrigued with their stories of spying and raiding throughout the New York Bay area. I got pretty angered of how the British and Loyalists gathered prisoners which included soldiers, militia men, and Patriots citizens. Many of these prisoners were kept in the Sugar Houses or on prison ships in Wallabout Bay in Brooklyn. We began to talk about how the whale boaters could gather their own prisoners to use in trade. That's what got me into the whaleboat militia," Marriner declared as he leaned forward on the table looking at his audience.

"My first expedition on the whaleboats was on June 11th," said Marriner. "I joined up with Captain Schenck and twenty-six men in two whaleboats. We set out on the Matawan Creek. It was an overcast night. One of our men became horribly seasick and I had to warn him that if he let out a sound, he would be tossed overboard. We could not afford to be discovered by the British. We landed on Long Island shore and left the boat hidden in the bushes with a guard. We had a list of Loyalists we planned to capture. The mayor of New York, David Matthews was our main target, as well as Jacob Suydam, Colonel Axtell and Theophylact Bache. They would make great exchange for the release of some of our officers being held captive." Marriner let out a huge laugh. "Who would have guessed that our targets were all out at parties," said Marriner, shaking his head.

"Didn't you capture anyone?" asked one of the men in the audience.

"Well, yes we did. At Jacob Suydam's house we found Captain Alexander Gradon, one of our officers, who was being held captive there. We rescued him. He was quite relieved to be unbound. Living next door was Theophylact Bache who was snug in his bed and sound asleep. We dragged him out of bed and didn't even give him time to change clothing. Miles Sherbrook was hiding in another house and we dragged him out and he didn't even have time to put on a pair of britches! They were quite a group," said Marriner, laughing as he described the scene.

"Where did you take them?" asked another.

"It took us a little over an hour to get the two boats to Keyport, New York, where we gave over our prisoners to be used for prisoner exchange." Andrew pondered how important the work was for the whale boaters. It did not take him long to make the decision to join with Marriner.

During the next week Andrew spoke with Marriner about his decision.

"Well, Andrew, are you ready for your first raid?" asked Marriner.

Andrew paused momentarily. What the whale boaters did truly did help with the cause. He knew his brothers would not approve, but he would still be helping the cause, and still be home to oversee the farm. "Yes, sir. When do we leave?"

"How apt are you in rowing? You know you would have to be able to handle yourself rowing for several hours." Marriner looked deeply into Andrew's face.

"I have been using a small skiff to go up Rahway River to get supplies. I have found it is easier to travel and get supplies and return them without being caught by the local patrols that are always on the streets. I think I'm pretty good," said Andrew.

"We will be taking out two boats tonight right before dusk. Meet in the bay area."

For Andrew, this was his first foray with the militia. He knew that there was always the danger that Loyalists or the

British could take aim or intercept them as they travelled, or even as they approached the Loyalist households. Andrew spent the next few hours cleaning his rifle and praying. As the light of day dimmed, Andrew prepared to meet the others.

Two boats left that evening. The men had darkened their faces and their boats were rowed close to shore with no lanterns burning in order to hide from view. No one was allowed to speak, and Marriner reminded them that anyone making any sound would jeopardize all of their safety and the offender would be immediately tossed overboard into the cold water. Sound was amplified over the water, so precaution was made to not talk, or even whisper. Andrew stifled a cough and focused on rowing. The men rowed in unison and someone not expecting an invasion would think it was the sound of a wave splashing ashore.

Andrew reflected on the stories that had been repeated about William Cunningham, who ran one of the prison ships in the bay, and bragged about the treatment of captured rebels. Once Cunningham was liquored up he would begin tales of starvation and neglect and how they were no doubt responsible for more deaths of rebels than those killed by British bullets and bayonets. Cunningham was a hated enemy of all the privateers. To be caught by Cunningham was the most fearful thing they could imagine. Andrew pictured Cunningham in his mind and made Cunningham's disappointment his mission. Every enemy they captured and traded with the British would leave Cunningham fewer prisoners to torture.

A Patriot's Price

Andrew and the men knew their targets were the wealthy Loyalists who had taken refuge on Long Island. The problem was that they lived near the British line of troops. A boy who knew the area well had served as informant to Marriner, giving him details of the houses and hours kept by the homeowners. Raritan Bay was almost completely inhabited by the British, so Nicholas Marriner had to settle for moving through the creeks and ravines to reach their target. Most of the men on the whaleboats had been trained to row strong, steady and silently. Andrew quickly adapted to their strokes and moved as though they were all connected. The men could move silently across twelve miles in an hour. Andrew concentrated and remained focused. He and the others carried pistols and within the boat were lanterns, blankets, grappling irons, pikes and hooks on poles.

Marriner motioned for the men to stop rowing. Andrew could feel his heart pounding in his chest and thought it was loud enough that someone would be able to hear it. Andrew strained to see what was ahead. He could see faint lantern light ahead and movement of boats. In the silence of the night he could hear the sound of men talking and the sound of their oars in the water. As Marriner's boat drifted forward Andrew could see that the British boats were in constant motion. There appeared to be two boats being used to unload supplies from the British ship and transporting the supplies to shore.

Marriner motioned the men to quietly begin rowing. In a swift and agile motion the whaleboats moved forward. The men pulled out the hooked poles and as their boat glided next to the British boat, they caught the side of the boat and pulled alongside it. The British barely had a moment to react. They were already out of the range of vision of the large ship. Some of Marriner's men immediately gripped a knife threateningly against the throat of the enemy. Immediately the lanterns were put out, and the strong men on the whaleboats bound and gagged their prisoners. The entire takeover lasted only a few minutes. The British were fearful of being drowned, so they did not resist. Andrew expected some retaliation from the British ship, however it was apparent they had moved off the alert and lost sight of the sloop. Andrew's job was to move the cargo into the whaleboat, which he did efficiently and without any noise.

Once the cargo was transferred into the whaleboats, several men took over the sloops and followed the whaleboats as they made their escape. In less than two hours they arrived at their destination, sold their cargo, and turned over their prisoners. Andrew was jubilant that his first time out with the whaleboat was so successful. With his generous payment, he would purchase much needed supplies for home and planned to join in the next raid.

Each time he went out they returned with either prisoners who were used in exchange for Patriot prisoners, or goods which sometimes overloaded their boat. A large portion of the monies was given to support the local militia, but Andrew was able to pocket enough to guarantee he could pay for provisions for his mother and family at home. There were only a few times when Andrew felt completely endangered; however the whale boaters knew the waterways and could always escape the British who attempted to follow them. Each time he returned, Andrew prayed and thanked God for sparing him and the others.

The British were constantly on the move in New Jersey. Andrew and a group of other New Jersey men, when not serving on the whaleboats, would fill their time gathering information which was secretly shared so new plans of attack could be made. Great care was taken to check the accuracy of information. To move on a false lead would result in an ambush, or death, or even worse, imprisonment on one of the prison ships. Such a fate was too frightening as the British treated the Americans in the worst possible manner.

Andrew sighed as he recognized the fate of American officers was now to be imprisoned on the prison ships which were far worse than any of the previous jails the officers had previously experienced. Andrew prayed his brothers would not see such a fate. Of course, not only officers were so detained, but any American who was captured would face the same fate, and Andrew realized this could be his destiny as well. Andrew recollected a conversation he had heard about how the British felt about the Americans. A Captain Mackenzie stated that the American rebels were nonpersons and could be used in any way that would end this insurrection. Those words always echoed in Andrew's mind as well as the other privateers as they set about their work. Andrew continued to meet with other privateers, and he quickly learned that the prison ships were the most dreaded reality for any American. Even Washington prior to the use of the prison ships, had filed a complaint with General Gage in 1775 that the British mistreated the American officers who were captured in the cause of liberty and their country. He argued that they were imprisoned like felons and not treated like prisoners of war with regard for the Rights of Humanity. Gage only laughed and said the American officers rank were not granted by the King, therefore they were only rebels and traitors and would be treated as such and that they would be "destined to the cord."

Andrew continued with the whaleboats throughout 1777 and into 1778. Much of the involvement of the whale boaters was dependent upon the weather. Washington's troops were encamped in Valley Forge during the winter of 1777-1778. Reports came to many about the horrible conditions the men suffered. Elizabethtown had the same weather conditions which Washington's troops suffered in Valley Forge. This kept the whale boaters from making attacks on the British. For

Andrew, it was a time when he was able to remain home with his family, and gather information that streamed out from the encamped British Army.

While home Andrew felt the sting of his father and brothers absence was always present. Abra would send rare communications, and was unable to travel home both because of safety concerns and because of the charge he and the other delegates had in making plans for a new government once the war was won. Abra was ever fearful that his letters could be intercepted and place his family in further jeopardy. The few letters he did send were coded as if he were away doing surveying work. Often his letters talked about the work he was doing which would lead to eradicating the present pitted roads and building better roads for Americans to follow. He wrote about how the roads would help move crops and products for trade to people in need. An intercepted letter would carry no damning evidence of betrayal to the King. Andrew thought that winning the war had to be the outcome; otherwise the war would end with Abra and others being hung for their involvement.

Abra was in constant turmoil over the lack of supplies being sent to Washington's men. Andrew understood his father's concern about the lack of supplies, clothing, and food getting to the troops. Andrew felt guilty knowing his two brothers were living in that nightmare. He considered the plight of the men who were fighting on the front lines, including his brothers. The guilt Andrew felt of being safe at home eventually overwhelmed him. By May, 1778 Andrew made a huge decision.

On May 30, 1778, Andrew became a private in Captain Daniel Baldwin's Company, under Colonel Matthias Ogden's 1st Regiment of the New Jersey line.

Chapter 3
The Brutality of War

Now
June 1780

In an effort to shake off the stiffness of his aching limbs, Andrew stood and walked as best he could without benefit of light. He had witnessed far too many men lie immobile then succumb to disease and death in this hell hole. To remain inactive was certain death. Often in fear of falling among the bodies strewn about in the bowels of The Jersey, Andrew would run in place, just to get the blood flowing into his cold limbs. Lack of proper nourishment would limit his stamina, but each exertion kept death at arm's length. Andrew was fortunate that he had his hammock and blanket which he tried to keep as free from filth as possible. Each morning he would carefully roll them up and keep them from touching the contaminated floor. There were large chests for each mess group where they could keep their belongings. It was up to each mess to collect their supplies and keep them in the chest and keep watch over the chest so others would not help themselves. While theft was not acceptable in real society, here in the hell ship, theft was survival and it was recognized as such.

Smallpox was a constant companion within The Jersey. Andrew heard several of the American officers talking about giving themselves an inoculation of sorts by taking the festering pus from a soldier who was contaminated with the fearsome disease, then using a pin to scratch the substance into the skin. Andrew quickly completed this task with others in his mess group. He felt his stomach flip as he scratched into the skin between his thumb and finger, and then quickly bound his hand to protect it from touching other parts of his body. By the next morning the skin began to fester. Fortunately, there was no other complication for Andrew and he felt blessed that he had managed to take care of himself so he would not succumb to the vile death others suffered from smallpox.

One morning shortly after the Americans were released from their below deck prison, Andrew's attention was drawn to approaching Hessian soldiers who were peering at the clusters of men who stood or sat huddled near one other trying to avoid the driving rain. Andrew had squatted down, attempting to shield himself, yet keeping his eye on the Hessian soldiers. The Hessians were unpredictable. At times they showed some mercy to the captives, at other times they derived some pleasure in using their power over them. The Hessians were put on duty when the

A Patriot's Price

British soldiers took leave of the Jersey for a day. When one of the Hessians drew near Andrew he called out, "Over here." Another Hessian joined the first, standing over Andrew. Andrew couldn't understand why he was being identified, and fear swelled in his chest. "Put this on, rebel" snarled the Hessian soldier, throwing a pair of boots and coat at Andrew. Andrew at first wanted to spit out in protest to being called a rebel. Such a term was viewed as derogatory as the Americans felt they had the right to protest against Britain, and to be named a rebel by such guards as those on the Jersey was demeaning. These guards were barely literate yet they placed themselves above their captives. "Now, rebel!" screamed the soldier, and Andrew awkwardly pulled himself erect and kept his hatred filled gaze away from the captor's view.

Andrew struggled to put on the stiff and filthy clothing and although the boots were of a better quality than those Andrew presently wore, they were too large for his feet. He stood upright once the task was completed and looked at the soldier. "Now pull that body topside, and don't be thinking about any escape, you Loggerhead," the first soldier said. Andrew looked to where his hand was pointing, indicating the man who had lain next to him. Now, in the dim light of day, Andrew could see that the man's eyes were soulless and his mouth agape. He must have died soon after coming topside, no doubt eager to be away from the deadly and stifling air below decks. Andrew was pushed toward the body. In his weakened condition and oversized shoes he lost his balance and fell across the dead man. His face stopped within inches of the dead man's face and his eyes locked with the death stare of his once fellow captive. The two men pulled him up under his arms and swore at him to get busy. Andrew reached down and pulled the arms of the dead man. Another prisoner was ordered to assist Andrew. The two struggled to pull the dead man up to the front of the ship. Andrew shook off the running faucet of rain running down his face and squinted against his inability to see clearly.

"Where do we take him?" asked Andrew of his fellow prisoner.

"To the side. They will tie him with rope and drop him down the side of the boat to be gathered up to be taken to shore. Nasty bastards won't spoil their hands to do this work." Andrew followed the man who had obviously done this ritual enough that he knew the drill. "Name's Lefton," said the prisoner.

"Andrew," said Andrew, constantly aware that he should keep his last name secret in case someone made a connection between him and his father. Suddenly the butt of a Brown Bess pushed against Andrew's shoulder.

"No talking, you two."

Andrew noticed that Lefton was wearing a blue coat with very ornate cuffs with gold buttons. There was ornate scrolling designed sewed onto the top of the large cuffs with multi-colored threads. When the two were out of earshot of the soldier, Andrew asked, "Is that the jacket you wore when captured?"

"Heavens, no!" chuckled Lefton. This was thrown to me when I was picked for this duty only a few weeks ago. Poor bastard that owned it is no doubt dead. Probably his wife did all the needlework to send him off to war with a constant reminder of her love." Andrew thought about how many men left for war with wives or loved ones waiting for them back home. He knew his own mother would be mortified to know he was on this hell ship. Little would the woman who had embroidered the ornate cuffs know that this coat would be thrown to a stranger who was outfitted for such miserable duty as this?

Lefton guided Andrew in first lifting the dead body onto his blanket, then sewing a quick seam around the dead man's blanket to form his death shroud. Lefton and Andrew then pulled the body to the side. Andrew quietly spoke with Lefton as he worked, always careful to keep their captors in view. "This man just told me a few days ago of his capture. He was one of 500 Americans locked in a barn in Connecticut and for two days they went without food. Finally, as if feeding hogs at their trough, the British threw a small number of moldy biscuits into the mix of the captives. They scrambled like animals to grab what they could, first removing the maggots, then devouring the scraps before anyone could take them away. The following day they were thrown raw pork which they had to eat uncooked. Many of the men were reduced to horrible cramping, vomiting, and diarrhea, yet the British lined them up to march them about twelve miles through the British and Hessian army where they were beaten, kicked and insulted. Many had their only belongings stolen as they passed through. They were called 'dammed rebels' and told they needed to be hung. This man survived that mistreatment, only to die such a death and to be buried unceremoniously from this hell ship," said Andrew. Lefton cautiously nodded.

A rope was tied around the body and Lefton and Andrew lowered it over the side to a yawl which was waiting below. Andrew could see that there were already three bodies in the boat. Two other prisoners and a soldier were also in the yawl. Lefton looked around to be certain the solider was not near. He whispered, "Today is a light load. Typically we are hauling up around five to eight men a day." As the body was lowered, the blanket shifted and the face of the dead man was exposed. Andrew continued to look into the dead eyes of the man whose face leaned back at an angle that haunted him.

Andrew tore his gaze from the dead man and looked around the bay. Although the rain made it difficult to see, Andrew knew that Wallabout Bay was a kidney shaped area directly across from Corlears Hook on Manhattan. The shores of the bay were salt meadows with cord grass intermixed with cold and brackish river water and the freshwater that streamed from Wallabout Creek. Andrew knew that the

British had selected the best site to situate the prison ships as escape would be near impossible as the bottom of the bay was soggy mud flats which would make mobility near impossible. Also, the bay allowed the British a way to bring fresh water and supplies to the ships while keeping a safe distance from the population so that the miserable disease and infections that were known on the ships would not spread to the towns.

He was startled back to reality when the Hessian said, "There's another in the sick bunks. Gather him up." Andrew and Lefton climbed back into the hole. They were once again directed toward another lifeless body. Andrew gagged as he went to grasp the feet of the dead man while Lefton pulled the arms. The ankles were coated in pus and crusted blood and bodily filth. Again the British soldier's rifle butt pushed against Andrew's back and pushed him forward nearly toppling Andrew onto the body. The soldier laughed and Andrew swung around to confront him. The soldier forcibly kicked Andrew in the stomach, and Andrew fell across the dead man and several other captives.

Lefton dropped the dead man's hands and went over to Andrew and pulled him upright. He looked at the soldier who was squaring up to further attack Andrew. "We've got this," said Lefton, and the soldier stepped back allowing Lefton and Andrew to do the task. Lefton motioned to Andrew to grab the blanket and work to wrap the body and stitch it. This time Andrew made smaller stitches near the head so it would remain covered. The two went to work and their voices heaved with their exertion as they pulled the body up the stairs and then toward the side of the ship. Once they got to the side of the boat to lower the dead man to the waiting yawl, one of the Hessians yelled, "There goes another damned Yankee rebel!" Lefton looked over his shoulder to be certain the Hessian soldier was not immediately behind them. He quietly said, "Andrew, you had best remember that you can do nothing to aggravate these bastards. I watched them pummel a man to death who used to do this duty."

"I don't know how I can do this," said Andrew.

"Do it, or die," said Lefton. "At least we have an extra layer of clothing on our backs and the movement and extra rations they will give us will keep us alive."

"Alive for what cause?" asked Andrew. "I see no salvation for us."

"You've got to keep hope in your heart, and look for an opportunity for escape." Escape, thought Andrew. Escape. Live to escape.

Then
May 1778

"Name?" asked a grizzled man sitting at the small rickety table in front of the line which had formed.

"Andrew Clark."

"City?"

"Elizabethtown," responded Andrew.

"Height?"

"Five foot, eight inches."

"Eye color?

"Blue."

The man recording the muster reports looked at Andrew and added, "Dark complexion" to the line. "Sign here and date it."

Andrew added his name to the muster roll. He was now a private in the Continental Army. It was May of 1778 and the stories of Valley Forge and the brave men who survived a horrific winter were well circulated to those in New Jersey. Andrew was satisfied that he was making the right choice in joining Captain Daniel Baldwin's Company under Colonel Matthias Ogden's 1st Regiment of the New Jersey Line. Everyone knew that Washington wanted men to leave the local militias and join the Continental Army. When the 1st Regiment entered into Valley Forge they had 261 men with only 151 who were fit for duty. By the time they left Valley Forge and brought in new troops they had 538 assigned with 396 fit for duty. Andrew was fit for duty, and he was ready to fight for the cause and end this war. Andrew felt he was in good hands as Colonel Matthias was his mother's cousin and Aaron Ogden, another cousin, was the Paymaster. There were many men from Elizabethtown who mustered. Andrew was proud of his decision to leave the privateers and what some were calling a self- benefiting service of capturing British skiffs with property and taking Loyalist prisoners for trade. Yet, he was fearful of what the Continental Army duty held for him.

Days were spent training immediately after his joining the 1st Regiment. Gone were the days when Washington let the men rely on their own resources in battle. Andrew actually liked the discipline of the training and it made him feel that the men had a better chance of beating the British. In the evenings the men sat around the campfires and talked about the various stories carried back into camp. It was mid-July when the story of Wyoming, Pennsylvania came to the attention of the men. One of the survivors of that battle was persuaded by the men to tell about the massacre.

"It seems that Colonel Denison received a report from the scouts that there were seven hundred Tories, Indians and British Rangers forming up. They were being led by a Major John Butler and the Seneca chief, Sayenqueraghta at Fort Wintermute. Denison sent word to Washington about the danger. Washington sent troops and orders to move the nearby families into the protected forts."

"What troops showed up?" asked Andrew.

"It was the 24th Regiment and they went to Forty Fort to plan their attack. Problem was the troops were new and untrained and had no business being put on duty to protect the people and their crops against such a large enemy camp.

Most of the men were either very young, or they were old and none of them had received any kind of training."

"Didn't Washington send any other troops?"

"Captain Hewitt's Continental Company and the Kingston Company came in and both of them were well prepared for battle. There were also many men from the First and Second Alarm List Companies under Lieutenant Lebbeus Tubbs and Flavius Waterman, as well as the Wilkes-Barre Company under Captain Rezin Gere also arrived."

This stopped the progress of the story as the men shared their connections to the various troops, knowing various family members, friends or acquaintances that were with those companies.

"What happened?" another man questioned, bringing the story back to their attention.

"Well, the British commander comes up under a flag of truce along with an Indian and a Ranger with a message demanding surrender. They brought with them prisoner, Daniel Ingersol, who they had captured at Wintermute. He was not allowed to open his mouth."

"What did our men do?"

"They refused to surrender. They went back and held a meeting to determine how to proceed."

"A meeting? With who?" asked Andrew.

"All of them. They were acting like it was a town hall meeting debating the advantages and disadvantages of attacking."

"Since when do military leaders hold open meetings with all of the men? Military decisions can't be made that way!" spewed one of the men.

The story teller continued. "Meanwhile the British are sending more troops. Our side felt that there certainly were other troops coming from Fort Jenkins and maybe Fort Augusta who could help them. They sat there guessing at how many Indians, Tories and British could possibly attack."

"Anyone who knows anything about the Iroquois would know they are good at warfare and there are lots of them," said another.

"Luzarus Stewart got all the young men riled up that they could win with the troops they had at the ready. When Zebulon Butler said they should wait for reinforcements, he was shouted down by the younger men as being a coward."

"Wait. They talked to their leader that way? That would lead to a court martial!"

Andrew sighed. "As much as I weary of the drills we go through I am decidedly glad we are all trained together so we are better prepared."

"I have a gut feeling this battle did not turn out well. What happened?" asked another.

"On July 3th there were about 375 men who marched out playing "St. Patrick's Day in the Morning" and carrying the new flag led by Colonel Butler. By the time they got to Abraham Creek, Thomas Bennet shouted that they were marching into a trap and that they would all perish. No one listened. Bennet left and returned to the fort. The troops continued marching and when they go to Swetland's Hill their scouts came back and said the enemy was in full retreat! Butler wanted to hold the line until reinforcements came but Lazarus Steward riled up the men and they continued their march. At the end of the day only 174 survived."

An audible moaning was heard from the men as they talked excitedly about how the men should have listened to their leaders. After about three minutes the story teller said, "That's not the end of it. The British were not retreating when they saw the troops arriving. Instead they set fire to both Fort Jenkins and Fort Wintermute so it would appear they were retreating. When the Americans boldly came into the open near Fort Wintermute they were met with a line of the Tories and British who had formed a line across the plain, with trees and bushes behind them and a swamp to the right so there could be little chance for escape by the Americans. The Americans advanced as close to six hundred feet of the British and began to fire. The Rangers remained quiet. The Rangers stood and stepped back, making the Americans believe they were retreating. The Americans broke line formation and that's when the Senecas attacked on the right. Their loud screaming of the Indians startled the young men who stood confused by the attacking Indians. Many panicked and turned to run, many leaving the left and right wings open for attack. Then the Rangers returned fire. To give credit to Colonel Denison and Whittlesey they wheeled back to form an angle to the main line of soldiers in at attempt at protecting the left flank. Captain Hewitt's men made a slight retreat but one of his men said, 'The day is lost. The Indians are sixty rods behind us. Shall we retreat?' To this Hewitt replied, 'I'll be damned if I do. Drummer, strike up!' The young drummer began beating the drum as Hewitt tried to rally his men to the attack. As his arm was raised in the air a bullet struck him and for a moment, as if time stood still, he silently slumped to the ground. His men looked on, and then as if prompted by a signal, they turned to run."

"I can only imagine how terrified those young boys felt when they realized the mess they were in," said one of the men. "What happened then?"

"This is the part that makes my stomach turn. The men were actually surrounded and very few died. Instead they were all now prisoners. The battle had lasted only thirty minutes. What happened after was horrifying. A survivor, Samuel Finch, who escaped was able to report what he witnessed. The Tories and Rangers stood aside and let the Seneca do their dirty work. Those who had been captured were tortured and killed by the Seneca in a massacre that lasted over twelve hours. Some people say that Queen Ester bashed out the brains of many of the captives."

"My God!" exclaimed Andrew. "Who is this Queen Ester?"

"She was actually a mixed breed and her grandmother's

family was English. Her family had intermarried with several of the Iroquois tribes. She was considered a leader among the Indians. The story is that her son, Andrew, had been killed by Americans shortly before this battle. They said Queen Ester had sixteen Americans rounded up around a huge stone that they are now calling Bloody Rock. She then smashed in their skulls with her tomahawk."

The men gasped when they heard this.

"Not only that, but she led the Seneca in taking 227 scalps from the victims and turned them over to the British for $10 a scalp.

"That's despicable! " Andrew was sickened by the depths of depravity in war.

"I heard a couple of different stories. Some said it wasn't her because Queen Ester dressed more conservatively and the woman who did this was dressed in multiple hats and layers of clothing and was drunk. Queen Ester did not drink."

"Whether it was her or not probably doesn't matter. The fact that a woman could commit such an atrocity is unthinkable," said Andrew. He thought about his own mother and could not imagine her committing such a massacre.

"How do things stand now?" asked one of the men.

"Articles of capitulation were signed and the settlers were forced to give up their weapons and the fort was destroyed. The residents were to be allowed to keep their farms without fear of molestation; however that did not last very long. The

Seneca immediately plundered the farms and many of the settlers ran for their lives. One woman died while fleeing the area and her body was found. The men that found her said there was a charcoal message stating, 'Here lays the remains of Hannah, wife of Josiah Rogers who died while fleeing from the Indians after the massacre at Wyoming.' Many other family members were lost in the swamps as they tried to escape. Story is that General Washington is not taking this massacre lightly. I heard that there are plans to clear out the Iroquois."

The audience of soldiers spent the next hours retelling the story, demanding justice, and plotting the kind of revenge that should take place. As the evening progressed, most quietly reflected on their own families and the fears they had of what should happen if their own families met such fates as those of Wyoming, Pennsylvania. Andrew was among this group.

Within the month of hearing this story there was yet another story of brutality. Just like the Wyoming, Pennsylvania Massacre there was a repeat of the atrocity when the Seneca and Iroquois Indians, the Tories and British once again attacked, and for the American rebels, a firm hatred of the Indians and British was felt throughout the camps.

Chapter 4
The Continental Army Experience

Now
August, 1780

Andrew's clothing and food was a blessing due to a mistake made by the British. Andrew was not certain how or why it happened, but he was allowed to keep the clothing that was given to him even after a new batch of Patriot officers were captured and brought onboard. Andrew was thankful that once the British recognized they had made a mistake they chose not to have to retrain someone to do the work Andrew was assigned to do. Perhaps it was just their laziness, or resignation that it was no matter as the prisoners did not last long, so the mistake would take care of itself once the conditions claimed Andrew's health. The Working Party, as they were called by the British, were mostly Patriot officers. They were made to bring up the dead, carry the sick to the bunks where many were transferred to one of the other hospital ships. They also had to haul up the excrement tubs which were filled with human filth from the night. Some were assigned to haul the dead to shore and bury them. Andrew had no idea why his captors thought he should be assigned to the Working Party since he was clearly not an officer. Perhaps it was because there had been a prisoner exchange shortly before Andrew was incarcerated so they had a shortage of officers. No matter. His imprisonment had not afforded him many opportunities to feel thankful, but he realized that being part of the Working Party granted him additional clothing, movement, and a full ration of food, albeit contaminated and moldy for the most part.

Each day at sunrise the British would call out, "Rebels, turn out your dead." The British would pull aside the grate that held the rebels captive below. Andrew and Lefton would begin their duties of dragging the dead from the belly of the Jersey topside, and later lowered to the boat below. For payment of doing this grotesque job, additional rations of food was given to Andrew and Lefton. Andrew often thought that this was a gift from God.

The daily schedule was always the same. Prisoners were to go to the Steward's room to collect their ration of food once a day. For Andrew and Lefton, they secured their increased rations separately from the rest of the men. The prisoners were divided into messes of six men. The six men would take their rations and have them cooked in the Great Copper. This copper pot was huge and was divided into two areas. On one side the peas and oatmeal were boiled in fresh water. On the other side the meat was boiled in salt water which was drawn up from alongside the ship, the same water which had received the filth dumped from the ship. The salt water caused corrosion in the copper which would make the food poisonous. Cooking time was measured, and if food was not yet thoroughly cooked, it made no difference to the cook. The food was removed and given to the prisoners. The taste was horrible, but prisoners soon learned to cherish their luck in having anything resembling food.

To be certain he could eat his own full ration of food, Andrew would cook his own food separately rather than put it in the community pot to be divided among all members of the mess group. Since Andrew still had his own mess equipment which he kept in his haversack, he would gather up splinters of wood so he could heat his own tin and cook his food separately. He would use only the fresh water used by the cook to boil the peas and oatmeal.

The prisoners were to receive two-thirds of what a British Navy seaman received. A normal ration was 1 pound of biscuit, 1 pound of pork and half a pint of peas on Sundays and Thursdays; 1 pound of biscuit, one pint of oatmeal, two ounces of butter on Mondays and Fridays; 1pound of biscuit and two pounds of beef on Tuesdays and Saturdays; 1 ½ pounds of flour and two ounces of suet on Wednesdays. The British did not give any butter to the rebels, instead giving them what they called "sweet oil, which in reality should have been called rancid oil. A full ration also allowed a half pint of rum each day. The prisoners received no rum, which might have made their pain more tolerable and afforded some the ability to sleep. As such, the lack of sleep, a much limited diet, and food which had been prepared in such a contaminated manner, would quickly take its toll of the men. It did not take long to see fellow prisoners mutating into living skeletons as their bodies suffered under the living conditions and poorly prepared food.

Andrew and Lefton were fortunate in receiving a portion of rum, which they relished and protected as other prisoners would stare hungrily at it. Andrew quickly transferred his measure to a small flask he carried inside his clothing. He was always cautious when consuming it to hide it from the other prisoners. Andrew also made it a habit of only taking a swig of the rum in the morning, and he would drink the rest at night, hopeful that it would calm his mind from the nightmarish surroundings and allow his body to rest and regain strength.

Andrew also recognized that his survival was because Lefton was alert and crafty. Lefton had bargained with the cook, who was himself a Patriot, to allow them to cook their rations in their own kettle which was hung by a string off a nail above the hearth. Lefton and Andrew would save a portion of their pint each of fresh water and put it into their kettle. They were always on lookout for splinters of wood they could secure to set fire beneath their kettle. Andrew was certain this manner of food preparation is what had kept both Lefton and him alive. Both were always complimentary of the cook so that he would never turn against them in their practice. Andrew was always thankful that Lefton had the knowledge of avoiding the Great Copper, so in a sense Andrew owed his life to Lefton.

While Lefton and Andrew carried the dead to the upper deck for removal, several other captives were given the task of carrying the excrement tubs, buckets of human filth and waste to the deck to empty overboard. When one of these men would fall sick, Andrew was made to do this duty as well. While he had grown up on the family farm and had often cleaned the barns and was used to the filth of animals, this task was hideous to him. Many of the Working Party were made to carry buckets of water, which was already dirty and contaminated from the foul and polluted bay, below decks to clean what they could below decks. The captors took delight in making the rebel officers do this duty, knowing it not only degraded their rank, but put them in harm's way. The floor was always besmeared with waste as many of the prisoners' bowels would empty against the unwitting or weak owner as he lie near death from the various diseases that ran rampant among the captives. The Patriot officers would typically assign someone beneath them to do these tasks. Those commanded to clean the floors would push the mops in hopes of absorbing the debris and watery waste into the mop, then would swish it in the pail in hopes of cleaning off the worse of it. They would wring the filthy mops with their bare hands. This business and the thought of it would cause Andrew's stomach to turn. He noticed that this duty of men would soon fall to illness and they would be among the dead hauled topside by Andrew and Lefton. The buckets were disgusting and Andrew had to force himself against retching as the contents sloshed around, being careful to hold the buckets as still as possible so he would not spill the contents on himself. Getting the buckets up the ladder without spillage was tricky business. Andrew was thankful that the captors would typically pull a replacement captive for this duty when the regular man fell to illness or death. At those times, Andrew would sit and consider why he was so thankful to be rid of that business. Hauling human filth, or hauling human remains. What he was being forced to do was demeaning and foul. For the first time since his capture he chuckled to himself that he was differentiating which duty was worse. Perhaps he was losing his mind. He had certainly not found any humor since being imprisoned and his audible chuckle startled those around him as well as himself. Perhaps those near him thought Andrew was beginning to take leave of his senses, which was not something unusual in Hell.

Andrew began to take note of the appearances of the various captives. The officers took the former Gun Room as their quarters. They became part of the Working Party as soon as they were captured and brought onboard, and as such received the full rations and often were given clothing to replace their own clothing when it became destroyed. Perhaps it was the daily exercise, or their additional food, or just their resiliency as officers to maintain better health. Whatever the reason, their health would inspire those rebels who could still identify with the officers and it gave them hope to carry own.

Andrew also noted that those in the lowest level of the ship were of the worse lot. When they actually had the strength to climb the ladders to retrieve their food rations, their appearance was frightening. Their hair was long and matted, their beards unkempt, their clothing, or what was left of it, was in tatters as they had no means to replace it. The longer they were imprisoned, Andrew noticed their hair stopped growing and began to thin from malnourishment, and their skin was a map of oozing sores and discoloration. Andrew thought that the next time he would see them was when their bodies would be brought to the forecastle for transport to the shore for burial. Even then, they typically would not have the decency of a blanket to be made into their shroud as it had either been stolen or lost when they failed to defend themselves.

Sometimes during the night Andrew would be shaken awake and told to pull a body out to the forecastle of the ship to be unloaded in the morning. These late nights were frightening as they moved by lantern light which was unsatisfactory and Andrew feared he would injure himself which would put him in the general population of those suffering in their nakedness. The British did not like going below decks any more than the prisoners, thus they avoided any task which required their attention there. It was only when prisoners screamed out and thrashed about when they discovered the body draped about them was now lifeless. The soldiers would open the grate and demand that the dead be brought up. Andrew and Lefton would proceed to do their duty. Andrew quickly learned to stay clear of the thrashing prisoners for fear they would pull him off balance in the fits of their madness. The fact that Andrew was a fellow prisoner would mean nothing in the insanity that befell the prisoners. The pulling the body free from the often times thrashing throng of prisoners was frightening. Pulling the body up the ladders to the deck was just as treacherous and dangerous. With visibility so poor it would be easy for Andrew to fall and injure himself. Andrew quickly learned that the deck would be slick from dew or frost, making his trek to the forecastle also dangerous. It was often with a sigh of relief when Andrew would complete the task and feel "safe" once again in his known torment below decks.

The irony of his prayers of gratification for his safety did not escape him. His prayers for his continued "good fortune" would later cause Andrew hours of questioning his faith. His deep commitment to his God was becoming increasingly difficult to uphold as his days of captivity continued. Andrew prayed and tried to stay focused as he mouthed the words of his prayer. *"We praise thee, O God: we acknowledge thee to be the Lord. All the earth doth worship thee: the Father everlasting. To thee all Angels cry aloud: the Heavens, and all the Powers therein. We worship thy Name: without end. Vouchsafe, O Lord: to keep us this day without sin. O Lord, have mercy upon us: have mercy upon us. Amen.'* The words were said, but Andrew did not feel the passion he felt in the prayer as he had in the past. Andrew tried to repel the thought that his God had forsaken him.

Each morning Andrew and Lefton would immediately go to their tasks and not draw the attention of their captors. Both men acted compliant and the British soldiers would resume their conversations while Andrew and Lefton did their work. Once above deck the two would talk quietly and share any information they had heard. Lately so many were dying that there were now two other men on the removing the dead duty and two more who helped take the bodies to shore. On one particularly clear day, Andrew's attention was drawn to the loud screaming of shore birds. He looked toward shore to see what was attracting the birds. Andrew saw bodies heaped on the shore. "Oh my God!" exclaimed Andrew.

Lefton elbowed Andrew and quietly said, "Don't stare. Obviously there is to be a larger mass burial at a later time. The men on that duty get the bodies ashore, but if the ground is frozen they cannot bury them. Or if there is a storm brewing, the bodies are left in a pile to be buried later when the soil or sand stands a chance of not washing away. Be glad we are not on that duty. One of the men went mad when he had to handle decomposing bodies and throw them into the mass graves. He came back to the ship, but the next day he was one of the bodies being removed from the ship. Don't know if he died naturally, or was helped along when he wouldn't stop moaning, screaming, and wiping his hands and the Lobsterbacks just helped him cross the border."

"This is filthy business," said Andrew. "I don't know how much more of this I can take."

"You'd best toughen up. If you show signs of weakness they will strip you down and you will once again be below decks until you are given our freedom from this life," said Lefton in a stern voice. "Set your sights on finding a way to escape. I look for every opportunity to run." Andrew considered this. Freedom. He needed to make a plan.

Each day at 9 AM the prisoners were made to haul up their possessions and bedding. They would then line up for food rations. Most would go above deck and often would stand shivering in the cold as they stood in their limited parcels of clothing. The provisioners were paid to prepare and deliver food to the prisoners. Andrew would look at them with disgust knowing that their greed put the prisoners in greater danger than the hateful conduct of the British. Because Andrew was already above deck and on duty before the call for food, he could see the food preparation. The water for cooking and cleaning was drawn up from the muddy and foul water along

one side of the ship. The buckets of filth and waste from below decks had been dumped over the opposite side of ship.
Andrew winced at the thought of this. The meat the men
pulled out of the packages and thrown into the large copper
kettles was often brown, rancid, and often times unidentifi-
able. It was no wonder so many became ill. The provisioners
would also have to go below decks to provide food to those too
weak to come above deck for their food. They gave smaller rations to those who were sick which further attributed to their
weakness. They also claimed to give food to those who were
already dead, thus increasing their tallies for payment. There
were between 700-1000 prisoners on The Jersey at any given
time, and the provisioners made their share of profit on them.

Whenever new captives arrived, the same procedures were
followed. They arrived in chains. The first day they would have
missed their food rations, so they would go without food for
a minimum of a full day or more. When the rebels would try
to talk the British soldiers would approach and strike them.

As days turned into weeks and eventually months, Andrew
filled his days doing his duties, trying to hide his mind from
the realities of his work. He learned to not look into the faces
of the dead. He learned to hold his breath as he first returned
below decks to the stench of human filth and waste until he
would again become numb to the odor. He learned to remain
silent until he and Lefton were out of hearing range of the
British. He learned to talk in muffled tones, all the while

looking for a way to escape this hell. When his duties were completed he would return below decks and settle into his spot, and close his eyes to the reality of his world. When sleep would finally overtake him his mind would look at what he refused to see during the day. Images of dead bodies, carcasses stacked on shore, buckets filled with human filth, men blaspheming God and their lives, sounds of the ill gasping for air, teeth chattering in the cold, men reduced to skeletons too tired to chase off the flies which tormented their bodies, and the constant nauseating smell. When these images would torment Andrew's dreams he would jolt awake and pray that God give him the strength to survive. There were thankfully some nights when his mind would drift to the days prior to entering Hell.

Then
September, 1778

Andrew had mustered with the Continental Army on May 30, 1778. His contract would pay $5 per year. He was a private in Captain Daniel Baldwin's Company, under Colonel Matthias Ogden's 1st Regiment of the New Jersey Continental Line. In June he was moved into the artillery. Fortunately the New Jersey troops were ordered to protect the mainland from the British trying to come across the bay from Staten Island where they were stationed. Andrew was happy about this position only because they were stationed in Elizabethtown and he was so close to home. He felt he was directly protecting his mother and younger siblings.

Andrew was always alert when stories would be repeated about other troops and battles. The stories always focused on their enemies who were the British, the Hessians, and especially the Indians who committed such savage acts against the Americans. For Andrew there was an array of emotions. As a child he had heard his father talking about the early treaties and land contracts that the Indians were forced to sign to give up their claim to properties which they had always owned prior to the arrival of the colonists. Abra Clark had always fought to protect those least likely to be able to afford proper legal protection, and for Andrew he had always felt the Indians were not given their proper due. Occasionally he would see members of the Delaware Tribe prior to the start of this war, but they were often treated with disdain and prejudice by the local townspeople. Perhaps it was Andrew's tender heart growing up that gave him such a mature insight to prejudicial treatment of those who could not defend themselves, or it could have been his admiration of his father's values and morals. Of course, now his emotions were filled with the remembrance of the brutal attacks against the soldiers and the mutilation and torture of the Americans. Andrew was torn with his feelings of hatred for the enemy, while at the same time a sense that this war had finally given the Indians an opportunity for revenge for the wrongs they felt had been thrust upon them. Of course, the British used that emotion in order to ensnarl the Indians into their role in this war. Andrew hated the British far more than the Indians.

In the late summer of 1778 the constant conversation around the campfire would repeat the stories of the Wyoming, Pennsylvania massacre as it was one of the worse battles any of the soldiers had heard told. Andrew said, "Didn't our men know there were that many Indians who were siding up with the British?

"No one imagined there were that many. I think that even the British had to be overwhelmed by the savagery of the attacks the Iroquois made on our soldiers. "

Andrew was speechless. He immediately thanked God that Aaron and Thomas's troops were not in that massacre. He then looked up, "Who is this Butler who was leading the British troops?"

"Word is that he is Colonel John Butler, a Loyalist from the Mohawk Valley. He formed with a band of American and Canadian Loyalists and pulled in Indian allies. They became known as Butler's Rangers. In 1777 they were fighting in New York and Pennsylvania, attacking Patriot settlements. I heard that they have fought as far away as Virginia and the Northwest Territory. He has also teamed up with Joseph Brant, an Indian chief, who has pulled in the Mohawks and other Indian tribes. "

"How could Butler allow the Indians to do this?"

The storyteller continued, "They say he lost control over them over time. The Iroquois were taking revenge for several of their settlements being burned to the ground by Continental rifle regiment and a Pennsylvania militia group."

Andrew was torn. While he had always sympathized with those less fortunate, a trait he learned from his father, he could not fathom the idea of the slaughter that ensued in retaliation by the Indians on the white colonists. His father had shared stories of how the military leaders took advantage of the various tribes in giving meaningless trade items for valuable land. Even Elizabethtown was gained through such meaningless trade. Now it seemed that the Indians, once easily manipulated, were now actively engaged in taking revenge, and doing so in a most brutal manner. Andrew secretly held the fears that such retaliation could be set upon his father and his family because of his father's traitorous acts against Britain. Once again he feverishly prayed for this war to be over.

As days turned into weeks, and weeks into months, Andrew continued his duties in the artillery. The regiment was called out any time scouts identified that British troops were on the move. Andrew often would stand guard near the bay with his friends. They would talk about their families and Andrew was most careful not to provide too many details about his father. This had been reinforced for years in fear that either his father or his family would be made victims by Loyalists, Tories, or British.

Toward the end of November another story of Indian attacks circulated through the camps. "It was a bloody massacre," the soldier said. "It happened in Cherry Valley. It was that Butler's Ranger group. This time they had Cornplanter and Sayenqueraghta's Senecas and other tribes involved. They went into about six settlements and burned the buildings to the ground and killed off their cattle.

"Who told you this story?" asked Andrew.

"It was a Captain Benjamin Warren who happened upon the carnage. He said that it was the most shocking sight his eyes ever beheld before of savagery and brutality. Those were his exact words! His men came upon a fort in Cherry Valley in New York and found what looked like a scene from hell. There were bodies of men, women and children, many scalped or heads crushed by tomahawks and rifle butts strewn about the area. Cabins, barns and human remains were in smoldering ruins. Warren found out that there were hundreds of Loyalist militiamen, Seneca Indians and a few British soldiers who appeared out of the fog and rain. The fort was taken completely by surprise. That Loyalist Captain Walter Butler and the Mohawk war chief, Joseph Brant, went on a terror of destruction. The town was surrounded. It was totally destroyed, but the fort itself survived. There were sixteen soldiers and more than thirty civilians killed, and two hundred left without homes and crops."

"Walter? I thought it was John Butler who led the Rangers?"

"Walter is John's son. He took over command of the Rangers."

"People are calling John Butler, 'Indian Butler' because he uses the Indians to attack white settlers."

Andrew had great difficulty hearing these stories. He was filled with a wide variety of emotions; however his overwhelming feeling was that the Indians were a threat which must be destroyed.

As winter arrived for the Continental troops, General William Maxwell received order for winter duty for his troops from General Washington:

Middlebrook, December 21, 1778

You are appointed to the command at Elizabethtown at which place you are to remain with the New Jersey Brigade; but should you be of opinion that the troops can be more conveniently quartered by removing part to New Ark, you may order a Regiment or as many to that place as circumstances shall require.

The principal object of your position is to prevent the enemy stationed upon Staten Island from making incursions upon the main and also to prevent any traffic between them and the inhabitants. In this respect I must request you to be very vigilant and to use your utmost exertions as great complaints have been made of trades being carried on so openly and to such a height, as to alarm and give great umbrage to the well affected. I am informed that considerable quantities of provisions are carried over to and good brought from Staten Island through Woodbridge and Rahway Necks, you will therefore either keep patrols or post small parties upon that quarter, as you shall judge most expedient and likely to prevent such intercourse.

The orders from Washington were repeated to the troops and Andrew knew there were those among them who were guilty of trading on the black market with the British soldiers and supporters. No wonder Washington wanted guard duty posted to nip this practice. Guaranteeing that the Americans viewed Staten Island encampment as enemy territory and alliance with the enemy was detrimental to the American cause was essential if this war was ever to end.

Maxwell was also told to gather intelligence about the enemy's movements into New York so that once the American troops broke winter camp they would be aware of where and what the British were doing.

Despite the orders from Washington that the Army behave as an army, despite being in their home town, there were those who sneaked off camp to return to their homes, which were certainly more comfortable and warmer and had better food than the Army camps. Colonel Ogden often left camp and returned home, as did many others who left camp without proper furlough to do so. Many of the local men would leave camp and it soon became apparent that protection of Elizabethtown from constant Loyalist interactions with the

British, and British invasions into the area was problematic with Staten Island being only six miles from Elizabethtown. The loose guard detail provided the British opportunity to undermine the American cause.

Everything came to a head on February 25th, 1779, when the Elizabethtown Barracks were destroyed. Andrew was asleep when he was awakened by rifle shots nearby. He clumsily grabbed for his weapon and stumbled toward the doorway of the barrack. Outside ran a melee of soldiers, both British and American. Andrew managed to shoot, not knowing whether he made his mark. Andrew stopped to reload his rifle. He took aim at a British soldier who was fast approaching him. Andrew pulled the trigger but his rifle misfired. The soldier continued toward him and lunged. Andrew tried to back up, but another soldier was trying to move past him and pushed him forward. The British soldier locked eyes with Andrew and suddenly a piercing sheet of pain traveled through Andrew's thigh as the soldier fell forward toward him. A smoldering hole was lodged in the back of the soldier, however not before his bayonet had penetrated Andrew's thigh. He stumbled backward and fell to the floor of the barrack, just as a flaming faggot was thrown into the room. Andrew fought to pull himself upright and stumbled toward the doorway to escape the smoke rising within the room. He climbed over the body of the soldier who had stabbed him and held tight to the exterior of the barrack as he tried to decide which way to move. His heart beat wildly as he held fast to his rifle with one hand, and moved his other hand to his leg trying to push the pain away. Suddenly from behind a rifle butt struck him across the head, and Andrew fell to his knees.

A shot was fired and the attacking British soldier reared forward with the impact, then held his shoulder and staggered away. "Andrew," screamed one of his friends. "Hold on!" A friend grabbed Andrew's arm and wrapped it around his neck and held Andrew around the waist and forced him to quickly move away from the craziness of the attack. They moved into the wooded area where Andrew was propped against a tree while his savior ran back to either fight or save others. Andrew could see his britches turning red and felt his head swimming dizzily and his vision narrowing into darkness.

Chapter 5
Discharged

Now
November 1780

*"**O be joyful in the Lord**, all ye lands: serve the Lord with gladness, and come before his presence with a song. Be ye sure, that the Lord he is God; it is he that hath made us, and not we ourselves: we are his people, and the sheep of his pasture; For the Lord is gracious, his mercy is everlasting: and his truth endureth from generation to generation. Amen."*

Andrew said his prayer; however the words were fast losing meaning to him. Why was God not tending his people, his sheep on this ship? How is God being gracious? There was no everlasting mercy from God as he sat in this wretched state, ever watchful, ever suspecting the worse, and increasingly feeling that death would be a welcome release from this hell.

Andrew, who was always quiet, was becoming even more withdrawn as the days dragged on in his imprisonment. The only one he spoke to was Lefton, and even then it was minimal. His constant focus was on escape or release from The Jersey. "Maybe we will be pulled for prisoner exchange," said Andrew to Lefton as they began a new day of bringing up the dead.

Lefton was more apt to talk to other prisoners. Lefton was a keen eavesdropper, always looking to stand near the British to overhear their conversations. "Not likely. I heard the Lobsterbacks talking about how Washington wouldn't do prisoner exchanges for the privates as most of us are only in the militias, and we are not valuable as he needs officers who have confirmed their commitment to the cause. The Brits say the rebels think we are actually detrimental to the cause."

"Washington really said that?" Andrew asked. "I fought with the Continental Army, then recuperated at home after a near fatal wound I received in battle, then went back to serve on the Sullivan Expedition. I was trying to get back to the whaleboats when I got picked up by a group of Loyalists. I served. I fought. I was wounded, yet I went on to fight again. Other men on the hell hole have the same kind of stories. I can't believe Washington wouldn't be fighting to get us off these prison ships. Leaving us here to rot is unthinkable." Andrew went silent as anger began to swell within him. He pondered the truth of what Lefton had told him, and how it affected his hope that he would get his release from this hell. He could feel an internal draining of energy as he considered how much longer he would have to survive this ship. He had to hope that what the British were saying was just hearsay, and meant to further cause hopelessness among their prisoners. He had to hold onto the belief their captors were lying.

The daily routine of waking and handling the dead was wearing thin on Andrew. He had always been soft spoken and quieter than his two older brothers, Aaron and Thomas. His life at home had been sheltered prior to this war. Gone were the days of waking in the morning to the sound of his mother preparing the morning meal and the chatter of family as they awakened. He missed the innocence of his youth when his father was only off the Clark farm when he was doing surveying work. He missed the gathering of the extended families of both his father's cousins, and his mother's family. He missed neighboring farmers coming to the Clark farm, and evenings filled with the men folk talking politics, the women cooking or sewing, and the children playing together or going to the river to fish. He missed his brother Aaron setting off to work in the fields, and Thomas charging around on his horse. Things changed. He tried to remember exactly when this began. Was he all of ten years old when the men visiting his father began to huddle together to talk more secretively? Certainly by the time he was twelve the nature of the adult talk had become more severe, stern and secretive. He was fourteen when he was allowed to sit nearby to hear some of the talk which focused on taxes, complaints about King George, and suspicion voiced about various neighbors and their loyalties. Andrew recalled his excitement about being allowed to sit nearby during these discussions, but at first he did not have an interest in the talk. It wasn't until his two older brothers began participating in the discussions, and hearing their urgent questions asked of the adults that Andrew's interest was sparked. That marked the end of his childhood as he knew it. His father left for Philadelphia by the time Andrew was sixteen. He was sworn to secrecy of his father's signing of the Declaration. He quickly learned that sharing this information or acknowledging it to anyone would become a threat to his father's safety as well as his family's. Andrew thought of his mother, who he loved more dearly than anyone on this earth, and he could not bear to think she could ever be harmed. When his father told him that he was now the "man of the house" and he must look after the family and farm as both Aaron and Thomas were mustering and training to be officers, Andrew felt a sense of pride and responsibility.

If only this war had not escalated. There came a moment when Andrew realized that if the war was not fought and won, his father would be hung as a traitor. Such a thought was unimaginable. Andrew's prayers became more fervent as he needed God's protection of the family, and the Army's ability to win this war. It was unthinkable that Aaron and Thomas could also hang. Andrew's nights were constantly filled with the reality that this was now a different world than the one he had enjoyed as a child. There was no turning back and there was certainly no denying that Andrew's role had changed. Andrew thought about this and sighed, shaking his head. Now, here he was, on a prison ship with no visible means of escape. He looked at his hands which were filthy. His clothing was mismatched and crusty. He no longer could smell the filth, which was, indeed, a blessing in itself. He ran his hand up through his hair and immediately pulled his hand away as his stomach nearly wretched at the sensation of his fingers feeling crusty blood from the parasites that fed on his scalp. How much longer could he handle this?

The two continued their work in silence, and Andrew's mood was somber and bitter. He closely observed the protocols of the British as new prisoners arrived. His captors would seek out officers among the prisoners no doubt to use them in prisoner exchanges. Since Andrew was just a private, he now realized there was no chance that he would be rescued through exchange. His face momentarily flushed with the anger that rose from within his soul. The harsh reality was the only way off this hell ship was by escape or death. Washington was not coming to their rescue. Andrew wondered if his father found out he was on this ship he could use his power to secure his son's release. Andrew began to tie his hope to his father working to arrange an exchange for his freedom. This glimmer of hope renewed Andrew's faith in survival, at least for now.

Andrew and Lefton whispered daily about their various plans for escape in the long dark evenings spent beneath these decks. If they were to escape, they would have to act promptly when the opportunity presented itself. So far neither had come up with a feasible plan. The closest they came was diving overboard in hopes that they could swim underwater to the shallows and not be shot by the British on deck. That plan would only work in the summer months as the waters in Wallabout Bay remained cold even in the spring and fall. Andrew also doubted if he would have the strength to swim any distance. Each day he noticed more changes within himself. His hair, once thick and smooth, was now thinning. His arms had been strong and taunt from rowing in the whaleboats and hauling equipment with the army. Now he struggled to haul the wretched and emaciated carcasses out of the bowels of this ship. He was careful not to let the British see him struggle as he did not want to lose this job, which he despised, yet needed so he would not fall into the madness many of the prisoners experienced. To welcome that which he hated was now his new reality. Nothing in his present condition made sense to him any longer.

Andrew thought about other plans he and Lefton concocted for escape. One was to pretend to be dead, and be pulled up to the top deck during the night. Once left on the forecastle, an escape could take place by cover of darkness. Lefton and Andrew shared strategies as often as they could, knowing that if one suddenly appeared dead, the other would keep the secret. Andrew nurtured this flicker of hope that he would one day escape.

A Patriot's Price

Each day was the same. Dawn would break and the British would pull the grate away and call for the dead to be removed. Andrew would reluctantly open his eyes, although typically sleep had long since escaped his grasp. The less he strained his eyes looking at the outlines of the damned moaning and moving in the belly of the Jersey, the longer he could block out the harsh reality that was his life. Each morning he prayed he would awaken and realize this had all been a dream, albeit a bad dream. Once reality was faced, he, Lefton and the others would walk through the galley of the ship looking to collect the dead in the dimly lit bowels of the rotting Jersey. Often it was the rotting smell of a dead body which was hidden near the walls of the ship that pulled Andrew and Lefton to the spot where a body was to be found. Sometimes they would be beckoned by a group to pull away one of their group. The survivor's faces bore the reality that time only stood between them and the same fate.

Andrew was revolted each day at the thought of handling the dead bodies, but he forcibly made himself do this knowing his reward was the clothing on his back and the extra rations. He and Lefton had fallen into a routine of putting the body immediately onto the man's blanket and stitching it shut. Often the dead man's mates would have already done this deed, and they would follow after Lefton and Andrew to request permission to be on the burial detail. Sometimes this was granted. As they pulled up the bodies the provisioners would already be on deck preparing food, although often what they were served would never be called food fit for humans. Many of the provisioners were forced into service by the British, and many were not necessarily loyal to the King, nor to the Patriots. They were loyal only to their own pockets. Strangely, war had made them mercenaries in providing the bare minimum of provisions, pocketing the profit. Andrew thought they were much like the Miller of Canterbury Tales who had the "thumb of gold." While death held a grip on the prisoners below the decks who were too weak to move topside for their rations, death also held a grip on those who could climb topside and received food which could lead to their ultimate end. Sadly this was done through the hands of those mercenaries who were against the King, yet lined their pockets at the expense of the helpless American prisoners. This was unconscionable.

Ever watchful as new prisoners arrived onboard, Andrew was vigilant to observe how the British proceeded in hopes that an opportunity for escape would present itself. On one particular night Andrew was awakened by the sound of the captor dragging a man into the "hole," which was a dungeon area of the ship. Andrew wasn't certain, but the voice sounded hauntingly familiar. He wracked his brain to find hope that he was mistaken.

Andrew did not sleep that night. He strained his ears to listen in hopes that his mind was playing tricks on him. When morning arrived Andrew and Lefton began their job of removing lifeless bodies. "Let's start below," said Andrew, trying to keep his voice from airing suspicion. Despite working daily with Lefton, Andrew could not afford to trust anyone. He needed to work in secrecy. When the two went below, Andrew signaled that he was going to move toward the back area. Andrew could hear a commotion coming from the locked room and he worked his way over to the door. This time Andrew paid close attention to the sounds coming from the locked room. He heard the voices of two British officers taunting their prisoner. "Write it. Write it now!"

"You misjudge my father's influence. He cannot meet your demands, nor would he," the prisoner said. The voice penetrated Andrew's heart as sharply as a knife. Andrew winced as he busied himself as if looking at the bodies strewn about the floor to identify any who were no longer alive. Andrew listened closely to the sounds of beyond the door. It couldn't be. He hoped to hear a voice that was not familiar to him. Suddenly he heard the sound of a fist impacting a face and the resulting sound of a man moaning and pleading. "Please, in God's name, stop this. My father cannot and will not renege on his having signed the Declaration."

Andrew's heart stopped. He suddenly realized that he had to get control of himself and continue in this facade of identifying the dead without drawing attention to himself. It was not hard to do as there was a body near the locked room and he began slowly pulling it free toward the stairs. He strained to hear more, but suddenly the door burst open and Andrew suddenly turned and looked at the open door. His eyes shot a look into the room. A lantern hung above the prisoner, illuminating his face. It was indeed Thomas who was tied to a chair and his face was bleeding and his mouth was agape, blood dripping from it. Andrew tried to not react but for an instant he was certain Thomas made eye contact with him.

"What are you looking at? Get this carcass out of here, now!" shouted the captor. Andrew fumbled about and pulled the arms of the dead man toward the stairs. The captor looked hard at Andrew, studying his face. Andrew made certain he carried a look of ignorance and shuffled away. He knew he had to keep from drawing suspicion to himself if he wanted to help Thomas. What if the captor recognized a similarity between their captive and Andrew? Everyone had said the two favored each other more than the other siblings. Andrew dropped his head down and twisted away as best he could to hide his face from study. Andrew's mind raced as he considered how Thomas' identity came to be known. No doubt someone used the information of Thomas' connection to one of the traitorous signers of the Declaration of Independence as a trade to provide for his own freedom. Andrew's father had drilled it into his children that they not talk about his involvement in the signing of the document, or his work in Congress. Because Abraham Clark was a small farmer, he did not draw a lot of attention to himself. Other signers, like Richard Stockton of

New Jersey, had a large farm and wealth. He became a target for the British. Abraham's common standing actually protected his identity from the British. The Clark children knew that bragging about their father's role would put him, and themselves in danger. Yet, someone had to have identified Thomas Clark to the British.

Andrew knew the British berated the men daily and offered them freedom if they were to turn over important information, or if they would join forces with the British. Andrew figured it had to be a fellow Elizabethtown citizen who knew Thomas Clark was the son of a signer. Momentarily Andrew feared his identity, too, would be revealed. He shook this from his mind as he reasoned that every day the rebels were berated by the British and told that they had been abandoned by their countrymen, and to save themselves they only had to sign on with the British. In the time that Andrew was there he saw very few men agree to this. In fact, their faces would typically fill with hate as they replied, "No!" to their enemies. The prisoners preferred to remain patriotic to the cause. While this made Andrew proud, it also angered him that their loyalty to the cause was not being returned by Washington's efforts in rescuing them from their tormentors.

Andrew shook himself to concentrate. He had to figure out a way of saving Thomas. He didn't know how long the British would torture him. Andrew finished his morning tasks, and then collected his rations of food, such as it was.

The day dragged on with the moving through the rations line, and the exercising the captors demanded the men do. The exercise typically was nothing more than walking laps around the top of the ship while others in the Working Party, or their designees, mopped the decks below. Such movement probably helped many keep alive, but for others it was just another chance of their being bitten by malicious insects, or falling on the slippery decks and succumbing to an injury which would become a death sentence for men imprisoned as they were. Others would take cold and begin fits of coughing, leaving them too weak to spit out the mucus from their lungs. Eventually their lungs would fill with fluid leaving them gasping for breath, and their bodies would surrender to death. For Andrew he was on constant guard against being near those who were overtaken by fits of coughing, or those unstable on their feet that could potentially pull him down with them in a fall. Today he was especially careful as he couldn't wait to get below decks so he could get to Thomas.

At the designated time, Andrew went back into the belly of the rotting Jersey where he worked his way below. He dared not get too close to the locked door as might be a guard within. He found a position nearby and sat himself down to listen for any information which might pass about Thomas' fate.

From above Andrew could hear the iron grate clamping into place. The prisoners were once again locked below decks for the night. "All's well," called out the British sentry.

"All is not well. God damn this ship. God damn the British. And, God damn Washington for not putting an end to this torture," thought Andrew. There was no sound coming from the containment room and Andrew hoped that Thomas had found rest. He closed his eyes as if to block out his hateful existence. Finally, exhaustion overtook Andrew and he fell into a deep and exhausted sleep.

Then
February 1779

Andrew awoke lying on a blanket which was spread out on the ground. It was February and fortunately there had been a break in the weather and the sun, despite the chilly temperatures, was warm on the skin. Andrew's head throbbed as he attempted to sit upright. He looked immediately at his leg, fearful to see if it was still attached. Thankfully it was. His britches had been cut away near the wound and his leg was tightly bound with bandage strips. Blood had seeped through the bandages, but it was no longer bright red. Andrew groggily thought that this was good as the bleeding appeared to have stopped. He momentarily thanked God for his narrow escape from death, and then lowered himself back to the ground. His slight movement caused Andrew to feel a burning sensation rising from his leg. He looked next to him to see if the injured solider next to him was awake.

The man next to him had a wound to his head. "What happened?" asked Andrew.

"Welcome back. I thought you were set to leave us."

"How long was I out?" asked Andrew, not aware of the lapsed time.

"It's been a day. We had a surprise attack from the British who came over from Staten Island. They were joined by some of the local Tories here in town. Can't believe the locals would fight against their fellow New Jersey men." said the soldier.

"Anyone killed," asked Andrew.

"Don't rightly know. Aaron Ogden was gashed in the side by a bayonet, and his father is being court martialed."

"What did he do?" asked Andrew.

"I think it is for not maintaining the troops. He's been gambling, and he hasn't kept the men in line. Too many were absent without furlough and Washington feels this attack could have been averted if proper leadership had been maintained."

Another soldier stopped by Andrew after checking on the injured. "So, you are awake, Clark. How are you feeling?" he asked.

Andrew responded, "A bit groggy and kind of burning up."

"We gave you a stout cup of rum before we stitched that wound. Might have had something else in it which would have put you under a bit. Let me take a look at that leg." The man turned the leg and Andrew bit his lip in pain. "Looks like you've got an infection going on in there. We'll come back and let go some blood which should clear it up."

Andrew took the opportunity to ask about the attack. "Do you know what happened here" asked Andrew as he tried to ignore the growing pain.

The soldier sat on his haunches. "Seems the 42nd and 33rd British regiments, about a thousand men, led by their Lieutenant Colonel Stirling, figured they'd pull a surprise attack on Elizabethtown. They had landed in the middle of the night on the Salt Meadows, about a mile from Crane's ferry. They headed out to Woodruff's farm which is right outside town. The guard at the ferry caught site of them and reported immediately that an invasion was happening."

"They first headed to the governor's house, but thankfully he was not home. His daughters, however, were there. The British took letters which had been intercepted from England, and took only the paperwork before leaving. Fortunately they left the girls unharmed. The British were as mad as hornets for not having the governor as a prisoner and they then went into town and burned down the barracks, the school house, and a blacksmith shop before retreating back to their boats. Our General Maxwell had gathered up some of the troops, not realizing how many Lobsterbacks were involved in the attack. They turned as if to attack and Maxwell had our artillery encourage them to reconsider an attack. Those British turned and headed to their boats, but the men they left behind to guard the boats had moved them about a mile up Newark Bay. They had to slosh through the cold water and mud to get back to their boats."

"Any killed?" asked Andrew.

"One private was killed, and Brigadier Major Ogden and Lieutenant Kencastle were injured as were the two of you, and two others. Ogden was wounded in his right side by a bayonet. We know two of their men were killed, maybe more."

"How did they know where the governor lived?" asked Andrew.

"Seems Cornelius Hetfield, Smith Hetfield and Captain Luce were the Tories who led them into the town.

A chill overcame Andrew and his body shook momentarily as he attempted to process this information. "How could they do this? They are neighbors, and distant relations of my own mother. This war is turning into a civil war among our own people," said Andrew with a sense of disgust. Again, he felt perspiration on his brow and a burning rising from his leg.

Andrew looked around and the camp's barracks were in various stages of ruin. "Anything else around here get destroyed?" Andrew asked, trying to shake off the pain that was beginning to envelop him, and hoping that the family homestead was not touched.

"What I told you was about all they had time to destroy. Thankfully they made a quick retreat when Maxwell began following them. We are fortunate they could not tell that we were far outnumbered by them! It could have turned out very differently."

Andrew tried to move his leg so he could stand. The pain chilled his entire body, and Andrew could see a bright red blotch of blood appearing by the wound.

"Better settle down there, young man," said the soldier. "You are bound to rip out the stitches the doc put in there." Andrew lay down and again a burning heat overcame him. "I'll bring back something to help you with the pain." Andrew watched him as he walked away, and then closed his eyes and blackness overtook him.

Over the next week Andrew slipped in and out of consciousness. Despite the colder temperatures, Andrew's body raged with fever. An infection had set in and Andrew was given a discharge as he was unable to be in active duty. A decision was made to have Andrew loaded onto a wagon and was transported home. Andrew mostly remembered being lifted and pain raging throughout his body. The thump of his body against the wagon floor was welcome relief from the pain of being moved. A blanket was laid across him, and Andrew knew people were talking about him, but all he could make out was that he was being sent home. Fortunately the Clark farm was not too far away. It was one of the Elizabethtown boys who brought Andrew back to the Clark farm. The reality was Andrew was fortunate to be a local boy; otherwise he would have remained in the infirmary which likely would have limited his chances of survival.

As the wagon made its way up the long lane to the Clark home, Abraham, Andrew's younger brother, ran out to see who was arriving. When he looked into the wagon he ran quickly back to the house calling for Sarah. Sarah came out, wiping her hands on her apron and calling orders to the other children and Elizabeth, Thomas's wife, to set up a bed for Andrew. Sarah thanked God every day that harm had not come to her husband or children, and now she thanked God that she would be able to attend Andrew's needs.

A foul odor emitted from the wound and the soiled pants which were removed from Andrew's body. Andrew's flux was identified immediately by Rose, the Negro woman, and Sarah as they tended Andrew. His loose bowel movements were filled with blood and pus. Initially Sarah searched her son's body to convince herself that a bullet had not entered Andrew's body. "No, Miss Sarah. This is flux from his cut. We need to get this diarrhea to stop," said Rose as she gathered the rags they used to clean the wound. "I'll burn these."

"Shouldn't we just wash them and reuse them?" asked Sarah.

"Mam, you do not want to be handling these rags. My mama told me the devil is in such wounds like this, and just like sin, we spread the sin when we touch other parts of a body with the sinful cloth. This young man has 'nuf evil in this wound."

Young Abraham stood by and listened intently. He immediately went off to set up a fire in the yard to burn the soiled rags, and then went in search of other cloth which could be torn into strips to use as bandages on his brother.

Rose pointed out to Sarah that Andrew's mouth was parched. "This boy will die of thirst if we don't get some liquids in him. Between his fever and bowel, he has lost all his body water." Sarah tried to get Andrew to drink water, but he immediately vomited it.

"Maybe we should have a blood-letting?" said Sarah, desperate for Andrew's fever to stop.

Rose shook her head. "I don't think that is a good idea, Mam. If he is already in thirst, why take away his body's blood. If a well is going dry, you don't drain off more water to fix it. That bloodletting would just make him weaker and have less wetness inside his body." Young Abraham stood by and thought this made perfect sense. He looked to his mother who was stressed with trying to decide the best plan of action. Sarah looked deeply into Rose's eyes and found comfort in Rose's confidence. "We'll do it your way, Rose. I pray God help us make the best choices for my boy."

Rose immediately started gathering the supplies needed to tend to Andrew's needs. The first thing she did was take charcoal and scrape it into a cup of water. Andrew was forced to drink this. Sarah had to put her trust in Rose's expertise. Once Andrew feel asleep, Sarah and Rose and young Abraham kept watch over him throughout the night.

Sarah and Rose had a good relationship. Their conversations typically centered on family, children, cooking and religion. In the late hours of the night Rose and Sarah talked about Rose's knowledge of medicine. "How did you come to know some of these remedies?" asked Sarah.

Rose sat winding bandages from the strips that were gathered by Young Abraham. "My momma would tell me the remedies she had learned from her mama. Back across the water where our people came from there would be sickness and the women would gather plants to stop the pain and fever. My momma would hide this from her master because he did not want her practicing witchcraft. Ain't no witchcraft. God gave us the plants to use for food and cure. Every momma would pass down to her children this information. Watched a little boy when I was little die from a blood-letting. My momma cried and begged Master to not do that. He sent her away. I stayed in the room and helped clean up. That little boy died of a fever that would not break. His well just went dry. My momma said it was a needless death." Rose's eyes filled as she recalled the memory. Sarah sat and offered yet another prayer that Andrew's fever would break and she was making the right choices.

Young Abraham nearly attached himself to his brother's side and any voiced need was promptly handled. Sarah, Rose and Abraham spent the next five days bathing Andrew with various herbs identified by Rose, and sought and gathered by Abraham and Rose's two sons, Tobe and Pete. Baum, hysop, wormwood and mallows were among the ingredients collected. The boys went in search of bark and nut-hulls of the Butternut tree. When Abraham and the boys returned with the gathered bark and hulls Rose boiled them making a broth which she forced Andrew to drink. The concoction kept Andrew from vomiting and stopped the dysentery which further strained his strength. It was the first time Sarah saw an improvement in Andrew's condition. Rose also made a poultice of the various herbs and bandaged it against Andrew's wound. Slowly the redness began to fade and Andrew became more and more alert.

One morning Sarah was sitting near the fireplace sewing and Rose was preparing food when Andrew appeared behind them, startling both women. He had only ventured to sit upright in the bed and had stood long enough to have the bedding and his clothing changed before he would return to bed. Young Abraham had cut two canes for him to use to prop himself up during these exercises. On this day, he had moved alone the short distance from the bed to the fireplace. "What is there to eat?" he asked, startling both Sarah and Rose.

"Land sake, child. You about gave me a start!" declared Rose. Sarah quickly moved beside Andrew and guided him to the chair which Rose pulled to the table. Sarah tried to assist him in sitting, but Andrew waved her off.

"I've got it, Mother. Thank you. I feel like I just ran down the drive to the highway, but it feels so good to be upright."

"Are you in pain?" asked Sarah, very concerned that he had moved too much in one day.

"Just pained that I caused this entire ruckus for you, Rose, and the family. I am feeling much better, but I need to start moving more so I can get my strength back. That will happen quicker if I can get some of whatever it is you've been cooking in here!"

The women laughed, shuffled about hanging pots in the fireplace, getting Andrew seated comfortably and pulling a plate of food together. "Where is my little Dr. Abraham?" asked Andrew.

"Your brother is off getting more herbs for Rose."

"Rose, you aren't going to make me keep drinking those potions are you?" laughed Andrew. "I swear I knew I had to get better before you poisoned me with those concoctions!"

"You keep laughing, Mister Andrew, but those remedies got color back in your cheeks and dried up that flooding river from your body."

Andrew looked seriously at Rose. "I want to thank you for all you did for me. I have had plenty of time to think about the shape I was in when I came home and if you hadn't doctored me up, I don't think I'd be walking anywhere."

Rose waved him off, and busied herself with her work, but her face displayed a smile that revealed her pleasure in her success and Andrew's compliment. Sarah looked hard at Andrew.

"You know that you still have to finish healing. There will be no running off to rejoin the Army," said Sarah with a tone of sternness in her voice.

"Mother, I don't think you have to worry for a while. I need to regain my strength before I go making plans to do anything." At that moment Young Abraham walked through the doorway, spotted his brother, and ran toward him. Suddenly he stopped before he embraced him, then thought twice, and extended his hand.

"So nice to see you up and about, Andrew."

Andrew laughed. "What? A handshake? You have become so formal. Should I be expecting a bill for your services, Dr. Abraham? Come here!" Andrew threw his arms open and hugged Abraham while they all shared a good laugh. "Seriously, Abraham. Thank you for being so faithful in tending me. You should really think about doctoring. I believe you have a calling for it!" Young Abraham beamed at the compliment from his brother.

During the next several months, Andrew built his strength and endurance. Each day he would walk around the Clark farm with Abraham. Eventually he would start doing some of the chores and it didn't take too long before his endurance was near to what it was prior to his war injury.

Chapter 6
In the War Again

Now
November 1780

Eventually Andrew's eyes closed and he drifted to a fitful sleep late into the night. His restless sleep was filled with anxious thoughts and fears. This tortured sleep brought with it visions of someone being beaten; feelings of panic in being lost in a dark place and fighting off rats and vermin; panic of footsteps coming toward him and having nowhere to turn. At some point he dreamed he was on the top deck and no one was near. He had carefully moved to the edge of the ship when the British soldiers came running toward him. He let himself fall overboard and he jerked himself awake just as he was about to hit the cold and contaminated water. His body was shaking both with the cold and the fright he had felt. He then remembered that his brother was being held within the dungeon area of the ship. Andrew looked about him as his eyes scanned the utter blackness of this level of the ship. The blackness was constantly filled with the incessant shuffling and movement of prisoners, moaning and screams of the damned, and dependent on the weather, either chattering of teeth, or gasping for a breath of air in the stifling hot weather. Blasphemy was a constant from those who had given up all hope.

Andrew knew he would be called upon to begin his daily task of bringing up the dead, but he carefully moved toward the doorway of the prison which held his brother. No guard was posted. Andrew carefully thought about what to do. He lightly scratched at the door waiting to hear if a guard was within who would yell out to clear the area. Nothing. He scratched a little harder. Nothing. He braced himself, fully anticipating the door to burst open, yet he carefully tapped the door. Nothing. This time he tapped a little louder and quietly voiced, "Thomas?" A pause, then he repeated the action. Andrew furiously thought they might have taken Thomas out of the room at some point during the night. Trying to calm the wild fear within his chest he quieted himself when he heard a sound within the room. Someone was dragging across the floor toward the door.

"Yes?" said a voice which Andrew recognized too well.

Careful not to alert others who were sleeping nearby, Andrew whispered, "It is Andrew."

Thomas said nothing for a moment, then replied, "Don't let anyone know we are related. If they find out, you will also be in here. Are you well?"

Andrew wanted to laugh aloud at being asked if he were well while residing in this hell hole of a ship. He quickly whispered his reply. "Yes, well enough."

Thomas said, "What time of day is it?"

"Near morning," whispered Andrew. It agonized Andrew to hear his brother's once confident voice filled with pain.

"Don't let anyone catch you here. Come back tonight so we can talk."

While Andrew didn't want to leave, he knew Thomas was right. The darkness in the belly of this ship, and the stifling and putrid air around him further revolted him. He would be useless if he, too, was barred inside the prison room. He saw that other men were beginning to move, and Andrew quietly and carefully began to work his way toward the stairs so he would be prepared for the morning work detail. He knew he could tell no one of his brother's presence on the ship, not even Lefton. How strange that he could no longer trust anyone. In his former life he had trusted everyone. It seemed unbelievable that in less than a year's time he had lost all sense of innocence in dealing with others.

Andrew moved up the stairway and beneath the grate which allowed the weak morning light to filter down into the hell-hole. Lefton was already looking for him. "Where have you been? I feared the worse when you didn't bunk down for the night."

"I had gone to the lower level, then felt weak and sat down to rest. The next thing I knew evening had passed. Sorry to have alarmed you," said Andrew, trying to keep his voice sounding as normal as he could.

Lefton cocked his head to the side and looked carefully at Andrew in the faint light. Andrew looked away. He was not a very good liar, and he felt uncomfortable as Lefton studied his face. "Well, we'd best start moving about to our work," said Lefton, not missing the discomfort Andrew showed in his face when questioned. The tension was broken when the captors came to the grate and pulled it free. "Rebels, bring up your dead!" one captor yelled. Andrew and Lefton went silently to their work gathering the dead and dragging them to the top deck.

When it was time for rations, Andrew took his full portion, and then looking around to make certain no one was watching, he pocketed half of his provisions. Again Lefton watched this in curiosity. Typically the two would wolf down their extra portions. It was dangerous business to pocket food as there were many prisoners who would violently pilfer their pockets for the extra food. Hunger made even timid men behave violently. Lefton looked at Andrew and knew something had changed in the past day to cause these changes in Andrew. He would keep an eye out.

Then
May, 1779

As Andrew continued to heal, he was anxious to return to his regiment. His strength and endurance had returned to him, and even though he had received a discharge upon his injury in February of 1779, he wanted to return to fight for the cause. His father, Abraham Clark, had always set such high expectations for his sons by his own example that Andrew knew he could not rest until this war had come to a successful conclusion. To think otherwise was too frightful to even contemplate. Andrew envied his two older brothers who had quickly trained as officers and were fighting for the cause and leading their men in battle. Andrew felt that his father and mother, and even his brothers, had protected him from the reality of war. By the time he was old enough to really participate and vocalize an opinion, his father had left for Philadelphia to serve in the Continental Congress, and his brothers had left to serve in the war. Andrew felt a sense of guilt that he had sneaked off to join up and somehow his near death experience and injuries were punishment for not obeying his father's wishes. Despite this, he felt a need to return to battle now that he was regaining his strength.

It was at the end of May; George Washington had sent orders to John Sullivan that they were to form an expedition to fight against the savages who had attacked both at Wyoming,

Pennsylvania and at Cherry Valley. General Maxell's troops were to be part of the expedition. Andrew listened to the talk of other soldiers who had been left behind because they were still recuperating. It was evident that Washington had enough of the Indian attacks and wanted to put this business behind them. It wasn't enough that they were engaged in a war against Britain, but the attacks by the Indians were causing more dismay than the actual battles being fought. The savagery of the attacks frightened most of the citizens, and even soldiers were anxious about interactions with the Indians, specifically after hearing about the torture soldiers had endured in the Wyoming massacre.

Andrew knew that the Iroquois Confederacy was comprised of The Six Nations. The British had aligned the Mohawks, Cuyugas, Onodagas and the Seneca, and the Americans had pulled in the Oneidas and the Tuscaroras. What had not been considered by either side was that by dividing the Six Nations they had created a civil war within the Iroquois tribes. "No one was thinking about the repercussions in splitting up the Six Nations," said Andrew to a group of soldiers who met at the Terrill Tavern to share talk of the war.

"Agreed," said one of the men. "I don't think anyone really understood how the Iroquois worked as a tribe. We don't understand their culture, and that ignorance is now forcing us to understand it through their actions. It became immediately clear to John Sullivan that a major Indian war was brewing and he had to squash the attacks before it left a permanent problem for any colonist. Now we have to send troops to fight the savages."

Andrew listened to the men talk about the major assaults which had happened last year. Much of the information he had heard before, but new details were shared. The soldier, an older man who, no doubt, had held a position where detail and truthful reporting, began retelling the tale of the Iroquois. "In July, '78, John Butler and the Rangers accompanied by a force of Senecas and Cayugas, led by Sayenqueraghta, made an attack on Pennsylvania's Wyoming Valley in Pennsylvania which was a Patriot grainary and settlement along the Susquehanna near Wilkes-Barre. In this battle they killed nearly 360 armed Patriots." Immediately all the men began talking at once as they shared stories they had heard from friends and family members and other soldiers about the attacks, their voices became slowed and deliberate. It was as if they were reciting the tales of some ancient civilization which was hard to comprehend. The men would gaze forward as if seeing the brutality once again.

Finally one soldier who was filled with a sense of bravado as if he was above being humbled by the beastliness of the stories, spat on the ground and leaned his back in his chair. "Yep, even though we got nearly massacred, we got our retaliation. In September, '78, Colonel Thomas Hartley and 200 soldiers burned nine to twelve Seneca, Delaware and Mingo villages along the Susquehanna River in northeast Pennsylvania."

"That's true. At the same time Butler's Rangers attacked German Flatts in the Mohawk Valley, destroying all the Patriot houses and fields in the area," said another soldier as he rubbed this legless knee as his eyes looked toward a distant and painful memory.

Another soldier with his arm in a sling and a soiled bandage encircling the crown of his head drew the battle lines on the table. "So, this here was where the Indians attacked, but the American retaliation was soon taken by Continental Army units under William Butler and John Cantine, who led in the burning Indian villages at Unadilla and Onaquaga on the Susquehanna River," he said drawing where the army had taken their revenge.

The legless soldier's gaze returned, and he thumped his fist on the table. "That's right. On November 11, that Loyalist Captain Walter Butler led two companies of Butler's Rangers along with about 320 Iroquois led by Cornplanter, including 30 Mohawks led by Joseph Brant, on an assault at Cherry Valley in New York. Indians began to massacre civilians in the village, killing and scalping 16 soldiers and 32 civilians, mostly women and children, and taking 80 captive, half of whom were never returned. Brant was blamed for the attack, even though he tried to stop the rampage. The town was pillaged and destroyed."

The barkeep had been listening closely. "Women and children? Scalped and stolen? What is wrong with the Loyalists?

These are their neighbors and fellow colonists. How in God's merciful heaven could they allow this to happen?" A silence fell as everyone visualized what had occurred.

The original story teller picked up the story and continued, "Now General Washington wanted an end to the brutality by the Iroquois, and he wanted an end to the alliance between the British and the Iroquois. It was when the British moved their military efforts on the southern colonies this year that Washington decided to launch offensive attacks on Fort Niagara. Major General John Sullivan was fifth on the seniority list, was then offered command on March 6, and accepted. Washington's orders to Sullivan made it clear that he wanted the Iroquois threat completely eliminated."

The men continued talking about what this would mean and what the possible outcomes of this expedition would have. Would it be an end to the Indian problems, or would it be yet one more battle which would lead to revenge? Andrew paid for his drink and walked back to the Clark farm thinking about the expedition. His fellow troops were on that mission.

Andrew had heard of the orders that were given to Sullivan. The orders read:

Orders of George Washington to General John Sullivan, at Head-Quarters May 31, 1779

The Expedition you are appointed to command is to be directed against the hostile tribes of the Six Nations of Indians, with their associates and adherents. The immediate objects are the total destruction and devastation of their settlements, and the capture of as many prisoners of every age and sex as possible. It will be essential to ruin their crops now in the ground and prevent their planting more.

I would recommend, that some post in the center of the Indian Country, should be occupied with all expedition, with a sufficient quantity of provisions whence parties should be detached to lay waste all the settlements around, with instructions to do it in the most effectual manner, that the country may not be merely overrun, but destroyed.

But you will not by any means listen to any overture of peace before the total ruinment of their settlements is effected. Our future security will be in their inability to injure us and in the terror with which the severity of the chastisement they receive will inspire them.

The Sullivan Expedition, was to be led by Major General John Sullivan and Brigadier General James Clinton against Loyalists and the four nations of the Iroquois who had sided with the British.

Andrew felt he needed to rejoin his regiment, so he secretly packed up his gear, left a note for his mother, and left in the early morning hours before his mother had awakened for the day. Since Andrew had already missed his regiment's leaving to meet in Easton, he travelled with several other soldiers who were set to rejoin with their troops. Although Andrew wanted to hurry to get back with his troops, he recognized he was still not at full strength. By the time Andrew caught up with his regiment they were already in route to Easton, Pennsylvania. There were supposed to be fifteen regiments in Sullivan's army. Promised enlistments never arrived, and some battalions had suffered so many casualties and enlistments had expired so they were short on men as well. In addition to these shortages, one legion was recalled to the main army before the campaign. Thus the promised 5,000 man army was only 4,000 in number. When Andrew arrived he feared that he would be turned away because he had not formally reenlisted. "No fear, young man," said the captain. "We need every man to be spared to accomplish what we are set out to do."

"What is it we have been assigned to do exactly?" asked Andrew.

"This will be a scorched earth campaign," said the captain.

"What does that mean?" asked Andrew.

"We will be destroying anything that would be of use to the Indians. We will destroy their homes, horses, and food. We will burn their crops. This way they will be totally dependent upon the British and the Redcoats will be left to find resources for them which should limit them in their fighting against us."

Andrew was quickly settled in with his company and warmed himself at the campfire that night. In hushed voices the men retold witness reports of Indiana attacks and the many horrific stories of scalping and massacres. The graphic details made many of the men look downward as they pictured it in their minds. Andrew found it hard to sleep that night, despite his exhaustion from travel. He knew he would be a part of the retaliation against the Indians who had unleashed these nightmares on the white settlers.

The expedition began on June 18, 1779 when the army marched from Easton, Pennsylvania. In the morning the men with Sullivan began their 58 mile march to a camp in Wyoming Valley of Pennsylvania. They arrived on June 23rd. Andrew and the other men had been marching with nearly nothing left in their haversacks as they arrived in camp. Provisions were supposed to be awaiting their arrival. The supplies never arrived. The food was limited to what could be gathered by the men. Despite limited rations, the men remained focused, and very few deserted. Andrew set out with several other men and they searched for anything which would be edible. Fortunately that first day they were able to catch a rabbit which was divided among the three men. This impossible situation continued as the men awaited orders to move again.

On July 31st the troops again headed out to Tioga and arrived there on August 11th. They immediately began building a temporary fort they called Fort Sullivan. Meanwhile Clinton had set up camp at Otsego Lake. Andrew enjoyed the fresh air and the scenery of the area, as well as the comradery he shared with the other men. He heard a great number of stories of the men's home lives, as well as the latest rumors among the soldiers as they pieced together the plans and news of the war.

Sullivan sent a guide, Lt. John Jenkins, with a scouting party to investigate a nearby Indian village. The report came back that the village was active and unaware of the Americans in the area. When word spread through the camp of the scout's report, there were animated speculations as to how Sullivan would plan the attack. In the morning the men stood in quiet anticipation to hear the plan.

Sullivan organized a large portion of the army to move to the site which the scouts had reported were fully operational, however when the troops arrived, they found the village deserted. One of the men Andrew had befriended went out on the scouting mission. When men were sent out to track down those who had left the village they were ambushed. Six men died and nine were wounded. One was the friend Andrew had made. His anger at the Americans not being able to outsmart the Indians was equal to his feelings that the Americans should know the Indians were well versed in warfare. That night the men huddled around their fire and shared stories they had heard of Indian savagery. Andrew knew that the Americans were equally capable of such behavior.

Each day there were more ambushes and more casualties. There was even one night when a rifle discharged accidently and killed a captain and wounded another. The men were becoming much discouraged at being outfoxed by the Indians. The discouragement of the soldiers did not go unnoticed by Sullivan. He knew that they had to start overcoming their own mistakes and thinking that their quest was a simple one. Clearly the Indians were not of such simple mindedness that they would be easily defeated. Sullivan took the discouragement of his troops in stride, but set to work on an aggressive plan in having villages destroyed. Grain and vegetable crops were to be first pilfered, and then the remaining plants were destroyed. This plan would replenish supplies for the Americans, while at the same time destroying the Indian's ability to survive.

Word came early in the morning that Clinton and his troops were on the move. While this news brightened the outlook of Sullivan's men, they also recognized that Clinton's 154 mile trek to bring the supplies stood a strong chance of being sabotaged by the Indians. The men with Sullivan began to fear that Clinton's men would be ambushed and the supplies would be taken, leaving the army without the necessary supplies needed to withstand the length of time it would take to wipe out the Indian villages. Sullivan heard the men's fears, and he, too, feared that the Iroquois might try to attack the two sections of the army as they were divided, so he sent 1,084 men with Brig. Gen. Enoch Poor to escort Clinton's men to Fort Sullivan.

Once Clinton's troops arrived safely at Fort Sullivan on August 22nd, the entire atmosphere of the American army changed. They became more confident, and the needed supplies were certainly welcome. In four days the combined army of 3,500 men and 250 pack horses left Fort Sullivan and marched into the Iroquois territory in western New York. The men felt confident as they surely outnumbered the Iroquois. Andrew found sleep at night easier to meet as he and the other men were well fed and secure.

As the troops marched along the trail, Andrew spent much of his time marveling at the beautiful surroundings. How very ironic, the thought, that such savagery and butchery and hate should happen in such a beautiful territory. Andrew daydreamed about being in this area without threat of war and enjoying the peacefulness of nature. He breathed deeply the fresh air and his eyes continually searched the area, appreciating its beauty. This was a welcome change from the reality of what they were expected to do and the uncertainty of their safety.

The newly combined American troops found it was easy to accomplish their mission. Only one battle occurred and that was at Newtown on August 29th. It was a complete victory for Sullivan's army as the Iroquois quickly retreated when they realized the massive numbers of soldiers.

That night, one of the officers, Major Jeremiah Fogg of the 2nd New Hampshire Regiment, noted in his journal: "The nests are destroyed, but the birds are still on the wing." He shared this statement with his men, and it was repeated throughout the camp. To Andrew and his friends, this news was welcome as there would be less likelihood of having to face the Indians in battle. Despite the expedition objective of ending the frontier war was hoped to be at end, Andrew and the troops feared that the British would continue to rally the Indians into more attacks.

The reality of the retaliation of the Iroquois came to them when news of the September 14th attack riled all the soldiers. Lieutenant Thomas Boyd and Sergeant Michael Parker were scouting the location of Little Beard's town when they were captured and taken prisoners in Little Beard's Town near the Genesee River. Little Beard had Boyd stripped of his clothing then he was bound to a sapling tree. The Indians taunted Boyd by throwing their tomahawks above his head into the tree, and running around him menacing him with their scalping knives. After unnerving Boyd and Parker in this manner, a small incision was made in Boyd's abdomen, and his intestines were drawn out. They tied it to the sapling, then unbound Boyd and marched him around the tree until all of his intestines were wrapped about the tree. They then beheaded him, and Parker, who had witnessed this torture, was also beheaded. Little Bear then led his people into hiding to escape Sullivan's men who were soon to arrive. Upon arrival, troops were told to quickly bury the remains of Boyd and Parker, but the stories of what they witnessed quickly spread throughout the camp. The troops went to sleep that night filled with hatred and fear of what the Indians might do to them.

Christian men were asked to abandon their ethics and destroy property which the Indians needed for survival. The reality of what the Indians had done to Boyd and Parker spurred many to want revenge. For others, like Andrew, all he could think of was what it would take for someone who had lived a life of peaceful existence, to turn to such barbaric behavior. On September 15, Sullivan's men laid total destruction on the Iroquois villages before they would return to Fort Sullivan at the end of the month. Sullivan knew that if Little Beard's people returned to the site once they thought it would be safe, there would not be enough food to save any of them. All they would find would be bare soil and timber, burned houses, and dead and rotting animals.

The constant discussion at evening campfire was the brutality that had been dealt with destroying the villages. Little Beard's tribe had never participated in the battles and had lived peaceably with the colonists and the British. Having been provoked and threatened, they fought back in a most barbaric manner. Andrew thought that he, too, was being forced to abandon his ethics and upbringing and become a savage in the demands of war. Andrew could not handle the wretchedness of what they were asked to do in war, and instead would let his mind drift to the beauty of the country side and the peacefulness of the area.

Sullivan's troops went on to destroy forty Iroquois villages throughout the Finger Lake region of western New York.

Thousands of Iroquois refuges were left without food or shelter. Many would be left to starve or freeze to death during the upcoming winter. Sullivan and Clinton knew that there would be survivors, however they would need to flee for safety in Canada and the Niagara Falls area of the New York territory.

Within three days of returning to Fort Sullivan, the army abandoned the fort to return to Morristown, New Jersey, and go into winter quarters. Sullivan sent a portion of Clinton's brigade directly back to winter quarters by way of Fort Stanwix, under Colonel Peter Gansevoort of the 3rd New York Regiment. On September 27th, near their origination point of Schenectady, the detachment stopped at Teantontalago, the "Lower Mohawk Castle" and carried out orders to arrest every male Mohawk. The soldiers were amazed at the houses and farms of this village. Gansevoort wrote "It is remarked that the Indians live much better than most of the Mohawk River farmers, their houses were very well furnished with all necessary household utensils, plenty of grain, several horses, cows, and wagons". Gansevoort had the male Indian population incarcerated at Albany.

Local white settlers who had become homeless after Iroquois raids, asked that the homes of Gansevoort be turned over to them. They were. Immediately within the camp there were debates by the men that the particular Mohawk group of Lower Mohawk Castle had not been involved in any of the fighting. They had not taken sides, yet they were being imprisoned, and the homes and farms, which some of the men admitted were in much better condition than their own, were taken from them. Most of the men felt that all the Indians should be punished, and the actions were fair and just, but others argued that there were those among the Iroquois who had fought alongside the Patriots. There was a definite division of feelings. Andrew found himself siding with those who felt the army had been unfair. His mind would drift back to discussions his brothers had had of early treatment of the Indians who had been cheated out of their land in order for the white men to establish their own city of Elizabethtown, New Jersey. When he voiced this opinion to some of men of his regiment he was met with such stern reaction from some of the men that he became painfully aware that prejudice was strong and when talking about Indians, any Indians, there would be no changing of mindsets. How strange that they, the Patriots, were fighting because of ill treatment by another clan of their own motherland, yet they could not see their own prejudice when dealing with the Indians who had tried to accommodate the invaders on their lands. It was a mystery which Andrew could not decipher.

The return home was slow because Sullivan suffered various illnesses, and the troops would be stopped to allow for him to recover. Sullivan's return was celebrated as an overwhelming victory for the Americans. It did not take long, however, for the troops to overhear various reports that Washington was not pleased as he had wanted Sullivan to take Fort Niagara as well. Supporters of Sullivan argued that if Washington had made this an objective, he should have outfitted them with the artillery necessary to overtake the fort. As it was, the largest artillery they had were six inch field howitzers which would not be large enough to overtake the fort. Some argued that it was Sullivan's fault that despite the creation of 5,000 Iroquois refugees who would be left to starve or freeze, there continued to be attacks by Iroquois warriors and Loyalists in the Mohawk and Schohanie Valleys.

Andrew was overwhelmed with the debates he heard among the soldiers. Were all Indians bad? In war was man to ignore the Christian ethics which had been instilled in them and name all Indians as the enemies and destroy them? Should women and children be made to suffer because of war? How could God allow such beautiful countryside to be littered with war and destruction? In all of this Andrew realized that he had not officially re-enlisted, and he was under no obligation to remain with his troops. He would have to make a decision as to what he wanted to do. It was obvious this war was nowhere close to being over.

Chapter 7
Back to the Whaleboats

November, 1780
Now

The next morning Andrew awakened from his fitful dreams before the light of day. For the first time he focused on the fact that he had a new purpose and that was to save his brother, Thomas. Andrew recognized that he had lost a tremendous amount of weight while imprisoned, and he could feel his cheekbones poking his thinning skin on his face. Today, however, he felt a new sense of vigor he had not felt since before his imprisonment. Being able to help his brother gave him the motivation to live and stay alive. He tenuously moved to the prison doorway where his brother lay imprisoned, first looking around to make certain no one was too close by to hear him. He was careful not to awaken the other prisoners nearby. "Thomas, can you hear me?" he whispered. He listened closely and heard movement behind the door.

"Andrew? Don't let them see you. Protect yourself. I do not want you to suffer as I am." Thomas' voice was strained and his speech slightly slurred. Andrew thought his lips were probably bruised and cut from the beating he had taken.

"What can I do to help," asked Andrew.

Thomas carefully whispered, "I don't know if anyone can help me. Marriner and I were captured after we captured the vessel called the Snow. It was loaded with British weapons. When we reached Brockleface Inlet in a storm, we were caught. Marriner and I had been imprisoned in the North Church in August. Marriner's luck, however, was cut short as he was tried as a traitor. What no one could quite figure out was that Marriner was released on parole after promising he would no longer serve on the whaleboats."

Andrew absorbed this information. "No doubt he paid off an officer. He certainly would have had the money to do so."

"That's probably true. For me, my imprisonment was bad, but it was tolerable. That didn't last long. While in the prison yard we were exercising when I saw someone pointing me out to one of the British guards. I immediately buried my face, but I was pulled over to where the guard stood. One of the Loyalists from Elizabethtown recognized me and announced that I was a Signer's son. Within two days I was being transferred here. They stopped my rations once I was identified. That was four days ago."

Andrew raised his voice slightly. "You have not been given your rations at all?"

"Quiet Andrew. They will not provide rations until I write a letter to father. I have refused. Father will not renege having signed the document and I would not insult him to ask him to do so."

Andrew thought for a moment. "Thomas, just write the letter. This should satisfy them for the time being and hopefully they will stop this torture. Even if father does not respond immediately, it should give you some relief. Father can ask his fellow delegates to implore Washington to work on your behalf."

"Don't be foolish. Father would never ask for special treatment, and Washington is far too busy to deal with a solitary soldier's mistreatment."

Andrew thought about this for a moment. He wanted to believe his father would do anything to protect his family, but he also knew how loyal his father was to the cause. Certainly his father would do what he could to help them escape this mistreatment. Washington only seemed interested in rescuing the officers, so getting Thomas' condition to the attention of Washington was essential.

Andrew heard movement amongst the men and he cautiously told his brother he would return later. "Eat this," said Andrew as he took a piece of biscuit from his pocket, broke it and rolled it into a cylinder shape, and carefully slid it into the keyhole.

"Thank you, Andrew," said Thomas as he pulled the twisted piece of biscuit through the keyhole. Andrew made several more cylinders of bread and moved them through the keyhole careful not to gum it up. Thomas quickly pulled each piece out and devoured it.

Andrew told him, "I've been imprisoned on this ship since I came back from the Sullivan Expedition. I went in search of you when I heard you were going to captain the whaleboats. That is when they captured me. I've been here for about six months, but it seems like years. You've got to keep your faith to survive here. Promise me you will do that, Thomas."

Thomas quietly said, "I will do that, Andrew. Be careful. You can trust no one."

Andrew quickly moved back toward the stairwell and moved up knowing the grating would be moved and the Working Party would be summoned to begin their morning tasks. Andrew quietly slipped next to Lefton and looked up to watch the grating as it was moved. Lefton had been waiting for him and looked suspiciously at Andrew, but said nothing.

"Rebels, bring up your dead," called the captors as they opened the grating. So another day in hell began.

Andrew looked at who was on duty. Typically the ship was run by the English, Hessians, and sometimes the Loyalists who were called the Refugees. Of all, the captives hated the Refugees the most. The commander of the ship would rarely allow the Refugees to be in charge as each time they rotated to serve on the Jersey, there was a sense of chaos. The prisoners would swear at them, and the Refugees would hold their bayonets in such a way as to form an obstacle for the inmates to pass around. Often the Refugees would offer His Majesty's pardon and favor if the rebels would swear allegiance and fight for the British. This would always bring forth additional chaos. The British had placed the Refugees in charge of the water. Each day about 700 gallons of fresh water was brought onboard. The prisoners were allowed one pint of the fresh water each day. The Refugees would guard it and would often show their power by not allowing some of the prisoners their share. Additional water could be obtained from the butts, which was often filled with sediment and contaminated matter. Andrew knew to drink from this source meant certainty of illness, however there were men desperate to survive and unable to secure water at the hands of the Refugees, so they would take their chances at the butts.

As to the Hessians, although they were feared on land as barbaric soldiers, they were far less offensive on the ships. Andrew remembered his constant fears for his mother and the girls left on the farm as the Hessians were known to plunder the farms and often have their way with the females. Andrew winced as he again felt guilt for having left his mother to deal with the farm on her own. He prayed they were safe and hoped that in his absence there had not been any advances on the farm or on his family.

Lefton and Andrew went to their work, and afterward lined up to receive their full portions of the day's food. Andrew again pocketed half of his biscuit. Lefton walked closely beside him. Andrew looked startled as Lefton continued to walk beside him. Lefton reached over and handed Andrew half of his ration of biscuit. "I don't know what you are doing, but if you need help I am here for you." Andrew was moved, but could not vocalize his thoughts to Lefton, and he merely nodded his thanks. Andrew and Lefton moved to join the others from their mess. Andrew and Lefton always cooked their own portions in their tins as they typically had larger portions than the others so they didn't want to lose this to the rest of their mess. After eating, both Andrew and Lefton walked around the top deck. The late November air was decidedly cold in the New York Harbor. Both Lefton and Andrew held the collars of their coats up to ward off the chilled air. Lefton finally broached the topic with Andrew. "Well, Andrew, are you going to tell me why you were stowing away this food and why you disappear sometimes all night these last few days?"

Andrew hesitated for several minutes before responding. "Lefton, there is a prisoner below decks that they are torturing and starving. I need to at least try to get some food through to him. I cannot believe that the British are so cruel."

"We shouldn't be surprised by what they do. Our experiences have shown us that they have little to no compassion for their fellow human beings. It is hard to look at them and feel as though we have been fellow countrymen to them and they treat us in this way."

"Even so," said Andrew, "starving someone and torturing them is hardly civil treatment. I know that as soldiers we shoot to kill in the fields but to treat prisoners in such a way is inhumane. I heard one officer say that more rebels have died on these prison ships that in the actual battles."

"I'd say that is probably a true statement," said Lefton. "As these winter months are coming upon us it seems we have more and more bodies succumbing to illnesses and smallpox. I think some have just given up their will to live under these conditions. Yesterday after the burial detail came back several of the men brought back turf from the shoreline where they buried the poor fellows. Everyone stood in line to hold the turf to their faces so they could smell the ground we once cherished and wished that we could return to."

"I just feel that I have to provide some assistance to the man being tortured below. I know if I'm caught I can end up with the same fate. So, I'm asking you, Lefton, to not tell anyone what I am doing."

"You know that I will keep your secret and I will try to share at least a portion of my biscuit ration each day. Hopefully the man will be released from his torture either physically or spiritually." At this, Andrew winced. The facial expression did not go unnoticed by Lefton.

As the men continued to exercise, a call was made that Dame Grant was coming aboard. This local townswoman ran a tidy business with the prison ships. She typically would bring aboard the ship items for sale to the prisoners every other day. Since the English had allowed most of the men to keep the contents they carried aboard, some men had money they could use to purchase items to make their life less stressful onboard the ship. Those who had tucked away money benefited from the visits of Dame Grant. Unfortunately, most of the prisoners had no money, so they looked longingly at the small bags of tea, tobacco, needles and thread, fruit, and soft bread which she sold at cost. Andrew considered what he could procure to help his brother. The problem, of course, was that it would need to fit through a keyhole as that was the only way Thomas could access it. Andrew asked Dame Grant for ground up herbs which would serve as pain killers. She provided him with a small bag, which Andrew secreted into his pocket. He would mix it in with the biscuit and this should, at least, provide Thomas some relief from his pain. It was a small matter, but it gave Andrew a huge sense of accomplishment that he would be able to provide some assistance to his brother.

The British never allowed men to come onboard, however Dame Grant was given permission. In the past Elizabeth Burgin had been given permission to board the Jersey. Burgin came with supplies and food to distribute to prisoners on the various ships, especially the Jersey. Andrew had never seen her but he had heard that the British had declared her to be a traitor and were on the lookout for her. Andrew heard the story that Burgin was approached by American officers and asked to spread the word to officers captured on the Jersey that an escape was being planned. The winter of '79 was brutal and the water surrounding the ships was frozen solid. Burgin set to work and on the given night the escape happened and 200 officers who were housed in a room above the dreaded hell hole, jumped from the Jersey onto the frozen ice and escaped. The guards were overcome and the officers quietly escaped by cover of darkness. Once the British figured out what had happened, they became even more cautious of any outsider coming onboard. Dame Grant always gave token payment to the officers on duty which allowed her to continue her business. For this, Andrew was thankful. He was also thankful to hear that Elizabeth Burgin escaped and was in hiding, much to the chagrin of the British! Funny how it was women who tried to help the Americans. He imagined that if his mother were in a position to help, she would be the kind of woman who would work to rescue soldiers on this ship. The thought of his mother warmed Andrew and made the constant torment of his mind subside.

The warmth Andrew felt surprisingly lasted for several hours. He continued to feel a sense of purpose with his trying to rescue Thomas, and knowing there were at least some people, albeit women, who worked to save them. He had a sense of thanksgiving. That evening he prayed long and hard for the first time in months. He had long given up on prayer as none of his prayers were ever answered. He now said all the prayers he had memorized as a child, and created more of his own. He slept with fewer night terrors that night.

Then
December, 1779

The return to New Jersey after the Sullivan Expedition, as everyone was calling it, was surprisingly quiet. Andrew and the others spent many of their hours reflecting as they returned to their familiar surroundings. One thing was certain, Andrew felt in no hurry to rejoin the Continental Army. Upon returning to Elizabethtown with the first New Jersey Regiment at the end of 1779, Andrew visited his home but made it known to his mother that he would quickly be leaving again. This time Andrew felt he needed to once again join the whale boats as this would afford him the opportunity to stay closer to home but at the same time allowing him a chance to make some extra money which would assist him in supporting his family.

A letter had arrived home from his brother Thomas. Thomas was sent to help organize the whaleboats into a more structured organization in order to help the Continental Army more efficiently. Washington had not approved of the way the whaleboats did their business in the past, so Thomas and others were sent to serve as captains of the whaleboats and bring order and decorum to their efforts at winning the war. Thomas was to be a captain alongside Capt. William Marriner. Andrew wanted to meet up with his brother and serve under him.

Sarah could not persuade Andrew to not go. He was a young man and had already seen the horrors of war. She gathered supplies for him and sewed into the hem of his shirt what little money they had reassuring him that they would be able to sell what they made off the farm to sustain themselves. Andrew promised that he would send money home as soon as he was established. Word was that Thomas was stationed in New York. Within days Andrew and several other local men set out to join the whaleboat captains. Andrew already knew Captain Marriner from his prior work with the whaleboats. He would attempt to join up with Thomas, but if not, he would join up with Captain Marriner. Andrew was comfortable in this decision and felt this was good use of his talents. Certainly if he were teamed up with his brother and Marriner, they could bring this war closer to an end.

Travel was risky as the British were still stationed on Staten Island. To get to New York Andrew and the others had to work their way around the British troops that were all nearby. Fortunately Andrew and the other men grew up in this area so they knew many of the by-passes, trails and streams, allowing them to travel somewhat safely. Andrew and his fellow travelers finally arrived nearer Long Island, safely out of view from the British ships. They met up with several other men who were also attempting to join with Marriner and Clark.

The morning brought an unusually clear day. Andrew took the opportunity to stand within the cover of a clump of trees to look out over the Wallabout Bay. He could make out several ships of disrepair. Several other men walked up behind him. "Best watch out for those ships in the Wallabout," said one of the men.

"What are these ships?" asked Andrew. His eyes looked at the poor excuses of British ships. None had sails, and what he could tell of the ship closest to them was that they were not in good repair. He could see a number of ships off in the distance.

"They are the hospital ships and prison ships. At one time the British used all of these as hospital ships after taking them out of their navy, but they have now converted these ruined remnants of their Navy to be prison ships. There are three hospital ships now in use: The Scorpion, the Strombolo, and the Hunter. The Hunter seems to be a place for the doctors to stay, and where medical supplies are held. I don't know how many of the sick are actually carted off to that particular ship. I have heard tell of Old David Sprout, who's the Commissioner of Prisoners, works on that ship. He gets great satisfaction in telling any prisoners taken to the hospital ships that they will eventually land on the prison ships. He points them out to the prisoners, "There, rebels, are the cages for you!"

"See that ship there?" said another man. "That one there is the Old Jersey. Several of the men that I traveled with talked about how below decks on the Old Jersey looked like a scene out of Dante's Inferno. I heard a story that on the Jersey there were about a half dozen men they called 'nurses' but were actually nothing more than common thieves. The sick were held in an upper deck where they built bunks for them to stay while they healed, were treated, or were readied for transport to the hospital ships, but most were sent to the shore for burial. Prisoners are allowed to keep their possessions when imprisoned on the ships, but the nurses make it a point to steal and pick their pockets while they are under their care. They did little to help them and instead of them being transferred to the hospital ships, they were transferred to the shore for a shallow grave. The English want to take all of the rebel seamen off of our waters and lock them up and kill them in a most inhumane manner."

Another man shared, "By late '76, the British had taken over 4,000 prisoners after capturing Fort Washington. They then started arresting private citizens who they suspected of helping with the rebellion. Eventually their numbers added up to about 5,000 prisoners. They quickly ran out of room in the regular jail houses. They started converting other spaces into prisons. Three large sugar houses, several churches, a hospital and even Columbia College were turned into prisons for the captured Americans."

"It didn't take long for small pox to spread, as well as other diseases which spread when men are put into inhumane conditions. There was never enough food, clothing or medicine for the prisoners. Perhaps the lucky ones were those who faced the gallows run by the Cunningham, the Provost. He looked for any reason to rid the prisons of those who proved to be problematic. It wasn't long after that when they started pulling in the old hospital ships, which were not fit for human habitation, and put them into service as prison ships."

"Don't forget the Whitby which was the first prison ship anchored in the Wallabout. Rumors quickly came to shore that there were no doctors to attend the sick, and the men suffered from lack of food, bad water and savage punishments. Within two months the shore was filled with graves of the dead who had finally reached salvation from their mistreatment on the Whitby. The Whitby was finally burned down when a replacement ship arrived to take over the prisoners. Stories came back to us that the most severely ill were left on the ship to perish in the fire." The story teller, as if overwhelmed by the vision created from his retelling of the story, sunk down in the sands to sit and reflect on the treatment of his fellow countrymen.

Andrew sat thinking about the fate of those who were imprisoned. Certainly the British would want to use the prisoners for their own good, exchanging them for those English captured by the Americans. He had already heard stories of the old Jersey. They called it "Hell." Some said that the Jersey held up to 1000 prisoners on board and that the death rate was unnaturally high. Andrew shook his head in disgust. How could their motherland treat its descendants so despicably? Where was God?

Andrew was nudged by the other men out of his reflections, and he turned to pack up his gear and to move on to where they hoped to meet up with Thomas or Captain Marriner. As the men walked, they quietly shared stories of both Marriner and Thomas Clark. Andrew was careful not to identify him as his brother. He had long learned the art of secrecy in order to keep his family safe from interrogation or retribution for the role his father played in starting this war.

"What do you know about this Thomas Clark?" one of the men asked in general to the others. "How is it that he is with the whaleboats? I heard he was with the artillery."

Andrew carefully answered the question, without identifying Thomas as his sibling. "Clark was the First Lieutenant of the Continental Army in '76. He then became Captain and commanded at Blazing Star for near five months. He was with Washington at the Battle of Trenton, and at the Battle of Princeton a couple weeks after that."

"He fought at Trenton? That is pretty impressive. You know that only one third of the army made it across the Delaware because of all the ice on the river. Those that made it across certainly turned around this war."

Andrew waited until everyone shared their stories about people they knew who had fought at Trenton, or were stranded on the shores of the Delaware, unable to cross, or those who marched into Princeton. Once the commentary stopped, Andrew continued. "He then went on to become Captain of Artillery in the Continental Army and fought at Brandywine, Germantown, and Monmouth. "

A general murmur of admiration was heard among the men. They were quick to recognize soldiers who had fought in the major battles. One soldier piped in, "I'll bet you never heard this story! I heard that Captain Clark was an expert horseman."

"That's true," said Andrew. "He knew the whole countryside around Elizabethtown, and he had a horse which no one could handle except him."

"That's part of the story I heard. I heard he was put on scout duty for General Washington. He got captured two times. The first time he and his horse were turned over to the New Brunswick sugar house jail. No one could handle his horses better than he, so he was released to care for the animals. He was under heavy guard the whole time. Now Thomas was charged with being a spy, and that was punishable by death. The British soldier put in charge of Thomas handling the horses took a liking to Captain Clark because he was so amiable. Together they put up a plan for Clark to escape. The guard told Captain Clark to let his horse get loose and head toward the opposite shore while the British officer distracted the other guards. Clark signaled his horse to move to the opposite shore, and then he quietly slipped into the water. By the time the British officers saw what was happening, Clark and his horse had gotten safely out of range. The British shot at them and tried to follow, but Clark and his horse were too fast and easily escaped."

The men all laughed and slapped each other on the back as they pictured the rebel officer outsmarting the British officers. Andrew had never heard this story, but his heart filled with admiration for his brother who was so very personable. He could see Thomas befriending someone, even an enemy, in order to escape.

The men traveled on, determined to meet up with Thomas Clark and Marriner.

Chapter 8
The Meeting of Now and Then

December, 1780
Now

The grating entombing the inmates was removed earlier than usual. The winter sunrise was hours from rising. "Rebels, bring up your dead and be quick about it," shouted the English guard. Andrew roused himself and knew something was amiss. He and Lefton met and quickly scoured the decks to bring up the dead. Andrew and Lefton stomped their feet and beat their hands against their coats to get the blood moving. Such was their only means of warming themselves up in the cold winter air. Once the two had removed the dead from below decks, a command that all the rebels were made to gather their belongings and move to the top deck quickly. Each prisoner looked startled as he tried to figure out what was happening. The Working Party was sent to do their duties below decks and warned to do an especially good job cleaning the decks. The provisions room was not ready to distribute provisions, and the cook had not gotten the Great Copper prepared for cooking. Andrew and Lefton kept looking around to see why their schedule had been changed. The distribution of rations ended up being over two hours later than normal and the men suffered in the frigid air. The top deck was being scrubbed, which was pointless as the water quickly froze. Finally, the men were summoned to line up for rations. The men were lining up with their mess when everyone was told to stand back.

"Maybe it is a late Christmas present," said one of the prisoners. "Maybe the war is over and we are about to be released." He sounded sarcastic, but there was a hint of hope within his voice.

"Yes, and maybe we were to ready this ship in all its cleanliness to be sailed back to Jolly Olde England," said another man. Although there was a short laugh at the gallows humor, the air was still baited with expectation as to what was happening.

The British were quickly moving to stand at attention for an oncoming guest to the ship. Andrew looked to see who was arriving and he did not recognize the guest. He looked at Lefton and raised his eyebrows. "Good God, it's Provost Marshal Cunningham," whispered Lefton. Andrew had heard the name before. He had also heard that Cunningham was cruel and inhumane when dealing with the prisoners. Obviously the crew wanted to make a good impression by having the ship cleaned and in order before his appearance.

Cunningham stepped onto the ship and the rebels were warned to be silent. Several of the prisoners began shouting, "Cunningham! Does General Washington know you are treating us unfairly? We demand that you allow him to see how we are treated on this ship."

Cunningham stopped and turned. He then nodded his head to two of the guards attending him, and they dragged the two shouters out to the center of the deck, stripped off their shirts and proceeded to flog them. One guard would strike on one side, one on the other. As the blood sprayed, a mist of heat escaped, and as the blood hit the deck, it froze in a reddish splotch. The prisoners tried to not cry out, but Cunningham was not putting an end to their suffering until one cried, "Mercy. Have mercy."

Cunningham looked around at the rest of the prisoners and asked, "Anyone else want me to deliver messages to your Mr. Washington?" Cunningham had purposefully pronounced "Mister," rather than "General," half expecting someone to challenge him. No one did. Andrew looked at him with hatred in his heart. The prisoners outnumbered the British on this ship and it would have been easy to overtake them, however none of the prisoners had the strength or the power to do so. Instead they stood with their heads bowed in submission.

After several minutes of silence, one man said quietly,

but loud enough to be heard, "That's General Washington." Cunningham's head snapped around to see who had mouthed this outburst. The guards quickly grabbed the offender and pulled him in front of Cunningham.

"Obviously you do not understand the protocols of the King. Washington cannot be a 'general' as he himself is a rebel of the King. He is a traitor and a rebel, but he is certainly not an officer, let alone a general. King George does not recognize colonists as being anything other than royal subjects to him. Those who are not or declare themselves to be officers in an organization set to disgrace him, well; they will be marked for the gallows." Cunningham nodded toward the officers and they stripped the man of his shirt, tied him to one of the barrels on the deck, and flogged him. Blood sprayed those standing near and soon the man's back was a mass of rips and tears. Finally the man passed out, and Cunningham ordered a bucket of salt water to be poured on him. The salt brought the prisoner to consciousness and he screamed in pain. Cunningham again had him brought before him. "Any more comments you care to make?" One of the soldiers grabbed the man by the hair and yanked his head back. The man said nothing. "I thought not." Cunningham jerked his head toward the stairwell into the hell hole and the soldiers pulled the man to the hole and let him fall below decks. Those on deck stood shock still, their eyes watching the open hole, wishing for a miraculous resurrection. There was none.

The hated provost then turned and said, "Now, then, where is the Clark man?" Andrew's heart stopped. The guards nodded to below decks. Bring him to my cabin," said Cunningham as he moved toward the cabin area. "The rest of you, resume your morning rituals."

Two officers went below decks to retrieve Thomas. Armed guards stood over the opening to the ladders with menacing looks that no one should try to follow. Andrew felt his stomach turn to ice and he looked at Lefton.

"Is that who you have been feeding?" Lefton quietly asked.

Andrew nodded. "Why do you suppose Cunningham came here to see him?" Lefton shrugged and shook his head.

"Maybe he has information that Cunningham wants. Andrew, don't look so painfully interested. You will draw attention to yourself. We need to go about our tasks." Andrew nodded, and followed Lefton, but his mind could not focus on anything except what Cunningham would be doing with his brother.

The men gathered together in their mess and the topic of Cunningham's reputation was discussed. "You know, said one of the men, in '76 it was Cunningham who executed Nathan Hale. The British were working to capture the harbor area of Staten Island so they could control New York. Their goal was to have British troops move from Canada down the Hudson so they could separate New England from the rest of the colonies."

Another man picked up the story. "It was working too, as in August a troop of British and Hessian soldiers crossed into lower New York bay area and took over Long Island, forcing Washington and his troops to retreat to Manhattan Island, and in September he was forced to leave New York City to the British.'

"How did Nathan Hale play into this?" asked one of the group.

"Young Captain Hale, who was from Coventry, Connecticut and was a Yale educated school teacher before the war, volunteered to cross into Long Island to spy, disguised as a Dutch schoolteacher. He had traveled behind the lines gathering information, and when the British were setting fire to New York City, Hale was trying to cross back to the Colonial troops. That's when he was captured. The report to Howe included information that Hale had sketches of the fortifications and made notations of where they were specifically located. This was used as documentation of his being a spy. General Howe ordered Hale to be executed. The task was turned over to Cunningham who, being a heartless man, was quite capable to handling the execution. When Hale asked to be attended to by a clergyman, Cunningham refused. When Hale asked for a Bible, Cunningham refused this as well. A British officer, Captain Montressor, provided paper and pen to Hale as Cunningham made preparations for the hanging. Hale wrote two letters, one to his mother and one to a fellow officer. His dying words were, 'I only regret that I have but one life to give to for my country.'"

"Howe then sent a British soldier who had witnessed the writing of the letters and the hanging of Hale to seek Washington, under a flag of truce, to report what had been done to their officer. Cunningham's intent was to show Washington the British meant business and would not tolerate further acts of treason, like Hale had done. What Hale could not have predicted was that the report provided an opposite effect. Immediately, young Hale was regarded as a war hero and the story of his bravery when facing death became the stories for all the troops. His dying words became a battle call for the Patriots." The storyteller bowed his head, as if paying homage to the war hero.

Andrew had listened closely, but what his mind held to was how Cunningham disregarded the last requests of Hale, even denying him a clergyman or Bible. Now this same man was interrogating his brother.

Lefton urged Andrew to act normally and go about their regular routines so they did not draw attention to themselves. "You will be of little use to that prisoner if you are under suspicion by these guards or by Cunningham." Andrew and Lefton secured and cooked their food, and stood as closely to the fire as they could to warm themselves. Andrew pocketed half of his and Lefton's biscuits, and transferred his portion of rum to his small flask. Andrew kept an eye on the opening to watch for Cunningham's return. It was nearly four hours before Cunningham climbed to the top deck and spoke quietly to the British officers. He then removed himself from the Jersey. The prisoners only had a few more hours of fresh air before they were sent with all their gear to go below.

Andrew quietly worked his way as close to the place where Cunningham had interrogated Thomas. He busied himself as close to the door as he could manage so he could hear any communications made with the guards on the Jersey.

"He finally signed," said one of the guards. "It took some gentle persuading, but he signed. " His guards chuckled at the word "gentle."

"That makes seven of the Masters of Whaleboats who signed. I am to address this envelope to the Honorable Congress at Philadelphia to the attention of the Honorable Abraham Clark. The return address is from the Provost Condemned Room, dated December 28, 1780. This ought to get their attention. "Andrew could hear movement inside the room and the shuffling of a chair as someone stood. "Remember, no rations for the Clark man below decks." Andrew's face twisted with hatred. Lefton was standing nearby and immediately pulled Andrew around, just in time as the British officer exited the room with the letter in his hands.

"Stop. Stop now!" whispered Lefton. "Come with me immediately. You are not going to be happy until you get flogged, or you end up in that dungeon below decks." Andrew allowed himself to be moved and kept his face lowered so no one could witness the pent up rage he was feeling inside.

The officer left the ship and Andrew walked in a daze, replaying in his head what he had heard. The December chill while they were forced to stay above had definitely put a chill in the men. Many were anxious to move below decks; however they knew that with the shortened daylight hours, their internment below decks would seem like an eternity. Andrew wasted no time in moving quickly below decks to the pitch black hole where Thomas was imprisoned. He felt his way to the dungeon door and listened closely. He listened, but thought there was no sound inside. Perhaps they had moved him somewhere else on the ship? Perhaps they had killed him? Perhaps he was within the dungeon, but dead from the abuses he suffered. Andrew's wild imagining was taking on a life of its own when he heard a moaning inside the room. "Thomas?" whispered Andrew. "Thomas?" No answer. After what seemed like hours, but in reality was only minutes, Andrew heard a retching sound. He knew Thomas had not eaten anything of substance, so it would only be bile produced in this dry heaving. Andrew whispered again. "Thomas. Come to the door. Take this biscuit." Andrew rolled the biscuit into a tight roll, and carefully pushed it through the keyhole, just enough that it would not drop to the floor on the other side. "Thomas. Please, come to the door."

Eventually Andrew could hear Thomas dragging himself across the floor toward the door. It had to have been a great effort as he heard the deep breathing of Thomas as he exerted himself. 'Reach up to the keyhole. Take the bread, Andrew pleaded. Finally, Andrew could feel the biscuit being pulled through the hole. He quickly prepared another roll and carefully inserted it. This process continued until Andrew was close to running out of bread. The last piece he dipped into the rum and quickly pushed it into the keyhole before it became too soggy to push through.

"Thank you, Andrew," said a shaky voice from behind the door. "Forgive me. I am weak and could not withstand Cunningham's demands."

"Don't worry about that, Thomas. Just rest. Sleep. Get stronger. We must wait to hear what happens in Congress."

"Nothing will happen, Andrew. Nothing can happen. I was made to ask father to renege on his signing the document and to pledge allegiance to the King. I was made to sign a document that had been signed by six other whaleboat captains telling Congress of the treatment we were receiving and our only hope was for them to surrender. Father will not do this, nor would I want him to, and Congress will not accept this blackmail that Cunningham has masterminded."

Andrew was stunned. How could his brother believe that their father would not push for his release; for their release? Andrew sat outside the door and put his mind toward prayer.

His prayers begged that his father, Congress and Washington would react favorably toward need of release from this hell ship. Andrew prayed that Cunningham would be punished severely for his treatment of Thomas. He prayed that this damned war would be over. "Thomas, pray with me," said Andrew.

Thomas' voice was sad as he replied. "I have lost my faith in prayers. Prayers, Andrew? I'm beginning to think God has abandoned us in this war. We hear reports that the British raid and burn our homes. The Hessians rape the women and even young girls. Our landscape is covered with blood and ruin."

Andrew bit the back of his hand as he heard his brother's response. He now feared what may have happened to his own mother and sisters. Where was God? Why wasn't he protecting them? Andrew drank the last of his rum and eventually nightmares and sleep became one.

Then
April, 1780

Andrew and the other men continued their march toward where the whaleboats were to be harbored. They were constantly on the alert as there was heavy British activity in the Long Island harbor area. Andrew knew that both Marriner and Thomas would have their boats secreted in the tributaries which were hidden away from the common paths. The trick would be finding them.

The army had dismissed the nine-month soldiers in March. This had served to lessen the number of troops serving in the New Jersey regiments, eliminating about 500 men from serving. Many of the men who wanted to serve sought out other opportunities, and many had decided to join the whaleboats. Part of the problem was that there was no money to pay for the troops. Another was there was no money to procure the necessary supplies to outfit the soldiers with clothing and food. The promise of the Whaleboat service was the possibility of gaining income from the spoils of war. Many of those who sought to join the privateers in the whaleboat service reasoned that as much as Washington disliked the militias and the privateers, he would have to recognize that they did, indeed, support the cause at virtually no cost to the Continental Army. The reality, however, was that nearly half of those in this service would be captured. The other reality was that the captives would be transported to the prison ships which had a death toll which far exceeded anything seen on the battlefields. Regardless, the men felt the gamble of serving on the whaleboats was worth the risks.

Andrew and his fellow travelers finally met up with Marriner's men. Andrew decided he would stay with Marriner as he wasn't certain where to find Thomas at this point. Marriner quickly welcomed the men and began training

the men in how to best work the whaleboats. When he saw
Andrew he immediately welcomed him. He was glad he had a
seasoned and experienced man to join this work.

"What have you been doing, Andrew?" asked Marriner.

"A little bit of everything. After leaving you, I joined the
Continental Army. I got shot and went home to recuperate.
I then left again to join up with Sullivan in the Finger Lakes
area of New York."

"Beautiful country there," said Marriner. "I heard about
the scorched land campaign. Effective, but you have to have
quite the backbone to have carried off that quest."

Andrew nodded, but said nothing. "Glad to see you back
in the whale boating. Your brother has been quite busy up
here. We try to spread out so our work is not observable by
the British. I find the men who join up here either become
satisfied with one large take and leave with money in their
pockets, or they become careless and clumsy and get caught
and hauled off to the prison ships. I am constantly training
new men for this duty."

"My plan is to stick it out. I'd eventually like to meet up
with Thomas, but for now I will work with you."

"Good man! We have a raid scheduled tonight. I am only
taking nine men with me. Want to join me?"

"Certainly," said Andrew, happy to be put to work.

When darkness fell on April 18, 1780, Mariner and nine
men went down the Raritan River silently in one whaleboat.

They crossed the bay to Sandy Hook. There they saw a three decker British ship named the Volcano. Next to it was a captured American brig named the Blacksnake which had been overtaken by the British and kept as a prize. The prized brig, Blacksnake, should have been protected by the Volcano, however Marriner had other plans. He was certain he could capture it and take it back for their own cause.

Marriner's boat moved silently in the water. They were undetected as they moved next to the Blacksnake. It brig was manned by Captain Cornelius French and twenty men. The crew was asleep and taken by surprise when Marriner and his men swarmed over the counter of the ship. Marriner's men disarmed the lookout and battened down the hatches so the crew would be imprisoned below deck. All of this happened within seconds and in complete silence. The adrenalin in Andrew's blood was pumping fiercely and he worked aptly at cutting the anchor cable and helping to shake out the sail. Marriner's men worked so quietly that the crew of the Volcano never awakened while Marriner and his crew quickly maneuvered the Blacksnake away from the Volcano.

Marriner and his crew celebrated their victory. They immediately planned how they would use the Blacksnake in continuing their streak of good luck. The Blacksnake had eight-pounder cannons which would appear to be frightening to any ship they approached. What the British didn't know was that there were only nine men sailing it, not enough to even work its sails. Marriner banked on the British not knowing he only had a skeletal crew operating the ship. He hoped his strategy would work.

Marriner soon spotted the British Morning Star in the darkness. The British ship was lightly armed but outfitted with a crew of thirty three men commanded by Captain Richard Campbell. Marriner decided to attack. Once again Marriner and his men silently maneuvered their boat through the water and brought the Blacksnake broadside, surprising Campbell and his crew. At first Campbell and the crew surrendered. However, once Campbell realized they were overtaken by only nine men, he signaled for his men to fight back. Marriner's men showed no mercy. Campbell and several men were quickly cut down and the rest quickly surrendered a second time. Marriner now had his whaleboat, the Blacksnake and the Morning Star, fifty prisoners, and all the supplies the newly conquered ships held.

"All right men, we need to get these ships into Cranberry Inlet and head to Tom's River. We need to do this as quickly as possible before the British realize these boats are gone and the prisoners below have time to plot a takeover." Every man quickly and efficiently worked the three boats and was fast in moving them to their destination.

Once safe, the men left behind on shore quickly joined the work. They gathered the prisoners to take them for prisoner exchange while Marriner and his nine crewmen took a well-deserved rest. The other men unloaded supplies, ammunition, and determined what would be sold and what would be saved for future endeavors. Soon their pockets were filled with their share of the winnings and those who had been on the whaleboat received the largest cut. Andrew was quite happy. He would have money sent back to his mother and he would hold onto a small amount for future use which he sewed into his coat.

Andrew remained with Marriner for the next month. He knew Thomas was now a Captain on one of the whaleboats, and could certainly use additional men who knew their way around the canals and rivers. Washington wanted to put an end to the privateers and wanted his own men running the whaleboats in a more structured naval structure. Andrew would go in search of Thomas. It was already the end of spring and summer was fast approaching. After traveling all night, Andrew selected an area in a wooded area to sleep. His exhausted body fell into a deep sleep. His mind was filled with memories of the days before the war, when his family was whole. The dream was broken when he heard a twig snapping underfoot. He jerked awake and reached for his musket, but it was gone. He looked around him and found he was surrounded by British soldiers who were aiming their rifles at him. Andrew became a prisoner.

Andrew and other rebels who had been gathered near the Long Island bay area were loaded onto a boat to be imprisoned.

A Patriot's Price

Andrew looked around to see where he was heading. It was the Jersey. "No!" he cried out loudly. One of the soldiers hit Andrew with his musket butt. "Quiet, Rebel. You will soon find your cage on the Jersey." Andrew's head spun and his senses blacked out.

Part Two
Hell and its Consequences

Chapter 9
A Purpose in the Madness
January, 1781

The first months of 1781 in the Long Island bay was freezing cold. Andrew continued to do his assigned duty of body removal for the Working Party. Each day the routine was followed. Andrew quickly moved beside Lefton to complete their work, gather their rations, exercise, and when ordered below decks he would work toward saving Thomas. Each day he went below decks to push a portion of his biscuit through the keyhole to his brother. Thomas's coughing at first was occasional, but Andrew recognized that the fits were lasting longer and Thomas' gasping for air sounded more and more excruciating. Andrew tried to encourage Thomas to stand and move about. Thomas would comply during his daily time with Andrew which gave Andrew hope that his brother would survive. For Thomas, each day his dark prison would envelope him, depress him, discourage him, but when Andrew arrived he knew companionship and felt his connection to reality.

Andrew was fearful Thomas' lungs would fill with fluid. He had witnessed countless other prisoners who would fall into fits of coughing, and they would sink into despair, refusing to push themselves to move around. Those prisoners would eventually stop rising and walking, and within days Andrew and Lefton would haul their bodies to the forecastle for removal. Andrew refused to let Thomas fall into this same fate. Andrew's sole purpose in living was to try to rescue his brother. "Stand up, Thomas. You must stand up and move about the room. Trust me. This will save your life."

"I know," said Thomas. "I know. It is hard to do and I feel so weak."

"Picture yourself walking toward Elizabeth and little Jonathan. Picture your being able to reach them. You have to walk." The image proved to give Thomas the motivation he needed to push himself out of his despair and to pace about the room. The pain in his belly from hunger would subside as his blood would circulate during this exertion. Andrew felt satisfied that Thomas had fought off death another day.

Each morning when Andrew went to the top deck, he would look to see if Cunningham or his men would return with a response from Congress. Nothing. How long could it possibly take for his father to respond? Certainly he would ask Congress to rescue Thomas. What Andrew could not know was that the letters sent to Congress had prompted action. Andrew did not know that the letter sent by Thomas to their father was not going to be addressed. Abra had made the decision to not ask Congress to act upon his son's behalf. He had shared the letter with Reverend Witherspoon and the other delegates from New Jersey, but he said he could not ask for special treatment for Thomas as other fathers had no recourse to save their sons from British mistreatment. Abra had sunk into a terrible depression over this decision, and was seen by his roommate kneeling in hard prayer with hopes for divine intervention on his son's behalf. Witherspoon and the others did not feel that Thomas was being treated like other prisoners, that this mistreatment was a direct attack on those of them who had specifically signed the Declaration of Independence. Witherspoon and the others secretly took the letter which Abra had slipped into his Bible, and decided to share it with others in Congress. It had its effect on them since they, as Congressmen, could become a target of the British and their families could be subjected to such punishments. Congress demanded that action be taken to stop the mistreatment of American prisoners, and specifically to stop the torture of Thomas Clark.

There was already history of George Washington reprimanding General Howe about the mistreatment of American seamen. He had written,

I am under the disagreeable necessity of troubling your Lordship with a letter almost wholly on the subject of the cruel treatment which our officers and men in the Naval

Department, who are unhappy enough to fall into your hands received on board the Prison ships in the harbor of New York. From the opinion I entertain of your Lordship's humanity I will not suppose that you are privy of proceedings of so cruel and unjustifiable a nature and I hope that upon making the proper inquiry you will have the matter so regulated that the unhappy persons whose lot is captivity may not, in the future, have the misery of cold, disease and famine added to their other misfortunes. You may call us Rebels, and say we deserve no better treatment, but remember, my Lord, that we still have feelings as keen and sensible as Loyalists and will if forced to, most assuredly retaliate upon those upon whom we look as the unjust invaders of our rights, liberties and properties. I should not have said this much, but injured countrymen have long called upon me to endeavor to obtain redress of their grievances, and I should think, myself, as culpable as those who inflicted such severities, were I to continue silent.

Now Washington once again petitioned a warning to Howe. On January 5, 1781, the Continental Congress resolved that there should be retaliation against British captives to match that which was happening to Captain Clark and other officers. The topic of the mistreatment of the American prisoners was becoming a topic which was becoming a household conversation. A Philadelphia journal published an eye witness account of the intolerable conditions onboard the Jersey. Old Daniel

Sproat quickly defended the treatment of the prisoners and the conditions on the prison ships as being fine. He stated that *"Very many of the captives are sick and die. It is true, however I will not allow that their disorders proceed from any other cause than dirt, nastiness and want of clothing."* Sproat then charged that when he put stoves on one of the prison ships for the comfort of the captives, they, *"willfully, maliciously and wickedly burnt the best prison ship in the world."* This, of course made no sense to Congress or Washington that the prisoners would set fire to the very ship in which they were imprisoned. Others indicated the fire was spread by accident. Sproat then went on to have prisoners on the Jersey sign documents that they were treated fairly on the prison ship and conditions were tolerable. Washington did not believe these propaganda ploys by Sproat, nor did Congress.

On January 25, 1781, George Washington wrote a letter suggesting that "an officer of confidence on both sides examine the prison ships and see what the truth was." Washington also wrote Sir Henry Clinton urging him to look into the matter. Clinton immediately claimed to have no authority over the prison ships. The matter was turned over to the Royal Navy. A Captain George Dawson, as senior officer, refused to permit a Continental officer to see the prison ships. He did send Washington a curious report of an investigation conducted by himself. He reported that the problem was the amount of food the Americans received. Their first concern was in feeding their own soldiers. Condemned rebel prisoners were traitors to the King and worrying about their comfort or dietary needs was not a priority. Washington promptly ordered retaliation upon captive British seamen. Washington ordered that the British officers would receive no more food than the American sailors onboard the New York prison ships obtained. Further, the treatment which Captain Clark was receiving would be issued upon the British officers. Such a threat had its impact and Captain Clark was removed from solitary confinement. The order for Thomas's release was over a month since the time he had sent the letter to his father and signed the letter with other whaleboat captains to Congress. A month living in such conditions certainly had its effect on the prisoner.

Meanwhile, each day Andrew would follow his daily routine, ending each day by pushing food through the keyhole to Thomas. A number of other men also began this practice. Andrew was uncertain if Lefton had asked them to do so, or if they just felt the need to help Thomas, which was a way to defy the treatment the British had laid upon him, and them. Andrew had started taking a portion of the meat and shredded it and wrapped it into the biscuit cylinder he would put through the keyhole. Such small supplements of food wouldn't keep a man alive for long, however Andrew felt that the companionship Thomas felt knowing Andrew would arrive each night kept hope alive in him. Each night Andrew would immediately find his way through the darkness to sit outside the prison door. "Stand up, Thomas. Stand up.

Pull yourself upright. You must move to keep your lungs from filling. Thomas, can you hear me?" Andrew was insistent until he would hear Thomas rouse himself and shuffle about the limited space. Andrew knew his brother had been in complete darkness and without benefit of lamplight until the British officer would send down a guard to take a small amount of water to Thomas and to remove the filth which would accumulate in the room. Andrew would try to engage his brother in conversation, but Thomas had stopped talking. Most conversation was answers of yes or no, but no real conversation. Andrew felt it was probably due to exhaustion, inability to fill his lungs to produce the breath needed for talking, or even pain in using his voice. Andrew's mind was always filled with the worse possible scenarios of his brother's condition, which in reality, he feared, was probably worse than he could even imagine.

The day finally arrived when a boat arrived and men from Cunningham's camp came onboard. Andrew recognized one of the men from the first time Cunningham came onboard. Papers were handed over and conversation was minimal, and the prisoners were ordered away from the ladder. Andrew quickly moved to the front. "Excuse me, Captain. Are you in need of someone helping you locate a prisoner? I am in the Working Party and I know the areas below decks." The guard look startled, then ordered another man to go with Andrew below decks to help retrieve the Captain Clark. The British soldier carried a lantern as they went below.

A Patriot's Price

When the prison door opened, a foul and putrid odor emitted from the room. At first Andrew could not see his brother at all. As his eyes adjusted to the dimly lit room, Andrew saw Thomas who was lying on the floor, tucked into the far corner of the room. It was the first time Andrew had seen him since that first glimpse he caught when Thomas was first brought onboard. A lantern was held up and Thomas was told to stand. Andrew moved into the room and held Thomas under his arm to help pull him up. Thomas staggered and was barely able to hold himself upright. Andrew quickly grabbed his arm to assist him when he realized he could encircle the entire arm with his thumb and forefinger. Andrew tried to not focus on the bitter hatred he felt for the British doing this to his once strong and healthy brother. Andrew knew that his encouragement to Thomas to stand up and move in the confined room had its benefit. Not only had it kept his lungs from completely filling with fluid, it kept some amount of strength in his legs. His malnourished state, however, caused him to be exhausted with each movement. Thomas had not seen lamplight or daylight for well over a month, nor had he had any food save for the small amounts pushed through the keyhole by Andrew and others who had taken pity on him. As they moved toward the stairs, Lefton appeared and handed Andrew a couple of blankets. Andrew helped his brother navigate the stairs and wrapped blankets around him to protect him against the winter winds. Once Thomas reached the top deck there were guards waiting for him. He was to be transported for prisoner exchange. Thomas's once strong frame was now bent and broken. His clothing hung in tatters around his skeletal frame. His coughing shook his entire body. Andrew feared he would not make it back to the shore in this condition. Andrew kept whispering words of encouragement to Thomas, imploring him to hold on and regain his strength. "Elizabeth and Jonathan are waiting for you at home. Mother will nurse you back to health." Thomas made no motion that he understood.

The British officers roughly grabbed Thomas under his arms and moved him to the ladder to the boat waiting in the cold waters below. Andrew rushed to the side of the ship to watch the progress of the boat to the shore, but the air was thick with fog and he could not see anything. After about thirty minutes, Andrew slowly sunk to the floor, exhausted, and confused as to what purpose he now had in living. Andrew tried to pray but the God he fervently prayed to so had betrayed him. He had lost any feeling of hope. Why had his father and Congress taken so long to help Thomas? Had there been immediate retaliation, Thomas would not be in this condition. God had betrayed him, and so had his father. Andrew grew warm as anger swelled in his chest and his face swiveled around looking for someone to attack. At that moment Lefton appeared and pulled Andrew toward the stairway. "Stop. Stop, Andrew. Don't do something that will keep you from reuniting with your brother. Stay strong." Andrew allowed himself to be led back to the hell hole where he sunk down in his usual spot and his body heaved as if sobbing, but there were no tears in him. His shoulders shook and his head pounded, but no sound escaped his lips. Lefton sat next to his friend and prayed for God to give Andrew some kind of comfort.

"Don't pray for me, Lefton. Your words are futile. God has abandoned us here on this hell ship." Andrew withdrew from Lefton's touch and huddled alone in his sorrow. It was no wonder that Andrew was feeling defeated. News would drift in from new prisoners, and none of it made Andrew feel any better about their situation. The prison ships had become a topic of conversation by many including Congress, state governments, and the people of the colonies. The British and the Americans were in a continuous battle over the condition of the prison ships and the treatment of the captives. The number of deaths continued to escalate, yet when questioned, the British were unable to provide the numbers of deaths. Nor were they able to provide the names of all the prisoners.

When Andrew heard about the mismanagement of records, it made him even angrier. His hatred for Sprout was reinforced when they heard about how lie were sent to Congress and Washington. It was expected that Joshua Loring, Sproat's superior, possessed the records, but no one was ever able to produce them. Reports would leak back to Congress and to Washington that such records existed, but no one seemed to know who had these records. Admission that the records existed would have been used by the Americans to implore other support for their cause against the British. It was considered to be a huge cover up to prevent the truth from being known not only to the Americans, but to the British citizens who believed their soldiers were fighting a good fight, and to the French, who already held negative relations with England. In wars across the centuries, there were always deaths on the battlefields, and yes, some prisoners died as prisoners of war, and often prison camps were harsh, but in no known history were there the number of fatalities as those that were caused on the British prison ships during this war.

Sproat continued to defy every entreaty to release or exchange prisoners. He demanded Washington trade American seamen for British soldiers. The problem was the privateers, who were the majority of the prisoners on the prison ships, were not part of the Continental Navy, thus they would have no allegiance to further serving in the war. The British therefore would have the advantage of having more men released who would be able to continue fighting. This was just a British ploy which Washington immediately recognized. Sproat would then taunt the prisoners that Washington didn't recognize the captives as worthy of exchange. This was meant to drive the prisoners to pledge their allegiance to the British in exchange for their release. That did not work either as the prisoners so hated the British they refused to ever support them. Even though there was logic in the information shared from incoming prisoners, Andrew was too angry to understand why Washington would not make the trade, yet he fully understood how Sprout was using this decision as a way to further inflict mental anguish on the prisoners.

One New York captive brought word of a Loyalist printer who was publishing stories of released prisoners, one being John Cooper, who went to Washington to beg for the seaman for soldier exchanges, yet Washington refused. "We have been deserted by our own countrymen," Cooper was quoted as saying, and the headlines further pushed the British propaganda. The prisoner actually had a copy of the publication he had tucked inside his coat. He shared them with the American officers and told many of the prisoners what had been written. The propaganda had the effect the Loyalists hoped to achieve. While the officers understood the propaganda, many of the men below decks expressed their anger against Washington and Congress. Andrew was one of them. The war was not being fought only on the battlefields, but in the prisons and in the newspapers. All of this manipulation, propaganda, and psychological war strategy was done, yet the prisoners onboard the prison ships continued to suffer and die. For the prisoners, like Andrew, the propaganda further depressed and isolated them. The feeling of despair was constant.

As the war continued, there was an increase in the amount of propaganda put into print. Sproat made a proposal that Washington release British soldiers and in exchange they would liberate the captive American seamen on the prison ships. In the Royal Gazette, Sproat put forth a public plea for help, supposedly penned by the Jersey prisoners. It was later discovered that no such letter was penned by any of the Americans on the Jersey. The letter read:

Friends and fellow-countrymen of America. You may bid a final adieu to all your friends and relations, who are now on board the Jersey prison ship at New York, unless you rouse the government to comply with just and honourable proposals, which has already been done on the part of Britons, but alas! It is with pain we inform you, that our petition to his Excellency General Washington, offering our services to the country during the present campaign, if he would send soldiers in exchange for us, is frankly denied. What is to be done? Are we to lie here and share the fate of our unhappy brothers who are dying daily? No, unless you relieve us immediately, we shall be under necessity of leaving our country, in preservation of our own lives.

This publication was followed days later with a document signed by twelve American ship captains and one doctor that the naval prisoners in New York were well-fed, comfortable and content. "Anything said to the contrary is false and without foundation." They complimented the Robert Digby who was commanding His Majesty's fleet for the "humane disposition and indulgence to the prisoners." The document went on to say that the sick were cared for "in wholesome clean ships.

Every man furnished with a cradle, bed, and sheets made of good Russia linen to lie in, the best of fresh provisions, vegetables, wine, rice, barley, etc." It also went on to say that Commissary Sproat and his men "conscientiously do their duty with great humanity and indulgence to the prisoners and reputation to themselves." Although the letter was reviewed with great distrust from nearly everyone, Sproat hoped the letter would keep investigators of the prison ships at bay. When the prisoners heard of this it was quickly revealed that many of those who signed the document had signed without having read what Sproat put before them in an effort to avoid being put on the Jersey instead of the promised release in prisoner exchange. Sproat's use of propaganda and falsification of letters appeased many that chose to believe that the prisoners were well treated. For the prisoners, reading such lies added further distress. Andrew's hatred had a new target as Sprout's name continued to come up in any conversation on the Jersey.

There were many outright lies by many shielding the public from knowing the truth about the prison ships, particularly the Jersey. Congress asked Washington to investigate the conditions of the prison ships. Washington contacted Admiral Arbuthnot about the "truly calamitous and deplorable" treatment of American prisoners on the Jersey. He asked that Arbuthnot allow an American officer to inspect the Jersey. Arbuthnot passed this request to Captain George Dawson who communicated to Washington that he and three other officers inspected the Jersey on February 2, 1781. They interrogated the prisoners and learned that "their situation was made at all times as comfortable as possible and that they were in no instance oppressed or ill-treated." The report went on to say that their weekly rations were no different in quality or quantity from those provided to the ship's crew. The report also said that two or three prisoners from each rank were allowed to go to shore every day to purchase whatever additional supplies they or their comrades might wish. As to the reported illnesses, Dawson assured Washington that it "arises from a want of clothing and a proper attention in themselves to their own cleanliness." Dawson closed the report stating that there would not be permission granted for American officers to visit the Jersey. For Andrew and the other men this further set them into despair as it seemed no one would be willing to step forward for their cause, and their personal Hell would continue.

So many of the newspapers in New York were run by the Loyalists who printed stories which supported the British cause. Dawson made certain the report was published for all to read and to assure anyone who might be suspicious of maltreatment on the prison ships that the prisoners were treated well, and such treatment had been documented and authenticated. Of course, this was war, and such propaganda was fair in the fight.

Many other stories were not shared in print, as they told a different story, one which would anger even the staunchest advocate of the King. A man named VanDyke who had been on the Jersey was released in an officer exchange shed a different story. He told a reporter that the stench on the Jersey was so strong; he thought the smell alone would kill him. He then shared that a typical meal was not nearly enough to share among the men of his mess. "I received a small piece of salt pork so small that my five messmates and I only had one mouthful each and nothing else for the entire day. Another meal was a soup which was merely brown water and fifteen floating peas, and this was to hold all six of us for a full day." Van Dyke was lucky as he and eighty other Americans were transferred to the hospital sloop, the Hunter. When he was finally released he returned home a broken man. When asked by the reporter what it was like on the Jersey, Van Dyke sadly recalled, "Pale faces, long beards, white pale eyes, and ghastly countenances. This dismal sight I cannot erase from my mind as long as God permits me to retain my sense." His story was never seen in print. Anger by the other officers on the Jersey when they learned that VanDyke's story had been ignored quickly made its way to the men below decks. They, too, felt this experience would never end.

Andrew began to wonder when his own death would occur. He had already outlived many of those who were taken prisoner the same time as he was. Would he die in a few days? A week or two? A month? Certainly he could not expect to live another month. He had been in this Hell for well over five, maybe six months. He had outlived his purpose. He had helped to save Thomas's life, he hoped. Although he did not know if Thomas was able to get home to recover, Andrew felt a sense of relief that at least Thomas lived long enough to escape Hell. Andrew's mind had nearly shut down. He no longer prayed; he no longer thought. He went through the motions that were expected of him.

Lefton recognized that Andrew was not engaging and knew that this was a certain sign of someone who would not last long. He tried to engage Andrew in conversation, but Andrew's eyes were becoming vacant and his face was blank. After two weeks of this Lefton pulled Andrew to the side and began slapping him across the face over and over again. At first Andrew merely stood there, allowing himself to be bullied and beaten, but eventually he sunk down and covered his face and began to sob. Lefton pulled him up by the lapels of his coat and shook him. "Andrew. You must remain strong. You cannot give up. You cannot let these Lobsterbacks win. Damn it! We have come too far. I need you to help me. If you give up, what do I live for?"

Andrew's body shook with his sobs, and as Lefton talked Andrew's eyes began to focus and his face came back to life. "I'm sorry, Lefton. I was so caught up with my own misery, I didn't think about you. You have been here for me since I first came onboard. You helped me get food to Thomas. You stood by my like a brother. You watched my back. I'm sorry." Andrew's voice began to calm but his body still heaved from the emotion he had allowed himself to feel. The emotion also seemed to heat his body from within and for the first time since Thomas left the ship, Andrew felt alive. He realized that Lefton had made him his purpose on this ship. Andrew's survival meant his survival. Just as Andrew had fought to keep Thomas alive, Lefton was doing the same for Andrew. If he gave up, Lefton would have no purpose in living.

That night Andrew tried to pray again. At first he couldn't even think of a prayer to say. Finally he found his own words. "God, I am not happy with you. I do not know why you have forsaken us on this ship. Please, if you are there, give me the strength to survive this test and let me live to set foot on land and find my way back to my home and family." Would God answer?

Chapter 10
A Daring Escape

February, 1781

The American officers continued to use the former Gun Room of the Jersey as their bunk place. The Gun Room was off the main deck. The officers were expected to be at call in a moment's notice when their captors had a task for them to do. What was meant to be additional punishment to them by making them perform the Working Party duties actually had an opposite effect. Because of their activity and full rations, most were able to withstand their torments. The Gun Room was also not as crowded, which Andrew felt kept many of the diseases at bay for the officers since the men were not on top of one another. Additionally, the Gun Room had more air circulation than the decks below, which provided the officers less torment in the stifling summer months, and fresh air which cleared out much of the putrid and contaminated air. Once an officer became too ill, he was immediately removed and placed in the hospital bunks where he would hopefully be moved to the hospital ships. It was believed that the hospital ships were less crowded and patients sent there would stand better chance of survival than being left on the prison ships. While Andrew understood that the officers were to be used in exchange for British officers and soldiers, the inequity of treatment began to wear thin on him.

Andrew had spent his youth listening to his father preach about equality and fairness. The longer Andrew remained on the ship, the angrier he became about everything which was unfair. Most of his anger was directed certainly at the British, then Hessians, and the Loyalists and Refugees who acted as the jailors on this ship. But Andrew was also angry at Washington for not working to protect them. He was angry at the Americans in New York and elsewhere who closed their eyes to how the prisoners on the prison ships were being treated by the British. Andrew was angry with his father for not using his influence to save him and the others. And most profoundly, Andrew was angry with God. Andrew had long since given up any pretense of praying. The God he thought he knew had deserted him. With each body he pulled from the belly of the Jersey, Andrew's anger grew.

In an attempt to draw his emotions into check, Andrew tried to pay attention to how the officers behaved. He hoped that if they had a plan for escape, he, too, would follow them. It was essential that he focus himself on what was happening on land and how the war was progressing.

As new prisoners were brought onboard the Jersey, the officers would pull in the new prisoner into the Gun Room and question him. Andrew had taken the habit of standing near the doorway to listen to what was said. He was alert for any who were from New Jersey. The news that was brought was typically about where the various troops were located, what battles had been won and lost, and general news they had heard before being captured. It appeared that many of the new battles in the war were shifting to the southern states. South Carolina had seen much action and the Americans had beaten the British at Cowpens. There was also news of the Pennsylvania soldiers' mutiny because of nonpayment of their wages. Once the officers had gathered the information from the new prisoner, the inmate was given an orientation, and the general rules which had been established by the prisoners for behavior onboard the Jersey was reviewed. The process for procuring food was reviewed, and then the inmate was sent to find a mess he could join.

After the new prisoners would leave, the officers would review the information gathered. The mutiny troubled the officers. They debated how this would affect the war and its outcome. Would the Continental Army be able to accomplish what they needed to do if lack of funding was going to plague the very men the government needed to employ in order to bring this war to an end? Although winning battles was encouraging, many feared the lack of money for supplies, food, and wage could undermine their quest. Other officers said that since most of the early battles were in the northern colonies, the southern colonies were able to hold onto their wealth a bit longer, and they would have the money to fight since the war was now moving to their property. The men would decide which information they would openly share with the other prisoners as they walked about the upper deck for exercise. They typically shared information which would be encouraging and bring hope to the men. Of course, there was nothing standing in the way of the new prisoners repeating other stories to the men, but typically new inmates were so overwhelmed with the harsh living conditions onboard the Jersey that they did not engage in lively banter with others. For those without stamina and resiliency, they quickly became another casualty of war.

Andrew noticed that the officers, too, had lost considerable weight and stamina. The officers were unable to do much in leadership roles on the Jersey as they were continually watched by the English, but their constant presence gave many men a bit of hope that should an opportunity arise for escape, the officers would lead them to safety. Andrew, too, needed to hold onto the hope that the officers would be able to lead them to escape.

Several recent prisoners were questioned by the officers in the Gun Room, and they said they came from the Elizabethtown, New Jersey area. Andrew immediately took notice. His body reacted most favorably in hearing the news as his heart beat faster and he felt color coming to his cold and chapped face. After the men were released by the officers, Andrew quickly met up with them. "You are from Elizabethtown?" Andrew asked. "When were you there last?"

One of the men, a young man who probably had not yet reached his eighteenth year said, "I was there just a month ago."

Andrew asked, "Did you hear anyone say anything about a Thomas Clark?"

"Captain Clark?" asked the young man.

"Yes, Captain Clark. He was onboard this ship and was to be part of the prisoner exchange. Did you hear anything about his making it back to Elizabethtown?"

The young man put aside his anxiety of being made prisoner of this ship and answered, "Yes. He was released and he was taken back to the Clark farm. Everyone was talking about his mistreatment by the British, and how Washington had fought to get him and other officers released. I heard he was in a bad way when he returned home and was quarantined to keep him from infecting others."

Andrew's face broke out in a huge smile, probably the first and only time he had done this since being captured. "Thank you, thank you," he said. "Any other news you have of his recovery."

"Not really. All I know is that when we were told about Captain Clark, a group of young men joined up to fight the British. Sadly, my mates and I were captured on our first mission." His face turned to look at his surroundings and the life within his eyes began to diminish. "I had no idea that I would end up in the same surroundings as poor Captain Clark." Andrew quickly thanked the young man for the information and invited him and his friends to join their mess. It was the least he could do to help them after they brought such valuable news back to Andrew.

Thomas was alive, albeit gravely ill. He knew that he was in the best hands with his mother, Rose, and Elizabeth caring for him on the Clark farm. He remembered the care he had received at their hands and how he had been nursed back to health by his mother, and his younger brother, Abraham, and certainly Rose, who used her knowledge of herbs to fight the infections war typically brought. Certainly Thomas stood a better chance of survival in their capable hands. For the remainder of the day, Andrew felt light-hearted, a feeling which he had not experienced in nearly a half year. Thomas is safe. That evening he sat reflecting his recent attitude. He realized that when he heard the news about Thomas he had silently thanked God. Andrew sat in prayer, asking God's forgiveness for his disbelief, and thanking God for delivering Thomas safely home to his family. Maybe God would show mercy and help his situation. Andrew felt that his luck had changed and certainly Washington would now work to exchange all of the men. He was filled with hope.

February, March and April slipped by with no sign of reprieve from captivity. Each day felt like a lifetime. Andrew's brief parlay with hope quickly ended, and he lived in an aura of despondency. Lefton noticed the change coming over Andrew each day, and the depth of his despair could not be shaken. Andrew had so tied his hopes into the prisoners being rescued that with each passing day his level of despair deepened.

News that came from new prisoners identified changes in government, but no hint of changes in the condition of the prisoners of war. In March Congress had finally ratified the Articles of Confederation. At first the men cheered that their government had made a bold stand in organization and was looking toward a restructuring of government. Andrew, however, did not feel the same. "It took this long to finally ratify it? It was proposed for ratification in 1778 and it took this long to finally get it ratified? How can we expect to be freed when it takes three years to approve something which was logical to do in the first place?" said Andrew scornfully as the men talked about the new document. "And just what did these Articles provide us with? Establishing our name as the United States of America? How are we united? Who is united in setting us free from this hell? United? All that entire document gives us is an agreement to be friendly toward each other. I don't see any friendship being extended to release us, their fellow citizens, from this monstrous ship. This friendship is supposed to work toward binding us together to withstand attacks on each state's people. Who is fighting for our need as we are attacked daily with the degradation of our health and safekeeping?"

Andrew's words were filled with the passion of someone who was betrayed. Andrew's words had an immediate effect on the men who had just seen a glimmer of hope. Many looked at Andrew with hatred because he took something that should have rallied their hopes and he shot holes in it. They needed something that could give them hope, and Andrew had closed the very glimmer of hope they had that Congress was moving to end this war. Lefton immediately feared that some of the men might beat Andrew for his outburst as they needed to believe in something and Andrew's bitterness was tossing this ray of hope away. What Lefton feared most was that a beating would be the death sentence for Andrew as he would continue to fall deeper into despair. It was the first time Andrew had come alive in weeks, but his hatred could end up causing his own demise.

Andrew recognized the looks of hatred coming from those nearest him. He stood and moved to the rail so he could look toward the shore. He desperately wanted his feet to once again walk on land. The shore, and the graveyard of so many who had perished on this hell ship, was at least a half mile or more away. Andrew found himself wishing he could just drop overboard and swim to the shore. He knew he did not have the strength to swim that distance, or any kind of distance in his current condition. He dropped his head, desperate to end his misery, and stared at the water beneath. That's when he saw it. It was some kind of a wood structure which was bobbing in the water. Andrew strained to see what it was.

Lefton moved beside Andrew. "What are you peering at?" asked Lefton.

"What is that?" asked Andrew, nodding his head toward the object floating in the water. Lefton looked around to make certain they were not being watched.

"I can't tell. Maybe a door or piece of furniture? It is hard to tell what it is from here."

"Lefton, I can't do this anymore. I am going mad. I'd rather risk the waters below and try to make it to shore than stay one more day on this ship. I can't do it. I just cannot do it."

"Don't be a fool, man. They will shoot you as soon as they hear the water splash when you jump. Plus there is no way you would be able to get to shore. It would take more strength than you can muster to fight the tide and make it to the shore."

"I don't care. I am going to jump. Bullets be damned. If I die, at least I will die free from this ship."

Lefton looked hard into Andrew's skeletal face. He knew Andrew had made up his mind and there would be no stopping him. He would rather believe Andrew could make it to safety than watch him continue to fade away onboard the

Jersey. Lefton looked at the water below. It was the side where the contaminated waste was dumped each day. The guards would be least fearful that a prisoner would jump off this side of the ship. There was also only an hour or more of sunlight left to the day, and the Jersey prisoners would be sent back below decks for another night of mental and emotional torture. Lefton also knew that this piece of wood, whatever it was, would not remain in the area another day. It was now or never for Andrew. "Wait. I will cause a distraction. Give me a few minutes." Lefton clapped Andrew on the shoulder and mouthed, "Good luck and God's speed, Andrew." The two men looked at each other. Such a bond they had made. Andrew knew he was abandoning Lefton who had done everything to help him survive. Even now he was willing to form a distraction to allow Andrew his escape. Andrew nodded at Lefton, and Lefton briefly smiled. He then slipped away.

Andrew turned to watch Lefton, but knew if a distraction was to happen he would need to act quickly. He moved himself to a more shielded area of the deck and waited. Within minutes a loud scream was heard. "Stop, stop, stop. Get this vermin off me! Help! Help! Help!" Andrew knew it was Lefton reenacting a scene of madness they had often heard below decks when a fit of madness overtook someone. The screaming became louder and louder.

Shouts of the guards quickly followed. "Gag that man. Tie him up before he sets all of these rebels into a mass hysteria."

Andrew took this moment and straddled over the side of the ship, then with as strong of a push as he could muster, he pushed himself off.

His descent to the water felt freeing as the air encircled his body. He entered into the cold water, feet first and went completely under water. A piercing shock was felt throughout his body as it sunk into the cold depths. Andrew sunk deeper and deeper, and he felt a release of the panic which had built within him. Death welcomed him, until suddenly his mind became alert as if it were his last moment to fight for life. Andrew fought hard to move his arms in a way to propel him back to the surface. There seemed to be a momentary tug-of-war between his body being pulled deeper into a watery death, and his lungs which had expelled his last breath yet wanted to gasp the cold air above him. With an awakened alertness, Andrew pulled his body upward toward the surface. His head bobbed above the water and he gasped for air, but quickly closed his mouth so not to swallow the diseased water. He momentarily listened to hear if there were shouts or gunshots. There were none. No one seemed to notice he was overboard. He tried to contain his panic and quietly move toward the object he had seen bobbing in the water. The frigid water chilled him to the bone, yet he knew he must not succumb to the cold.

It seemed to take an eternity to reach his floating lifeboat, and once he did he carefully stationed himself to the side of the object so he would not been seen by any onlookers climbing atop it. He recognized his savior was a broken tabletop. The legs had already been knocked off or removed, and the tabletop itself was broken across one end. To climb atop would have been the safest thing to do, but Andrew knew that while he was still near enough the ship this could be easily seen by the guards, or even other prisoners who might point and draw attention to the waters below. He would just have to hang on as best he could and wait to get some distance from the ship before he tried to climb atop the flat surface. The water was still very cold, but the taste of freedom and the shoreline which seemed to stretch forever away was close enough that Andrew felt hope within himself that he could actually save himself. His heart was pounding so fast that Andrew could feel it within his chest. Perhaps his accelerated heartbeat gave him inner heat which warmed him internally as his extremities fought the cold water. Whatever the cause, Andrew was able to slowly move with the floating tabletop toward the shore.

The cold of the water was beginning to have its effect on Andrew. Although the waters in this early May were warmer than normal, they were still considerably colder than Andrew's body could tolerate. Andrew knew that the waters did not warm up until well into summer, so his safety depended on getting to shore as quickly as possible. His boots were weighing him down and since they were already at least a size too large for his feet Andrew kicked them off his feet. The salt water was helpful in giving Andrew some buoyancy in the water, which let him exert less effort in staying afloat. Andrew's mind raced as he thought about the many seamen who died in the whaleboats because of exposure to the cold waters. He evaluated his circumstances and determined that the cold, yet not freezing water, his weakened body condition, and the distance from the shore were all contributing factors to his potential freedom. He looked back at the Jersey and realized that he was now a moderate distance from it. If he tried to climb atop the table, perhaps the moderately warm sunshine and lessening panic would allow him to reach the shore.

Andrew tried to climb atop the wooden structure, but each time it bobbed in a way to knock him off. Andrew was fast becoming exhausted. Finally he decided to just rest his arms and upper torso on one end of the table. This raised the front of the table too high for Andrew to see above, so he had no idea the direction he was moving. Fearful of not having the strength to once again pull himself back into that position, Andrew began to paddle his feet, praying that his newfound vessel was aimed at the shoreline and not out to sea. As darkness began to descend, Andrew was still moving slowly toward his unknown destination. This agony continued until Andrew's foot hit something soft and he realized he must be near the shoreline. The moon was mostly hidden so there was little light for Andrew to see where he was, but he knew he was soon approaching the shoreline. Andrew attempted to stand upright, but his feet were sucked into the muddy bottom.

Pulling himself free took much energy. The muddy bottom was impossible to stand in, and the brush separating him from the shore was thick. Andrew thought that anyone who tried to escape the Jersey could certainly perish trying to maneuver through this obstacle course. Andrew again climbed onto the tabletop. His best bet was to try to navigate to an opening. He had to act quickly as the sky was fast darkening.

What if he had paddled his way right to a British camp? Would they fire upon him? Would they arrest him and prepare him to return to the Jersey? Andrew's mind whirled with fear. When he finally felt secure footing, he pushed off his craft and tried to quietly make his way to the shore without making too much noise. This was most difficult to do as it seemed Andrew's arms and legs were not cooperating.

His feet finally touched the shore and Andrew fell to the grassy shoreline and kissed the ground. Home. I am home, he thought. He breathed in the salty air. He smelled the turf as deeply as he could. The salt had run its course through his nasal cavity and it seemed to empty the contents of months of filth and disease which he had breathed in while imprisoned. He pulled the fresh air into his lungs and breathed deeply. Then, exhaustion overcame him and Andrew fell into a deep and dreamless sleep.

Chapter 11
Kindness

May, 1781

Soft sea breezes and sunshine, and the gnawing pain of hunger in his belly finally awakened Andrew. It was fortunate for him that the air was unseasonably warm. He was uncertain as to how long he had slept. He ran his hand through the turf and breathed in deeply. The clean untainted air filled his lungs, but he then fell into a fit of coughing which he tried desperately to hold in for fear that perhaps there would be a nearby British soldier who would hear him. Andrew quieted himself and his eyes burned. He suddenly heaved a huge sob and again caressed the turf he had slept upon. As he gained control of himself Andrew strained to cautiously raise himself to his knees which were now weak from his desperate push to the shore. He was careful to look around to ascertain whether he was in a safe area. He looked back into the water to see where the Jersey was and realized he had paddled not straight toward the shore, but had moved a considerable distance from where the bodies of the dead had been buried. He could see a farmhouse located not far off from where he knelt. He hoped it was the home of a Patriot, yet this was New York, and many Loyalists had moved to the area. He tried to calm his fears by rationalizing that the Loyalists would have moved to the city limits, whereas the shoreline would be inhabited by families who fished for a living. They might be more supportive of the Patriot cause considering the British had placed so many regulations on their fishing and taxes they were to support. Despite his rationale, Andrew's fear persisted that it would be a Loyalist family living on the shore and they would end up sending him back to the ship. He certainly did not look like a traveler. His clothing and his appearance could only be someone who had escaped the hold of a prison ship.

Again, Andrew scanned the area to get a better bearing on where he was. Could this be the house of the Old Dutchman, a miller who ran a tide mill on the shore line? He heard some of the Officers of the Working Party talk of the house, and the Old Dutchman's daughter, who no one actually ever reported seeing. They said she kept a record of the number of dead who were buried in the shallow graves each day. He strained to remember whether anyone had said whether the Old Dutchman was Patriot or Tory. As he pondered this, he thought it best not to move toward the house until he was certain it was safe. Perhaps the talk of the Old Dutchman was just fanciful thinking of men who were imprisoned and destined for death.

His first need would be food. What was it he could secure to stop the growing pain in his belly? Andrew crawled
slowly through the thick boggy shrub along the shoreline,
slow enough not to draw attention to himself. That's when
he saw activity coming from the house. The owner came out
to feed the farm animals. Andrew watched and listened from
his hiding space. The grasses became alive with chickens
who bustled toward the man as he threw feed out upon the
ground. Andrew concentrated his stare at the Red Dorkiing
chickens as his belly growled. How he longed for the meals
his mother would make for her large family. The Clarks
rarely ate chicken as they needed the chickens for eggs, but
his mother would certainly use seafood and wild game as
meat dishes and the basis of many stews, along with baked
beans and pease porridge and dark breads. The food was
never elegant, but it was filling and satisfying. Andrew now
longed for such meals. The man disappeared back into the
house and came out again with a bucket of scraps which he
dumped into the pig pen. The pigs squealed their thanks,
and the farmer then went into the barn area, probably to
milk the cow, Andrew thought. As the man disappeared,
Andrew crept quietly to the pig trough and reached in to pull
out some of the scraps and hungrily devoured them. Peelings
from vegetables and some stale bread were the mainstays of
the scraps, but to Andrew it was fresh food, something his
body had not had for nearly a year.

"You! Who are you?" a voice bellowed. Andrew was so busy that he had not remained alert to watch for the man's return. Andrew attempted to pull himself upright, but his legs were not strong enough and he fell to the ground. He tried to crawl away but the man quickly apprehended him, pulling Andrew back. It was not much of a struggle. Although he felt fire within him to help him escape, his body was too weak to cooperate.

"Please, please!" cried Andrew. "I am so hungry. I meant no harm to you."

The man towered above him, looking intently at Andrew. Andrew tried to return the stare, but the man was outlined by the sun which burst around him. Andrew could not look into the face to determine if it was good or evil. "Are you from the ships?" the man asked, in a voice that was neither demanding nor stern.

"Please, I beg you, have mercy. Do not return me there. Good God, man, please, I beg you. Kill me if you must, but do not send me back to Hell." Andrew fell into a fit of coughing.

The man stood over Andrew, waiting for him to catch his breath. "Do you have a name?" asked the man.

"Andrew, sir. "

"Well, Andrew. You have landed on my property. I know many of the British and Hessians who oversee the burial detail down the shoreline call me the 'Old Dutchman.' My name is not important as I would not want it repeated to anyone who might seek retribution for the services I provide."

"Sir, are you a Loyalist or a Patriot?" asked Andrew, fearing the answer.

"Let's just say that my people have not been well regarded by General Howe. It was heard that he said, 'I can do nothing with this Dutch population; I can neither buy them with money nor conquer them with force.' We have sought to remain as neutral as possible; however we recognize by our own ancestry that governments derive their just powers from the consent of the governed. There is no such thing as 'the divine right of kings to rule.' God does not grant kings the right to betray their people and turn them into slaves." The Dutchman stopped to allow Andrew time to absorb what he said.

Andrew was perplexed. He could not really follow everything that was being said, perhaps because of his fear, or perhaps because of his weakness, or perhaps because of his hunger. Andrew tried to concentrate on what the man had shared. If he understood it correctly, this man was set to help him. With that, Andrew blacked out.

When Andrew awoke he was laying on a bed. A bed. How long had it been since he had slept in anything other than the filthy floor boards or in a hammock on the Jersey? The filthy clothing of his escape had been removed and he was now in a clean night shirt. It took his mind a few moments to remember he had escaped his hell and that an old man had found him trying to pull scraps from the pig's trough. Andrew feebly looked around him, and saw the old man was sitting in a chair near the fireplace. Andrew's movement stirred the old man's attention. "Ah, you have decided to remain among this living," said the old man. "Now tell me, Andrew, how is it that you have escaped?"

Andrew attempted to sit up, but fell back. The old man quickly came to the side of the bed and helped Andrew sit upright. Andrew nodded his head to the old man in thanks, and felt he needed to respond to the questions put forth to him. "Sir, I survived the Jersey only because a friend watched out for me and guided me into survival. We served in the Working Party, carrying the dead to the forecastle each day. For this we received full prisoner rations and sturdier clothing which certainly helped in my survival. I would think the daily struggle of bringing the dead aboveboard also kept some of my strength. A shipmate caused a distraction and I threw myself overboard without drawing attention from the guards. A floating piece of furniture became my savior. I awoke on your shoreline. I am now at your mercy."

"You need not worry, young man," said the host. "You will be protected on my watch. Now let's get some proper food in you." Andrew stared at him in disbelief. Was this man going to treat him humanely? Was he to be saved? "Wait here," said the man as he disappeared from the room. Andrew looked anxiously after him, fearful that he might return with a musket to order Andrew back to the British. Andrew looked feverishly around him to see where he could run for escape.

His legs were in no condition to move him, so Andrew awaited his fate. The man soon returned with a bowl of food. "Now eat slowly. If you have not eaten properly your stomach might not react well to food. This might well introduce your body to food without sickening it." Andrew gratefully took the bowl. It was filled with crushed berries." Andrew looked at the man questioningly. "The juices of the fruits will give your body a chance to get some energy back. After a bit I will give you meat broth. As your body adjusts, we can introduce more food." Andrew was so thankful for something fresh he did not question the man. Anything was better than the foul slop he had consumed on the Jersey.

The man pulled a chair close to the bed and sat next to Andrew, watching him as he hungrily ate the crushed berries, and running his finger alongside the bowl to gather every trace. "I will get you some fresh clothing. It may not fit perfectly, but I believe you will be more comfortable than you are now. I hope you don't mind but I we should burn the clothing you arrived in as they not even fit to clean and reuse." The man dug through a trunk and pulled out shirt, trousers, old jacket and some boots which looked to be close to Andrew's size. "You can put these on when you are strong enough to dress yourself," he said. "Is there anything sewn into the garments you wore that you need or want? "

"No. There is nothing I want to remind myself of the Jersey." The old man merely nodded in his understanding.

"I must admit, that I have not heard of many stories such as yours. We have had bodies wash ashore, but it was believed they had attempted to swim ashore, but were overtaken. You, Andrew, have certainly had God on your side."

"Sir, I don't know if it was God. I fear I have lost my ability to pray." Andrew proceeded, but at a pace that was agonizingly slow. It was like he relived each inequity as he shared the story with the farmer. "I am very sorry, sir, but I have many questions of a God who would allow nearly a thousand men at a time to wail within the bowels of the Jersey, lacking proper food and clothing. In the summers it was sweltering. They provided no awnings or canvas wind sails to direct air below the decks and the summer nights were spent baking in the heat, gasping for each breath, and fearing that each breath was contaminated with the illnesses of those surrounding us. Men would strip down to try to withstand the intense heat, only to be covered in the vermin which ate away at our skin. In the winters there was no warmth, no additional clothing, and no fires to keep us warm. We had only what we had carried onboard ship with us. Fortunately most had a woolen blanket which we had carried onboard with us when we were incarcerated, but it was never enough to withstand the bitter cold. Our shivering became our internal heater, but so many became so weak they could not shiver, and in the mornings we would find them deeply asleep and unable to awaken, until a day or so later we would take their lifeless bodies to the forecastle for burial. Our food was cooked in contaminated water in a contaminated copper pot. Our fresh water was limited and we had to ration it for both drinking water and for cooking our food. Having a bit of money afforded us a chance to purchase the few extras from Dame Grant, or from the ship's Sutler. Such things as needles and thread were purchased. Dame Grant would sell at cost, but the Sutler would set his own price for what we needed, looking to profit as much as he could. The majority of the men onboard did not have spare money when they came onboard so there was the agonies of seeing their faces filled with envy as they watched those who purchased our meager items and enjoy momentary ease of imprisonment. What God would allow for men to treat fellow men in this manner? And what God would allow men to suffer daily and beg for death with no release from their torments?"

The man listened to Andrew, and then quietly said, "Andrew, it had to be divine intervention which allowed you to survive your trip to shore, and to allow you to come to this location in order to be protected."

Protected? Andrew glanced up into the man's face. He looked fatherly and caring. Andrew was completely overwhelmed and his body heaved a huge sob as his crumbled into shaking, tearless cries. The man cradled Andrew in his arms until Andrew fell into a deep sleep.

Andrew looked around himself trying to remember what all had transpired in the past day. He hoisted himself up and put his feet on the floor, but when he tried to stand, a groan emitted from him and he crumbled back to the bed. The man quickly appeared and looked at Andrew. "Perhaps you are not meant to be up and about just yet. You had slept nearly a day and a half. You must be hungry now." Andrew nodded his head. The man disappeared and came back with a bowl of crushed berries again. "Let's start with this, and I will warm up some broth for you." Andrew gratefully took the bowl and consumed the fresh fruit quickly. When the broth was brought in he greedily held it in his hands and sipped from it. The man sat in a chair nearby and watched Andrew.

"If your stomach is up for it, in about an hour we will try some stew. I've heard too many stories from the local Irishmen who had starved in Ireland and what happened when they began eating rich foods too quickly. Some became so ill their bodies retaliated and killed them."

Andrew nodded as he was just thankful that he was clean, dry, clothed and had something in his belly that wasn't made in the filth of the Jersey. "What are your plans, Andrew, once your legs decide they want to join with the rest of your body?"

"I'd like to go home. My brother was also on the Jersey, and he was put into prisoner exchange after he had been put into torturous conditions."

"More than what the rest of you dealt with?" asked the man.

"Yes." Andrew pondered whether it was safe to tell this man everything. He felt it was safer not to mention anything about his father being a Signer. "My brother was a whaleboat captain and he was forced to write letters to Congress asking for intervention."

"Quite a fuss over those letters. Seems that Congress did react to letters that outlined especially harsh mistreatment of officers. It rallied up a lot of public opinion on both sides. Seems there was a whole propaganda campaign launched by the Loyalist printers who made it look like Congress didn't care about the prisoners."

"Did they care?" asked Andrew all too quickly. "How could public opinion have mattered? How could the citizens of New York who knew what was happening on these British prison ships not reach out to help us? Were they all hard hearted Loyalists? Did no one care how we were being mistreated? As to the letters my brother signed and wrote, they were sent well over a month before any action was seen onboard the ship. During that time my brother was starved and beaten. I don't know if he had the strength to survive by the time he left the ship. How could the Congress forsake him and the others? How could Washington turn his back on us and not do prisoner exchanges? We were taunted every day by our captors who said that the British had offered American seamen for British soldiers and Washington refused the exchange. How could he do that when we were left rotting on that ship after we had put our lives on the line for the cause? How could my father not act on Thomas' behalf?" Andrew stopped. He had said it.

"Your father? Why would your father have any control over what was happening on the prison ships?" the man said as he studied Andrew's face.

Andrew reddened. He had not meant to say anything. This information could cost him his life. Andrew knew that if this man had any allegiance to the British he could be turned over to receive the same treatment Thomas had received.

"Who is your father?" the man asked.

"I've said too much. I should not have said what I did."

"Young man. You don't understand war. You do not understand that nothing happens quickly in war. If your father, indeed, had any power to make an impact, such decisions are debated upon from all sides. Don't hold this anger in your heart against your father. I fear you misjudge him in having the ability to have rescued your brother, yourself and the others. These prison ships have been out in this harbor for over a year now. News does not travel very quickly during war, and certainly few, if any, prisoners escape or are even traded from these ships. Those who are traded are typically put immediately back into service so their ability to share information is limited. Also, many of those who are imprisoned on these ships are in the militia, or they are privateers, so there is very little information documenting their whereabouts.

I fear that the severity of just how many die daily on these ships is unknown to most, especially those in power. I watch every day. I can see the number of bodies being buried in the shoreline. In just over a year I have witnessed well over two thousand bodies buried and they are mostly from the Jersey. Each day a detail comes in with at first no fewer than five, but now at times there are up to twenty bodies a day. I imagine there are graveyards in other parts of the bay as well. I dare say that there are more perishing on these ships than on the battlefields, yet no one really knows this. Your father, whoever he is, cannot possibly know the severity of these ships."

Andrew felt he had said too much already. He felt a burning inside him. It was a hatred. A hatred toward his captors. A hatred toward this war. A hatred toward, dare he think it? A hatred toward Washington, his father and God.

The man looked at Andrew and he could see his face contort with whatever thoughts were plaguing him. He shook his head as he rose up. This poor young fellow. He had much healing to do. He said a silent prayer as he walked back to the kitchen to fetch a bowl of stew for this tortured soul.

Chapter 12
Return Home

June, 1781

Andrew found his host to be quite mysterious. The
man, who never did reveal his name, looked after Andrew and
would sit with him nightly trying to encourage Andrew to talk
and to pray. Andrew was horrified that he had shared personal information about himself with this man, albeit a kind
stranger. Their conversations were mostly about things which
would have been normalcy before the war. The man tried to
steer clear of any topic which would once again pull Andrew
into the angry and unforgiving state he was in that second day
after his arrival. The man would start each day in prayer, but
Andrew did not participate, but sat stern faced staring into
the distance as if seeing the real life hell he had experienced.
The man who was not dissuaded, continued his prayers each
morning, and before each meal and again at night. He prayed
that Andrew would be able to find forgiveness in his heart and
begin to heal.

After several weeks, Andrew was able to eat again and was able to stand erect. The host would talk to Andrew about news he had heard, staying clear of the realities of the prison ships. One story that captured Andrew's attention was that of the winter of '79-80 when the British had tried to take Washington's encamped men at Morristown. The host was excited to share a story that might take Andrew's mind off the war itself. It seemed all young men liked stories of intrigue and potential treasure hunting. The host hoped the story would give Andrew something to think about other than the war itself. "The Narrows and Upper Bay were frozen solid. The British ship, Lexington, tried to invade New Jersey, but it sank in the East River in sixty-six feet of water. The report was that the ship had lost $1,800,000 in materials, provisions and gold and silver." He paused to let the information savor in Andrew's mind. Andrew's face, for the first time, was filled with curiosity.

The Dutchman continued the story. "In November of '80 a new three-masted frigate with twenty-eight guns called the Hussar tried to move through Hell Gate, but the 114 foot ship got caught in a current which forced it broadside and it sank in sixteen fathoms of water. Story is that there was gold and silver worth between two to four million dollars. It was never recovered." Andrew listened intently and his mind imagined all the treasure hunters who would go in search of the lost treasure.

The host smiled as Andrew, for the first time, talked a bit freely about how he could imagine young men trying to find the lost treasure. The stories of the various British ships which were lost was a safe topic of discussion and the Dutchman and Andrew could talk without fear that Andrew would fall back into his fits of despair. The Dutchman looked for other such stories to share with Andrew, in hopes that he could pull the young man out of the black hole where his mind seemed to exist.

"In late October of last year the twenty-two gun HMS Ontario, an 80 foot long warship, disappeared. The ship was the largest ever built by the British and was recognizable as each mast had two crow's nests on them. And the bow stern was beautifully carved. None of the sixty British soldiers, forty Canadian crew members, or thirty American war prisoners survived. Only six bodies floated to shore of the 130 who perished. The ship never saw battle as she had only been launched five months earlier. It was their biggest ship and its loss was kept secret for as long as they could muster to keep the American soldiers and Washington knowing about the loss." The Dutchman waited for Andrew's reaction, and was pleased that much of the worry that was a constant on Andrew's face faded, at least for these few moments.

Andrew imagined that there would be plenty of people who would take up treasure hunting once the dangers of being near the rivers because of British patrols were over. Such imaginings helped keep Andrew's mind off the war. His host noticed, however, that whenever he did not engage Andrew in a discussion, Andrew was lost in his own thoughts and his face would often contort with the demons which haunted his memories.

Time passed slowly as Andrew healed, and there came a day that the host believed Andrew was beginning to heal emotionally. Surprisingly, Andrew had asked his host to help him walk to the shoreline on Wallabout Bay after dusk so he could pay his respects to the many men buried there. His host cautioned him that they would need to be careful. He doubted that there would be people coming to this area because of the smell and the sight of the burial grounds. Still, Andrew felt he needed to do this.

As evening approached, Andrew and his host arrived in the old man's wagon at the spot where Andrew remembered straining his eyes to see while imprisoned on the ship. There was a light fog which hid the Jersey from sight, and there was no sound of activity on the beach except the sea birds which sorted through mussels and crabs on the shore. In the fading light Andrew walked toward the beach area. There was the familiar smell of death mixed in with salty breeze off the bay. The host cautioned Andrew to not walk too close to the clearing as it was not safe. "If you look about you can see skulls lying about as thick as pumpkin in an autumn cornfield," he said. Andrew stopped and allowed his eyes to scan the area. There, for as far as Andrew could see, were mounds of freshly made graves, as well as graves which were destroyed. Bones, skulls, pieces of clothing were strewn about. He saw birds pecking at remains, and the sight quickly sickened Andrew. After controlling his gagging reflex, Andrew was quickly overtaken with emotion. "I, too, could have been one of these dead. How disrespectful that these men who had suffered at the hands of the British should further be humiliated with such shabby burial. They are disrespected in death as they were in life. Their lives had no value in this war effort." The host said nothing. Clearly Andrew's anger and grief were deeply embedded in him. "How many do you suppose are buried here?"

The host said, "In the beginning I would see five to eight bodies daily rowed from The Jersey to the shore. Every day there was a burial detail. When weather was too difficult to navigate the skiff to the shore, the following day there would be double the load. There have also been bodies which washed up onshore either from escapes, or from the British just ridding themselves of them and tossing them overboard. The Jersey only went into service a year ago. Since you arrived, I looked at my log which I tried to keep with my daughter. My estimate is that there have been nearly 2500 just from The Jersey" Andrew looked at the scene. He probably handled most of the moving of these dead to the forecastle for burial detail. So many. So neglected. And now, so forgotten. Anger began to swell again in Andrew's chest. He felt tears come to his eyes and he coughed to force himself to reach some kind of composure. The host respectfully said nothing and turned away to allow Andrew his grief. The two quietly moved away from the scene.

Andrew dropped his gaze and noticed there was a newly dug grave near where he stood. An arm was protruding through the sands and Andrew's eyes came into sharp focus. The cuff of the coat on that arm looked strangely familiar. Andrew's belly turned and he felt bile entering his throat. Andrew looked again and recognized it as the cuff of the coat worn by Lefton. "No!" Andrew's voice cracked. "It cannot be." The old man tried to move Andrew away from the grave, but Andrew pulled away. He fell to his knees and looked closer.

"What is it, Andrew?"

Andrew's voice faltered momentarily. "This coat looks like the one my shipmate and helpmate wore."

"Perhaps it is a coat similar? Perhaps someone took it from him?" offered the old man.

Andrew nodded as if his agreeing would make it so. After a few moments, he shook his head. "No, I have to believe it is him. I cannot leave him here exposed for vultures and animals. He saved my life on the Jersey. He watched out for me. He helped me save my brother. We never spoke it, but he was a true friend to me."

"Andrew. That may not be him."

"Even so. I have to give him some kind of proper burial."

"I have a shovel in my wagon," said the old man. He left Andrew kneeling beside the exposed arm. Andrew reached as if to touch it, but he feared he would be sucked back into the dark night of the Jersey. When the old man retuned, Andrew took the shovel and weakly dug sand as best he could to cover the exposed arm. The old man offered to help, but Andrew insisted on doing the job himself. When he finished, the old man stood over the newly covered grave and prayed. Andrew remained silent. When the old man finished he asked Andrew if he wanted to add any words, but Andrew's face screwed up into hatred and pain.

"To thank God? To beg God? I did that on the ship. I praised God all my life. God did not help me. He abandoned me. He abandoned my brother. He abandoned my friend. He left us to rot on that ship. He allows that ship to continue to turn mortal men into remnants of their former selves. You ask me if I have words. My words are only those which I never voiced aloud to my friend. He was the reason I survived. And then I abandoned him. I thought only of myself while he caused the distraction which allowed my escape. What if my escape caused him to be tortured by the British? What if they withdrew the few morsels of food they gave him because of my escape? What if I was his reason for living, and my escape gave him nothing to hope for? I may as well have killed him myself."

Andrew fell across the newly covered grave and shook and his silent cries heaved from his body. The old man stood helpless watching him. Darkness had finally descended, and when Andrew eventually calmed himself, the old man helped him to his feet and led him back to the wagon. That night the old man did not pray out loud. His prayers went silently to God asking for healing for this poor tormented young man.

Andrew slept late into the day. When he awoke the old man had made a meal for him. He stood quietly waiting for Andrew to talk, not knowing if Andrew was still in the depth of despair or if he would try to move forward.

"You said your daughter? Where is she?" asked Andrew, trying to steer away from the harsh reality of what he experienced the night before.

The Old Dutchman bowed his head. "She died of dysentery. I believe our water supply became contaminated. She just withered away in a few short days. I made a promise to her that I would try to protect anyone who came to shore from those ships. She was mortified at what she witnessed every day." Andrew quietly bowed his head. The stories were true, then, that the Old Dutchman did have a daughter, and she, too, became a casualty of war. The poison of the Jersey had to be responsible for her death as well. Again, the heat from his anger overcame him and he forced himself to look down and not into the eyes of the old man. He wanted to offer condolences, but he feared what horrible things would gush from him. This man had been his savior. He had not thanked Lefton, but he would no longer push onto the old man the hatefulness which was in his heart.

The week after his visit to the burial grounds, Andrew surprised the old Dutchman. "I believe it is time for me to find my way home," said Andrew. "I want to thank you for your hospitality and for listening to me. You've rescued me from hell, and from myself. I apologize for my outburst, but I cannot help what burns inside me. I was not this way before I was plunged into the bowels of the Jersey. I do not know that I can ever rid myself of the torments I experienced there, and the hatred for my selfish escape."

"Andrew, you must not condemn yourself for wanting to survive and escape. I am certain your friend knew what you were going through. That is why he helped you escape. No one knows what burdens the other carries within their own heart. Your friend might have looked at you as a brother who he was saving, just as you said you worked to save your brother."

Andrew said nothing as he thought about the old man's words. "Where is it that you want to go?"

"I need to get back to Elizabethtown, New Jersey. I need to see if my brother is alive and well, and to check on my family."

The host thought for a while and finally said, "You are lucky as much of the war effort is now moving to the southern states. There are far fewer patrols in the northern colonies than there were in the past few years. Seems that since '76 we have been the main focus of the war. Five years of constant battles and army troops in and out of towns, and wintering of troops in the dead cold of the northern states has had its effect on all of us.

With Staten Island being used as the main headquarters for the British, much of the war activity has been local. I believe I can get you safely to the Hudson River passage. From there you will need to find your own way home."

Home, thought Andrew. Home. If he could find his way home he knew he would be able to heal.

The Dutchman left the cottage the next day and returned late in the evening. He had gone to make what arrangements he could for Andrew's departure. Late in the afternoon the host packed food, blankets and extra clothing and loaded them into a backpack for Andrew. They planned to leave so that they would arrive at the harbor in the late afternoon. The host had made plans for a man to row Andrew across to the New Jersey shore but they would need to do this under the cover of darkness in case patrols were still out. The two traveled mostly in silence. The host prayed that Andrew would find forgiveness in his hardened heart. Andrew, however, replayed all of the hideous experiences he had lived through. It was his fervent hope that when he arrived at the Clark farm it would allow him to finally rid his mind of these nightmares and torments. Once he would get home he hoped that he would be able to find some sense of normalcy in his life.

The Old Dutchman helped put together the items he could afford to give to Andrew. A wool blanket, dry pants and shirt, a plate and cup, and a knife were packed into a knapsack. He also had a small pouch of coins he gave Andrew. Andrew protested, but the old man was insistent. As they were about to leave, the Dutchman said, "Wait. I have two final things for you." He reached into the back of the wagon and handed Andrew a flintlock pistol and a powder horn, and a Revised Book of Common Prayer. "Sorry, Andrew. The Book of Prayer is filled with prayers for the monarch, and since that would be traitorous to the American cause, some printers made revised books of prayer. Regular bibles are too large to carry. Besides, the English did not allow the Americans to print their own Bibles and demanded that we only secure copies from England so we can pay the additional taxes on them. Word is that Washington is working on having small Bibles printed though a printer named Aitkin for all of the soldiers, but they are not ready yet. I want you to have this book so you have something to help you learn to pray again."

Andrew looked at it and did not reach out for it. "I cannot take this. It belongs to your family."

"Please, Andrew. It belonged to my daughter. She would want you to have it. I feel you will find some solace in these pages when your heart is ready. Just take it and I pray there will be a time when you will be able to open it and find the peace your soul needs."

Andrew slowly took the book and humbly thanked his host, but he did not look into his face. He was fearful the host would see the doubt in his heart. He felt that he would never feel inclined to read God's word since God had not done anything to save those two thousand or more men left forgotten on the Wallabout Bay shoreline. Andrew tucked the book and pistol into the backpack and hoisted it into the wagon.

The two men sat on the wagon seat and headed toward the designated spot where Andrew would meet with his next rescuer. The two did not speak as each was filled with memories, regrets, and fears. Soon after reaching the New York Harbor, the host pulled over the wagon. Andrew pulled out the knapsack and followed his host.

The Dutchman walked with Andrew to a local tavern where they met with the man who was to take Andrew across the river. The contact was an old fisherman who would not draw too much attention to himself by the British. Nevertheless, they would travel in darkness. The three sat quietly at a table in the tavern, each drinking a tankard of beer, but no words were said between them. Andrew was careful not to look around the tavern, for fear it would draw suspicion from the others.

The old man stood to leave and Andrew looked at him and opened his mouth to thank him, but the old man nodded his head lightly as if he understood what Andrew was about to say, then patted Andrew's shoulder, and turned to walk away. Andrew watched him as he disappeared through the doorway. Andrew and the fisherman continued to sit at the table in the corner of the tavern to wait until it was time to leave. Neither spoke. A meal was served to the men and Andrew cautiously ate the stew and bread. Andrew cautiously looked around the tavern studying each face for a chance that there was betrayal. The other customers appeared to be other fishermen who had pulled their boats in for the evening. They were eating their late meals and talking about news they heard about the war. It seemed that war was the only topic Andrew could remember anyone discussing. What would they talk about if this war ever ended? Would they ever be able to talk about their families, their farms, their hopes and dreams, or had this war killed that as well?

The fisherman looked at Andrew whose face was beginning to show anger and said, "Steady, man. Don't draw attention to yourself." Andrew obeyed, but he couldn't help wondering if his trust was misplaced in this fisherman who might be turning him over to the authorities. Perhaps the fisherman and his host had conspired all along to turn him in. It had been so long since Andrew was able to trust anyone, and he did not think he could put his life into the hands of a complete stranger. The panic within his chest made his heart beat so hard that Andrew could feel its force within his chest. He forced himself to get control of his emotions. He had no choice but to trust this man, although he would feel better once his feet were on the shores of New Jersey.

Just as promised, the old fisherman stood up, dropped money on the counter for the meals, and then quietly moved toward the door. Andrew cautiously followed him, making certain his eyes did not come in contact with the tavern keeper or the other customers. As he followed the fisherman he kept a constant vigil to be certain he would not be ambushed. He wasn't. They arrived at a dock a short distance from the tavern and the man prepared the boat to be launched into the water. Andrew carefully boarded it, and did not breathe easily until they were away from the shore. At first, Andrew's stomach began to turn as he entered the boat and the familiar movement of the boat regurgitated the memories of his imprisonment. Andrew fought to tame his panic. To escape he had to remain focused. Andrew was used to traveling under a code of silence in the whaleboats, so he had no problem maintaining silence as the two moved across the river. Andrew kept a lookout for any movement of other boats, and as they neared the New Jersey shore for any movement there. He saw none.

Upon disembarking from the boat, Andrew went to reach in his pocket for some coins to pay the man, but the fisherman held up his hand. "No, young man. I understand you have already paid your price in service to the cause. Your debts are paid." The fisherman handed Andrew a sack. He quietly turned and got back into the boat, and pushed off to return home. Andrew stood momentarily looking after him. He didn't know how to react to the words that had been said. Could it be that there were some who understood the price that was paid, especially by those who had been mistreated by the British? Andrew looked into the sack and found bread, meat wrapped in a cloth, and some fruit. As Andrew watched the fisherman move into darkness he stifled a heavy sob, and then quickly looked about himself to be certain he was alone. He took a deep breath and began walking south. It was time to return home, to Elizabethtown, to his family.

Andrew walked in the shadows, and within tree groves ever cautious of his surroundings. The host was right. He saw very little military personnel compared to what he had experienced prior to his imprisonment. As he walked he looked at the destruction left behind by war. Houses were abandoned, barns burned, and property was unkempt. With all the menfolk off to war it made sense that no one was tending the fields. If this war ever ended there would be years of repairs and rebuilding that would be needed. Andrew then thought of the thousands who perished on the prison ships. In all likelihood, many of these farms could be theirs. He wondered if their families even guessed that their husbands, sons, brothers were in shallow graves, forgotten by their government and their God. Again, the anger swelled within Andrew. He thought to himself, "Will I ever feel whole again?"

Andrew's trip back to Elizabethtown was uneventful. He was ever careful to remain out of direct sight of anyone, ever fearful of being spotted by the British or their Loyalist informers. It was not such a long distance to Elizabethtown, but Andrew had to travel back roads, or in wooded paths. Nights were spent walking as much as he could, and once he became tired he slept in wooded areas where he selected spots protected by fallen trees or rocks. He was still not at full strength, but the clean, fresh air and the gifted food which filled his belly went a long way to strengthening his body and spirit.

As Andrew approached Elizabethtown he was overwhelmed with the changes he saw. The courthouse had been burned down, and many of the houses were in disrepair or stood abandoned. With the British stationed on Staten Island, it made sense that many people left the area. As Andrew looked at all the familiar places of his youth, his heart grew more and more fearful as he worried about the state of the Clark farm. The family farm was between Elizabethtown and Rahway, which was not a far distance. Andrew continued his hike, filled with anticipation of seeing his mother, Thomas, and his younger siblings. Despite his desire to see family, Andrew was fearful that his reunion would be filled with shock and dismay. His mind created images of all the losses his mother and family could have suffered during his absence.

Andrew neared the Clark farm, and as he approached it he suddenly had a strange feeling overtake him. Instead of the promised joy he had expected to feel as he approached his home which he had longed for throughout his imprisonment, he now felt a sense of dread. Although Thomas would certainly understand what he had been through, how could he vocalize to the rest of his family the horrors he had encountered as a prisoner on the Jersey? How could he open his heart and tell his mother how angry he was with his father, with Washington, with Congress, with those who knew what was happening on that hell ship yet did nothing to relieve their suffering? How could he tell her that her prayers and thankfulness were to a God who had no love for him or others on the prison ship? Andrew stopped and stared at the entrance to the Clark farm. He could not bear to move forward. The feeling of filth, disgust, and hatred overtook him. Suddenly the experiences of his imprisonment came flooding over him and his mind could once again see the bodies of the dead piled on the forecastle, the buckets of waste and filth being dumped overboard on one side and water being drawn from the opposite side of the ship, the horrible food the prisoners were given to eat, the shivering in the winter and the sweltering heat of the summer while locked beneath the hated grate, the moans of the ill and dying, and the dead stares of those who surrendered to death. And, he thought of Lefton, who he had abandoned. Andrew bent over and vomited and a wave of hatred once again overcame him and he sobbed at his remembering his nightmare.

"Mr. Andrew?" a voice startled Andrew. He grabbed for his pistol and swerved around to see Tobe looking at him. Tobe reached his hands out toward Andrew showing him he had nothing in his hands. "Mr. Andrew? It's me, Tobe. Mr. Andrew, sit you down here and I will fetch some help!" Tobe carefully stepped toward Andrew, but Andrew stepped backward away from him. His pistol was still aimed at Tobe.

Tobe's eyes moved from Andrew's face to the pistol, then back to Andrew's face. Andrew could see Tobe's frightened look and slowly lowered the pistol.

"No, Tobe. Please don't touch me, and do not fetch anyone. Please sit nearby while I try to collect myself." Tobe obeyed and sat near enough Andrew that he could help if needed, yet far enough that the pistol could be kept in sight. Andrew finally fell to the ground and sat with his head resting on his knees. He remained quiet for at least ten minutes. He finally raised his head and asked Tobe, "Did my brother Thomas make it home safely?"

"Yes, Mr. Andrew. Mammy Rose has been tending to him with your mother and Captain Thomas's wife. Your brother, Abraham, doesn't let Captain Thomas out of his sight. Mammy Rose doesn't think Captain Thomas will ever be his old self, but he will live all right."

Andrew nodded and showed relief in his face. Andrew looked at Tobe, and studied his worried face. Again, an agonizing anger swelled in Andrew. His father had served with the War Department in Congress and must have known about Sullivan's mission to destroy the Indians. His father also said he was against slavery, yet here was Tobe, and his brother, Pete, and their mother, Rose, who were purchased at the start of the war as slaves. Andrew knew his father had signed a document to free Rose and her sons when his mother died, but here again was a sign that his father contradicted what he said he believed in. Andrew could remember his father talking about how the land which became New Jersey was obtained by cheating the Indian tribes. He had sounded so sad, yet he was a part of Andrew being sent into Indian country to demolish the Indians. He said he was against slavery, but here was Tobe, Pete and Rose, slaves on their farm. He said he loved family, yet he did nothing to rescue Thomas and him from the terrors of The Jersey. Anger swelled and Andrew's face became hot as he thought about this.

Tobe interrupted his thoughts. "Master Andrew? You all right?"

Andrew fixed his gaze on Tobe. "Tobe, how has your life been on our farm?"

Tobe did not know why Andrew was asking such a question. He immediately became fearful that Andrew was going to make some change on the Clark farm which would disrupt their lives. "Well, Mr. Andrew. We treated right well by Mrs. Clark and the children. Pete and me work hard with the younger children to keep food on the table and keep the farm running as best we can. I was too young to remember much 'bout where we lived before, but we treated much kinder here."

Tobe was only about twelve years old, but Andrew was certain he knew what slavery meant. Perhaps they were not mistreated, but they were still slaves. Andrew remembered his father bringing Rose and her sons home prior to his leaving for Philadelphia. Andrew was surprised that his father would bring two little boys to the farm and wondered what his father expected the children to be able to do on the farm. He eventually understood that it was Rose his father wanted so she could help with the house and children. His father didn't want to split up Rose's family. Still, even though he might understand the motives behind his father's actions, it was still slavery. Andrew's emotions were so mixed he could not think straight. All he knew was that he did not want to see his father at this time.

"Tobe, I want you to not tell anyone that I have returned home. I will find somewhere to sleep tonight, and I will return to this spot tomorrow at about the same time. Can you bring me some food and any news you can gather. I am not of a good mind right now to see my family. I must come to terms with what I need to do."

Andrew's voice was quiet and stern, and Tobe, wide-eyed and bewildered, agreed that he would not tell anyone of Andrew's return. Tobe remained seated and watched Andrew gather himself up and continue down the road. Tobe waited until he could no longer see Andrew, then turned and ran back to the Clark house.

Chapter 13
Unreconciled

August, 1781

Tobe arrived early the next morning at the designated spot. He brought with him a variety of foods he had gathered without drawing attention to himself by his mother or others on the Clark farm. Tobe watched as Andrew unpacked the sack of food, carefully handling each piece as if relishing it was made at home. Tobe eyed Andrew and his face saddened as he looked at Andrew's drawn face and thin hands. When he last saw Andrew he was a healthy and strong young man. Tobe remembered Andrew's laughter and the way he joked around with his younger siblings and nephew. This was not the same man who had disappeared almost a year ago.

Andrew sat quietly and ravenously ate some of the food, then carefully packed the rest to take with him. Andrew had starved for so long on the Jersey that he never wasted any morsel of food set before him. Before rising to leave, Andrew asked Tobe if he had any news of his family. Tobe shared, "Mammy Rose is in the house all day with Mrs. Clark. Me and Pete don't go into the house much because we work on the chores with master Abraham, while your sisters, Sarah and Abigail feed the chickens and help Mammy Rose hang laundry. Once we finish choppin' wood and doin' the work by the house, me, Pete and Master Abraham take off for one of the smaller fields we planted in the spring. Now that a lot of the soldiers aren't coming around we might get some good vegetables this summer. Last year everything we planted was stolen. Lucky for us we planted another field deep in the woods. We planted some hay, and some wheat, corn and pota-toes. We can't do too much because all the men are off fightin' he war, but what we do collect helps with the animals and we can bury some of the potatoes in the cellar to help get us through the winter. Master Abraham helped sell some of the grain and wheat we were able to get for trade for flour. Mammy Rose brings out lunch to us around noon. Once chores are done, Pete and I take off fishin' in the Rahway River. Sometimes Master Abraham comes with us. If we catch anything Mrs. Clark gives us treats from the kitchen and we all get fresh fish for dinner."

Andrew listened intently as his mind pictured all the normal day activities of his family. It made him sad to think of Abraham, Tobe and Pete all working so hard so the Clarks could survive. Andrew asked, haltingly, "Is my father still working?"

"Mister Clark is home now," said Tobe in an excited voice. "He got home three days ago. Lots of neighbor men have stopped by to see him yesterday. Everyone is talkin' about the war. We don't see too many soldiers around here right now, not like we did the last couple years, but the war is still goin' on. I heard one of the gentlemen say they is fighting south. Mister Clark says he is leaving again in a few days."

When Andrew heard his father was home, his back stiffened, which surprised Andrew as he did not anticipate this reaction. Andrew stood and gathered up the food Tobe had brought him. "Tobe. I need you to keep secret about my being here. I am not ready to see my family yet. I need to sort some things out in my mind." Tobe nodded as he watched Andrew rise with the help of a stick he had at his side. "Don't tell Thomas or anyone else I am here, understand?" Andrew added. Again Tobe nodded. Andrew walked away, and Tobe watched him disappear into the woods. Tobe then ran back to the Clark house. He was certainly going to be late for morning chores.

This ritual continued over the next few days. Tobe would bring food to Andrew and answer any questions Andrew would ask. Andrew was careful to stand along a treed edge of the Clark farm so that he could detect any motion from the Clark house. He was determined not to be seen by his father who had not yet departed for his return to Philadelphia. He asked Tobe a great many questions about his younger siblings, his mother, and Thomas, but he never asked about his father, other than to ask when his father would be leaving.

Tobe dutifully answered, although every time he tried to add information about Abra, Andrew would raise his hand and shake his head. After several attempts, Tobe learned not to make any comments about Mister Clark.

Andrew learned from Tobe that Thomas was becoming stronger, but his lungs were still weak from his experience onboard the Jersey. Each day Thomas would force himself to move a bit further in distance. His mother and Elizabeth would take turns working with Thomas as he struggled to gain his strength and independence, and when they were resting or tending to other needs, young Abraham would step in.

"How is Elizabeth doing? When I left she seemed to be pretty frail in her dealing with this war," said Andrew to Tobe.

"No, sir, Mister Andrew. That Missus Elizabeth was pretty smart. After you left, Missus Elizabeth started going to the tavern to drop off baked foods to earn some extra money. British soldiers would be sitting at tables in there, and Missus Elizabeth would offer to clear the tables and help out. She would listen to what they were discussing and then she would write out messages to the American army officers and tell them what was being discussed by the British."

"What? She was spying?"

"Yes sir. She said it was the least she could do to help her husband get home safely. It sort of just happened one time, and then she would make it a habit. The British officers paid her no mind while she worked at the tavern. Probably never thought a woman would be smart enough to gather information," Tobe said. "She would do this once or twice a week and never once did anyone ever stop her."

"Well, I'll be!" said Andrew. Andrew thought about the many of the local women, especially the wives of indentured men hereabouts, who followed the troops. They had no real homes of their own as their husbands were not property owners. They followed the camps and served as cooks, seamstresses, laundresses, maids and nurses. They would earn 25 cents a day and get a day's rations for their work. For some of them, that was the only food they would have had as their menfolk had left for the war. Andrew even heard stories of some women posing as men to fight with the troops. Once caught they would be arrested, but their work was important to the army. Andrew smiled to himself in thinking of Elizabeth doing such work, especially with young Jonathan to care for.

"Your mother would take care of Jonathan. She knew what Elizabeth was doing, and she said that if it would bring you boys home from the war safely, it was worth the risk." Andrew pondered this and sat is disbelief as he realized his mother and sister-in-law had become part of the war effort. Gone were the days where the men protected the womenfolk. Now the women were sharing the burdens of war and trying to successfully bring this war to a conclusion.

Tobe continued, "And, Mister Andrew, you need to know young Master Abraham has been studying up on medicine.

When the chores are caught up on the farm he goes down to help with injured soldiers who have returned home. Once Mister Thomas returned, Master Abraham stayed at his side helping him recover. He is getting right good at gathering the herbs and roots to make poultices to ward off that pus on the sores." Andrew dropped his head as he remembered how dedicated Abraham had been while he was recovering from his wounds. Poor Abraham, thought Andrew. His childhood is steeped in training to cure the sick and healing the injured instead of enjoying the end of his childhood. Damn this war and all it has done to destroy the world he had once known. Tobe cautiously tried again, "And, Mister Clark has been worried sick over you and Aaron who is still out there...."

"Stop, Tobe," Andrew said as he raised his hand up as if to ward off the words Tobe was trying to say. "I do not want to hear about my father." Tobe looked hard at Andrew and could see the anger rising in Andrew's face. He was confused why Andrew was so bitter.

Tobe waited while Andrew ate the food he had brought and kept watch for anyone coming close to the area. Andrew looked at Tobe and felt sorry that this poor boy who had spent his childhood as a slave, and during the war as a constant lookout for the Clark family. Tobe was constantly fidgeting and every sound caused him to jump a little as it could be the enemy approaching, threatening his safety, the safety of his brother and mother, and the Clarks. He, too, had no childhood. Without realizing it, Andrew's face burned with anger yet again. The finger of blame needed to be pointed at something, someone. This war had taken lives. This war had stripped so many of their youth, their childhoods, and their safety. The price was too high.

Once Andrew collected himself, he rose to leave. "Thank you, Tobe. I will be by tomorrow."

"Mr. Andrew, where are you staying?" asked Tobe.

"Not to worry, Tobe. I have found shelter nearby. The old Cory barn is still partially standing, and I've been able to keep out of the elements there. Do not share that information with anyone, but should you need to get me, that is where you will find me, or somewhere near there."

Tobe nodded his head, and then gathered up the feed sack he had used to transport the food, and headed back to the Clark house. Andrew watched him until Tobe was out of sight, and then moved again toward the Cory farm. While in search of a good hiding place Andrew had found a root cellar which was still intact; however after having been held captive on the Jersey, Andrew could not bear to hide within the burrow beneath the ground which felt like a jail structure. He felt safer above ground and where the morning sunlight and fresh air were plentiful during the day, and the nights were not filled with the agonizing moans of prisoners. Instead he found an intact section of the loft which had not been damaged by the fire that had ravaged the majority of the structure, probably set by the British or the town Loyalists. Although it was a struggle for him to climb the ladder, he willing did this in order to find sleep and some level of comfort.

Andrew's own strength was still not totally restored, and sleep was often elusive as his nights were still filled with visions of the Jersey experiences. Andrew spent his days trying to look at the positives of his life, yet his mind continually remained focused on the negatives of the hellish environment of his prison. He was happy that Thomas was safe and healing, but he remained angered that his father had not rescued them. He was angered that Thomas' life was valued as an officer and worth saving through the prisoner exchange, but he was left to rot on the Jersey. To know that the privates who gave up their home lives in order to help win the war, yet were not valued enough to be rescued when imprisoned pushed Andrew to an anger and disgust that he could not control. He felt dirty because of the work he had done on the Jersey, and he was too filthy to ever stand in the presence of his mother and younger sisters. His hands had handled the dead, their vile and decaying and soiled bodies. He had threatened to kill those who laid hands on him in an attempt to steal his food or boots when they thought he was asleep, or dead. He had not been able to pray since he escaped, although he tried repeatedly. Where was his God? Where was the God that he prayed to for so many years when he needed nothing, yet in his darkest hour that God did not save him? Andrew mourned the loss of his youth, his love for his fellow man, and his feelings of inclusion with his family, his faith, and his respect for his father. At times it was almost too much to bear and Andrew considered several times whether taking his own life would be preferable to living the repeated nightmares of his poisoned memories.

Each day Andrew promised himself he would start anew, however his promise quickly faded. Andrew had not been able to sleep through the night without awakening numerous times jumping at any sound which he heard in the barn. His sleep was not restful, and once daylight hit his eyes he would surrender any attempts at sleep. His mind was constantly in a replay of one scene or another of his imprisonment. He tried to force himself to remember the joys of his youth, but those memories became overshadowed when a glimpse of his father would rise and Andrew would again be filled with anger that this man, who he loved and admired more than anyone, had not done anything to protect him.

Andrew was walking back to the meeting place with Tobe when he heard a wagon moving down the road. He moved off the road and tried to get as close to the tree line as possible, but he was in a stretch with very few trees. As the wagon approached him, Andrew's heart skipped a beat and his body shook uncontrollably. He could tell by the posture it was his father sitting on the bench alongside the driver. Andrew stopped and stared directly at his father, frozen momentarily in time. Abra had been talking to the driver when he glanced at the road ahead, then stopped talking and stretched his neck forward. "Andrew?" he mouthed. He leaned closer. A yell left his lungs. "Andrew!" Andrew stood frozen, hearing his father's voice, seeing the recognition in his father's face. Andrew's mind was locked and he was torn with emotion. Then, without acknowledging his father, Andrew turned and walked completely into the field and quickened his struggling pace with each step until he found himself staggering and running away from the wagon. He could hear his father's voice calling, pleading after him, but Andrew did not stop.

Darkness as approaching by the time Andrew found his way back to the abandoned Cory barn. He felt numb and profoundly overwhelmed with what had happened. He had not planned to react the way he did. It was as if his body was possessed and he had no control over himself. He just needed to escape from the possible confrontation with his father. He tried to reason to himself that his father truly wanted him to stop and he wanted to talk to Andrew, but Andrew knew life had changed him. His reaction told him that his mind had already been set. He could never go home again. He could never again embrace his mother. He could never say his goodbyes to his mother and siblings, even Thomas. He was unclean. He was not to be trusted in embracing family. And, it was obvious now that he completely blamed his father for both Thomas' health, and his own experience on the Jersey.

A Patriot's Price

Andrew tried again to pray to find comfort and peace, but the words would not form and the anger would not subside. At some point, Andrew finally drifted to sleep and perhaps because he had been so emotionally charged, he spent a thankfully dreamless sleep.

Chapter 14
A Purposeful Farewell

August, 1781

Andrew awakened when he heard a wagon approaching the Cory farm. His brain, which had been so sleep deprived, left him dazed and confused. Andrew tried to shake off the sleep, then when the realization that the wagon had stopped outside the barn, Andrew's body jolted into panic mode. He picked up his pistol and prepared to defend himself when he heard Thomas' voice.

"Andrew? Andrew? Are you here? It's Thomas."

Andrew's arm went limp and he stumbled out from his hiding place, shielding his eyes from the morning sun. "Thomas? How did you know I was here?"

Thomas carefully slid off the wagon seat, and with the help of Tobe he exited the wagon, using two sticks as canes to help steady himself. Andrew crawled down from the loft and cautiously approached Thomas. Andrew motioned to Tobe to remain at the wagon, and Andrew helped Thomas over to a fallen log which lay neglected outside the barn. Thomas breathed heavily as he walked the short distance with Andrew holding his arm to assist him. Andrew helped lower Thomas to sit on the log, and then stiffly lowered himself next to him. Andrew stared at his brother to determine the amount of damage his experience had caused. Thomas had lost a lot of weight, and his face was very much drawn. His coloring was not the robust complexion of his past, but pale and yellowed. Thomas was also staring at Andrew, measuring the same marks of imprisonment on Andrew's face. Gone was the youthful and stubborn young man he had left to tend the farm at the start of the war. Now there was a man sitting beside him. Andrew's eyes were hollowed and shadowed, no doubt as they had seen and witnessed much of war and pain. Even on the Jersey, Thomas was never able to fully see Andrew because of the darkness below decks. He knew it was Andrew who had saved his life. Likewise, Andrew knew it was Thomas who kept his hope alive so he could survive. Without Thomas' presence on the hell ship, Andrew would have given up and died with the rest of those who surrendered to the ease and peace of death.

"Father thought he saw you. He was heading back to Philadelphia and saw you. At first he thought it was his mind playing tricks on him, but when he called out to you, you took off without even acknowledging him. He returned home and told me. Mother overheard only a part of the discussion, and thought there was a runaway slave. She said that she knew Tobe had been taking food each day from the kitchen. She never confronted Tobe as she could not bear for someone to go hungry. After Mother left, Father called Tobe and questioned him, and Tobe unwillingly confessed that you had returned to the area. He said he did not know where you were staying, but after Father left to search our outbuildings, I questioned Tobe and he confessed to me where you were. I told Father I needed to seek you out myself." Andrew looked and saw that Tobe was sitting on the wagon bench with his head lowered, ashamed that he had broken his promise to Andrew.

"How did you escape the Jersey?" Thomas asked.

Andrew paused and weighed his words carefully. What should have been a quick reply was delivered in a haltingly labored manner. Each sentence was a struggle for Andrew as he relived each moment and memory. "After you were released for prisoner exchange, I confess I began to give up. I was filled with anger and hate. I lost my belief in God and mankind. At some point I saw an opportunity to try to escape. I knew full well the foul waters surrounding the Jersey could swallow me whole and put me to an end of my misery. A floating tabletop became my ship and I somehow managed to reach the shore despite feeling too weak to push myself forward. One kind man took me in. I never even asked his name, so far removed was I from civility. He nursed me back to some semblance of health, then helped me to escape Wallabout Bay and set me on my way to return home. My problem was that the closer I came to home, the more I realized I could no longer be part of this life."

Andrew paused, and Thomas dutifully waited for his brother to compose himself. "Too much has happened to me. I have changed. I have done the filthy work of the British. Daily I gathered the dead. Daily I handled the filth and disease ridden and decomposing and starved bodies of my fellow men. I dragged them topside. Daily I lay like a refugee, guarding my morsels of bread and morsels of food against those who would kill for food. I admit that I have beaten men for trying to steal the little food I had, and I carried no remorse for their condition. Daily I remained on guard against those who would steal the very clothing I lay in to protect them against the cold of winter. I cannot touch our mother or my sisters with these hands that have been defiled by death. I cannot see happiness, even in my escape, as there are those still suffering on that ship. Each year over two thousand souls are dumped into shallow graves on a beach. Most do not remain covered, and their bones wash out to sea to be tumbled about un-mourned and unknown."

Andrew paused for a long time, reliving his discovery on the beach. "Although I cannot be certain, I believe the only man to befriend me on that hell ship, the man who helped me to escape, he, too, met his end." Andrew was overcome with emotion, and Thomas sat silently letting Andrew regain his composure.

"Everyone turned their backs on those of us damned to be on the Jersey. The people of New York had to know what was happening, yet they did not intervene. Washington and Congress did not intervene. We were not worthy of saving as we did not have a value as non-officers. Our own leaders did not find any value in our being rescued, despite nearly every man on that hell ship having fought for the freedom of this country. Not even God intervened. I prayed. I prayed. I prayed. I recited every prayer, every Bible passage I could recall, every proverb, but God did not hear me. He shut me out. But worse of all, our own father did not intervene on our behalf. How can I return home to a family which still embraces the bounty of God and fellow man when all I feel is betrayal and hate?"

Thomas recognized many of Andrew's nightmares as he, too, had shared them, albeit for a shorter span of time than Andrew. Thomas could only look at his brother. Andrew's pain was deep and could not be healed with the herbs and roots and poultices young Abraham and Rose would apply. It could not be healed by the loving embrace of a mother who mourned daily for her children to return safely from this war. And it was most obvious that Andrew could not forgive his government or his father for their part in the British ill treatment of the prisoners of the Jersey. "Maybe you should talk to Reverend Caldwell. Maybe he can give your mind some peace."

"I doubt that even Reverend Caldwell can help me. He has to know how difficult this war has been, especially since he signed on as chaplain with the troops, and then as Quartermaster when father requested he take on that role. He is a spiritual man, but I feel nothing spiritual in my heart. At least he has a family he can look at that he does not resent as I do when I think of Father."

Thomas considered whether to share the news that broke the hearts of everyone in the Elizabethtown area. Andrew looked at Thomas' face and knew he was holding something back. "Thomas? What is it?"

"I hesitate to tell you, but Reverend Caldwell's family was to move to Connecticut Farms while he was off with the troops. Mrs. Caldwell refused to leave as she felt the British would have no cause to harm a woman with her children. When warned to go into hiding, she refused. In fact she dressed in her best and challenged those who warned her that the British could come, and she would not make way for them. A group of British soldiers came through the area and one peered into the parsonage window and spotted Mrs. Caldwell nursing her baby. He shot through the window and she dropped down dead."

Andrew stared at Thomas in disbelief. Thomas continued, "The British refused to remove her body from the house for a while, and wouldn't let the people take her and the screaming baby and children to safety. It was assumed that when the soldiers realized what they had done, they didn't know what to do next. Finally they dragged her body out into the middle of the street, but wouldn't let anyone touch her while they burned down the parsonage. She lay there exposed for hours before they finally left, allowing people to collect her body for burial. Her children were divided up into different families to be cared for after her burial. Poor Reverend Caldwell could see the smoke rising in the distance and thanked God it wasn't his home. Little did he know it was his home and his wife that had paid the price of this war."

Andrew stood up and began pacing back and forth. "How could they be so barbaric to do this to a woman? Where was God in protecting her? What God would allow the wife of a man of the cloth to be butchered in such a way? Damn this war! Damn the British. Damn God." Andrew's face was torn with emotion. Mrs. Caldwell was a good woman, a church going woman, a mother devoted to her children. All he could think of was that God had failed her, just as He failed him. Andrew eventually dropped down next to Thomas. "Where is Reverend Caldwell?"

"He has returned to work for the Army. Father picked the right person to be Quartermaster. Caldwell is now even more dedicated in securing the supplies our soldiers need to help them in fighting this war. He calls to the local men to fight beside him, and help him seek revenge for his wife's death. Reverend Caldwell is honest and dedicated and would never line his own pockets with funding that was meant to help our soldiers." Andrew held his head in his hands and felt an even deeper sense of despair for the Caldwell family. Poor Reverend Caldwell. He had put his faith in a God who was not protecting him or his innocent children.

Finally Thomas asked, "What are you going to do, Andrew?"

Andrew looked at Thomas, his face filled with uncertainty. "I don't know, Thomas. I don't know. The only thing I do know is that I am no good here for anyone. I cannot follow the troops to the South. I know that once I am fully well I am expected to rejoin. But I fear that my mind will never be fully well. I have this hatred inside me that I cannot shake. My anger at Congress and Washington in not rescuing those imprisoned on the prison ships in Wallabout Bay will never be put to rest. How could I serve an army that I feel deserted me and others? Two to three thousand men a year from the Jersey alone die forgotten and abandoned? How many more years will this go on? How many more lives will be lost rotting on that hell ship, not even in battle on our sacred soil, but wasting away in a rotting ship, being fed contaminated food that isn't fit for animals, and neglected and abused by their captors. You, Thomas. Look what they did to you. Starving you and locking you in total darkness so you could not tell day from night. Beating you into submission. How can you forgive them, let alone ever forget? I was on that ship for nearly a year. A year of my life, which I will never regain. They stripped me of my dignity as a man, my trust in man, God, our leaders, and even my father. No one should have to pay such a price. I could not bear the sight of Father when I saw him in that wagon. His voice calling to me was like a nail being driven into my very heart. I do not trust myself to see our mother as I know she will beg me to stay, and I would forever be a reminder of the damage done by war. I could not bear to have her look at the man I have become. I have changed, Thomas. I do not know that I can ever be the Andrew who once walked through this town, loving his life and loving his father the way I did, or worshiping a God who has turned his back on us." Andrew lowered his head, and allowed the tears to roll down his cheeks.

Thomas sat speechless at his side. He knew what Andrew said was true. He remembered his feverish state onboard the Jersey, wishing death would just take him to end the torment he felt and the abandonment and desolation in his own soul. But he had been kept alive by Andrew's sacrifice and others who shoved pieces of food through the keyhole to be grabbed and swallowed like a starved dog in the darkness of his cell. At least he had been released and exchanged. But Andrew had remained onboard the ship, surviving the torment every day and watching others be released of their pain by exchange, or by death. Even in his cell, Thomas could hear the moaning and wailing of those in the darkness outside his door as they blasphemed their captors, and their God! It must have been the hell Dante described in the *Inferno* as the tortured souls realized their torment would never end. How many of them died with curses of God on their lips? Thomas understood

Andrew's state of mind. He could not fix it with words. Perhaps even time would never heal him.

The silence lasted for a long period as each brother thought about the torments of the Jersey. For Thomas he was back in the arms of his family and his mind was healing because of the love of his wife, his son, and his mother. Andrew's torment lay deep in his soul, and the door was locked against the embrace of family and even God. Thomas at last said, "How can I help you, Andrew?"

"Help me? I don't think anyone will be able to help me. A man helped me when I first escaped. I could only look at him with distrust even as he tried to reach out to help me. A fisherman brought me to the New Jersey shore and asked nothing in return, yet throughout our silent crossing to New Jersey, I sat convinced he was setting me up to turn me over to the hated British. My paranoia runs so deep I doubt I will ever trust again. I was unable to shed the bitterness of my soul even when these two strangers helped me. I know I cannot stay here. Elizabethtown holds too many memories from the past, and it will only cause me further pain to look at it and realize that I can never return in heart and soul. I cannot join the troops as I will mistrust my commanders and even fellow soldiers, and I do not have the heart to face war again, especially if I were to be captured and sent back to the prison ships. I think my only recourse is to leave this place and go where I can live in solitude and try to reclaim my life."

"Andrew, the government is talking about land deeds for those of us who fought in the war. I understand what you are saying about Elizabethtown. I share that feeling because I, too, know that I can never look at this place the same. Father talked about the land deeds and I believe after the war is over, and we declare victory, I will take advantage of it and move my family to a new uncharted territory."

"Thomas, I cannot wait for this war to be over. What if it isn't? What if the British continue their brutal treatment of us, and escalate it? And, if we do win this war, I cannot take from the government something which I feel I did not earn."

"Did not earn? I would say you served the army well. Your imprisonment alone should make you a worthy candidate for compensation."

"No. I want nothing from this government but to be left alone. I certainly want nothing to do with anything our Father has done. I can never forgive him for abandoning us on that ship."

Thomas proceeded cautiously. "Andrew. He couldn't. He had to follow his ethical code of treating every man equally, and that included himself."

"He put his loyalty to the government ahead of his loyalty to family. I can never forgive that," Andrew shouted.

Thomas looked into his brother's reddened face. "Andrew, I pray that one day you will be able to see why Father acted the way he did. It had nothing to do with his love of our family. In fact when he heard I was released, he came home to see me."

"A little too late. Look at you, Thomas. You were the strongest of our lot. You were an expert horseman and healthy as an ox. You can't even navigate a short ride down the road without someone holding the reins. I'm sorry, but it is true. Will you ever return to your former health? I pray you do, but I fear you will always carry the reminders of you time in hell."

Thomas sighed, knowing that what Andrew said was true. "Regardless of my health, I understand Father's stance. I never expected him to use his influence to change the course of my treatment. You know that he has fought his whole life for the better treatment of every man, regardless of his income or place in life."

"We will have to accept that we disagree on this, Thomas. I doubt, no, I know I will ever be able to forgive him. That being said, I must leave this place. I would be considered a deserter for not returning to service once I am fully strong, but I cannot do it. I have had my fill of war and what it has taken from me and from my family. I want nothing from my government. I still fear that somehow Britain could win this war, although it seems the little news I have heard makes it sound like the Americans are gaining momentum and could possibly win. However, if the south takes the same kind of beating we have taken here in New Jersey, the war could continue for many more years. I cannot be part of this."

"But where will you go?"

Andrew sat quietly contemplating an answer. He tried to think about where he could go. "Thomas, in moments when I force myself to stop thinking about the Jersey, I tried to think about Elizabethtown, but the pain of knowing I would never see it as wonderfully as I did as a child forces me to stop thinking about it as well. That is when I let my mind remember the beauty and open lands where I travelled with Sullivan in cleaning out the Indian villages. Nasty business, but the land was so peaceful. I believe I will try to find my way there and live in solitude as best I can. I could likely do hunting and trapping and keep myself alive there."

"But how will we know where you are and how to reach you?" asked Thomas.

"I have not thought about that. I feel like I need to make a clean break of my past if I am ever to heal inside. Revisiting my memories will never let me heal completely."

"When would you leave?" asked Thomas.

Andrew again stopped as he had not thought about this. Now that his father was convinced he was in the area he knew that he would not stop looking for him until they found him and brought him unwillingly to the family homestead. As welcoming as that thought might be, Andrew knew it would be futile. He could never go home again. "I believe I will need to leave immediately. I will take my time in my travels and allow myself to heal along the way, but think it best that I not dwell here too long as I will be discovered and forced to face father. I would not want him to hear what is in my heart, so it is best that I leave."

Thomas knew in his heart this would be Andrew's answer. He also knew that if Andrew saw his mother and younger siblings he would be forced to stay, but it would do little good for his emotional healing. Perhaps one day Andrew would return home, both mentally and physically healed, yet Thomas knew that once Andrew put time and space between him and his memories, he would not allow himself to revisit the past. "I will gather up supplies for you and what money I can get to help you on your way. I wish you would reconsider, but I know you believe this is the right path for you. I will be back tomorrow."

"Thomas, do not tell Father where I am. I will not talk with him. And please, do not tell Mother or the children that I survived the Jersey. It is best that they believe I am a casualty of war, which, in essence, I am. I would rather they rest their minds in believing I am no longer among the living."

Thomas nodded. The two brothers embraced and reluctantly moved apart. Thomas, using his two sticks as canes, moved to the wagon where Tobe helped him onto the seat. Andrew watched as Tobe pulled the wagon around to head back toward the Clark farm. Andrew watched as the wagon disappeared around the bend of the road. Andrew sat alone thinking that his despair and isolation would be his constant companions, yet it was far better than facing his family and having them learn of the life he lived on the Jersey. He would never want his mother and siblings to witness the hatred in his heart.

Thomas was true to his word. He had gathered up a horse, supplies, and some money for Andrew. When he returned to Andrew's hiding place the two sat together in silence for a long time, knowing this would be the last time they would be together. Andrew's mind was set and there would be no returning. Each man's thoughts skirted through time, mostly the good memories, but in the end, both could only recall the realities of war.

"Andrew, I want to thank you for helping me survive on the Jersey. Had you not been there to talk with me, or to give me the morsels of food, I would have surely perished. You gave me the will to live."

Andrew looked into his brother's eyes as if memorizing them for eternity. "It was a fair trade. You gave me reason to live. Prior to your arrival I had all but given up. I had no reason to live. Saving you gave me a purpose."

"I will forever be grateful to you Andrew. You put your life on the line for me."

"Did you tell mother and the others?" asked Andrew.

Thomas looked at the ground knowing that his mother's heart would break if she knew. "No, I kept my promise. In time Mother and the others will believe that you did not survive the war."

Thomas looked at Andrew and decided to proceed. "Father wanted to see you at least one more time, but I told him you just could not bear to see him, that the war had hardened your heart and you saw no end to the pain you have suffered. I told him you had a plan, but it would not include returning home. Times are changing, Andrew. There is talk of many who want to escape the memory of war on their farms. Father has heard this talk from many other families, families who have deep roots in Elizabethtown. Too many lived daily for years with the British, the Hessians, and their former friends and neighbors who were against them. Many of the Loyalists have already moved out of the area to separate themselves for the role they have played in destroying their home town. Our buildings are destroyed, our farms are scarred, and our memories of the peaceful times is forever changed. Many men who came home from war injured in body and spirit are waiting for the war to end so they can collect on their promise of land out west to make a new beginning, far from the haunted memories of war. I know Mother retires to her room each night where I know she cries and prays. She has remained so strong throughout these war years, taking care of the family and protecting them, and trying to keep food on the table. Young Abraham is only fourteen and Mother fears he will sneak off to join the war effort in hopes of finding you. Abigail is only eight, and I don't know that she has a strong memory of you. Sarah is already twenty years old and she has been helping as a nurses' aid with the soldiers who are locally housed. I think she does this thinking she will one day find you among those brought home to heal."

Andrew nodded his head. "It is wise to not tell the younger ones of my decision. Perhaps one day they will reconcile themselves with the thought that I perished in the war and they will be able to forget about me."

"Perhaps. As to Father, he is devastated by your decision. He wants you to understand his position."

"His position?" Andrew asked, recognizing that his voice had risen. Calming himself he continued. "I'm sorry. What were you saying?"

Thomas proceeded cautiously hoping not to trigger Andrew's fragile emotions on the subject of their father. "Father understands your need to move on, but he is not happy about your wanting to go into the Indian lands, even though Sullivan rid the area of most of them. He would rather you wait until the end of the war and secure a piece of land which all veterans will be offered as there will be no money after paying the war debts. Your leaving is like desertion."

"Would he rather that I stay and risk being captured again and returned to the Jersey?" asked Andrew in a voice that was most challenging.

"I am quite certain Father does not want you to return to the prison ships. I don't know that he knows what the alternatives are."

"I will make this easy on him. I disown him and he has no reason to worry about me. I never plan to return to New Jersey. I do not know what the future holds for me, but I do not want father holding out hope that I will one day return. I will not be the prodigal son. I am carrying too heavy a burden that I can foresee ever being totally rid of it. I hope one day I will be able to come to understand his unwillingness to rescue us. My mind understands his words of ethical politics, but my heart demanded a father protecting his young. I may never come to peace in his decision. All I know is that I will never heal my heart here. I will always be filled with this rage which I cannot control or erase. Tell Father to write me off as a son. Do not include me in any wills, as I would never return to stake claim to anything left by him. My mind is made up. I will leave and bid New Jersey a final farewell. I will always hold you and my siblings and mother dear, but it is best that everyone forget me."

"Andrew, I pray that you can find God again in your heart to help you come to terms with these experiences."

"Pray? Why? I prayed on the Jersey. I begged God to help me. He turned his back on me and left me there to rot." The fury had again risen into his voice, and Thomas knew there would be no changing his heart at this time.

Thomas and Andrew sat for a long period of time and neither seemed to want to say their final goodbyes. Tobe had already left the wagon to feed the horse and stood waiting for Thomas to move toward the wagon to return to the Clark farm. Finally, Thomas struggled to stand up. Andrew stood beside him, and the two embraced tightly. Finally Andrew patted Thomas on his back. "Take care, brother. Get healthy and have a good life. You and Elizabeth should have a house full of children. I wish you well and I will always hold you dear to my heart. When Aaron returns home, you can tell him of my decision, or allow him to think I perished on the hell ship. Do what you think best. "

Thomas was moved by emotion, filled with sorrow that this younger brother, now a man, had lived such hardships at such a young age. Andrew was only twenty-two, and his heart carried a burden much heavier than any man should have to carry. Tobe helped Thomas onto the wagon, and led the horse and wagon to turn around to head back to the Clark farm. Thomas looked at Andrew for the last time and the two waved a solemn goodbye. Andrew watched the wagon and his past life disappear down the country road.

In the morning Andrew ate the food Thomas provided, and then packed up his supplies into the saddlebags. It was the end of summer in 1781, and Andrew headed his horse toward New York. Every step was a step further from his past and toward his future which lay unknown ahead of him.

Part Three
Rebirth

Chapter 15
On the Road to Find Peace

August 1781

Andrew traveled slowly from Elizabethtown toward the western New York territory. It was through his childhood knowledge of the rivers, and his war experience as a privateer and his frugality as a soldier that Andrew was able to set camp. He would fish and hunt in order to provide food for himself. He chose not to travel through settlements as his instincts guarded him against possible capture and imprisonment. Instead he traveled cautiously, following mostly the path Sullivan had used during his invasion into the Indian Territory. At first he travelled without really thinking of anything, other than what he needed to do to survive. He did not think about the past, but only the present. Each day he felt a little stronger. He knew he was far from where he was prior to the Jersey experience, but he fought hard to eat daily, and to rest. Sleep would help him heal, although he never knew when his sleep would instantly cease when his mind returned to the bowels of the Jersey. When this happened he bolted upright, and reclaiming sleep was often impossible.

As Andrew traveled, his mind drifted back to the conversations he had with the scouts for the Sullivan Campaign telling the men of the history of this region. Andrew recalled sitting around the campfire mesmerized by the stories. The scouts were knowledgeable about the Indians as well as the formation of the lakes. One scout in particular was brilliant. He was a learned man who spoke of things Andrew and the other men never heard before. "Scientifically we know the region was the result of great glaciers which crossed the land. As the glaciers moved south, deep trenches were ground out. As the glaciers retreated over time, the melt water filled the newly formed lakes. Many waterfalls from the gorges hung above the lakes and the waters cascaded down into the lakes below," the scout said.

"How do we know glaciers were in this area?" asked Andrew.

"There are those who study the geography and recognize rock and land formations which were caused by the earth being ground up by a massive force."

"Amazing. Simply amazing," said Andrew. Not all of the men cared to hear about the creation of the lakes. They were more concerned about their safety and the cunning savages they were sent to destroy. But Andrew enjoyed the diversion from their present worries.

The scout continued his story. "The Indians called this area the fingerprints of the Great Spirit who had reached down and touched the land. Because the Great Spirit had touched the earth, it became sacred land."

"I spent my entire childhood going to church and learning that God created this earth, however I cannot say that I have ever seen anything in New Jersey as magnificent as this area," said Andrew. "It takes my breath away."

The scout nodded. "The Indians protected this sacred land and considered the lakes and the fresh water here to be blessings from the Great Spirit. When the Tuscaroras joined the other tribes in 1722 they had formed a confederacy of Six Nations called the Haudenosaunee, or 'People of the Longhouse,' which included the Senecas, Onondagas, Mohawks, Cayugas, Oneidas and Tuscaroras. The Senecas were looking for a peaceful place to settle having escaped from the warlike Massawomeck tribe. Living in this area promised to be peaceful and blessed by the Great Spirit. The Iroquois prevented white men who came here to explore the area and from their establishing settlements. The few white men in the area who were allowed to live here did so with the permission of the Indian tribes. Such settlers had to be non-threatening and respectful of the resources."

Andrew nodded in understanding. The scout continued. "Map makers began calling this area the Finger Lakes as they resembled long fingers stretching across the landscape."

The scout took a twig and began drawing the resemblance of a map in the dirt near the fire pit. "The two largest lakes are in the center of the finger-like shapes. There are a total of eleven lakes that sit within the Finger Lakes area. Cayuga Lake and Seneca Lake are both the longest and the deepest of all of the lakes." The scout then pointed to each of the dirt drawn lakes as he named them. "The others are Canandaigua Lake, Canadice Lake, Conesus Lake, Hemlock Lake, Honeoye Lake, Keuka Lake, Otisco Lake, Owasco Lake and Skaneateles Lake. Oneida Lake is considered to be the "thumb" of the finger formation." The scout pointed out the location of each of the lakes and Andrew studied the sketched map of the area. Andrew was in awe that this man possessed such knowledge.

"Tell me this. What do you know of these Indians?" asked Andrew. They were being led to destroy them, but Andrew suspected that the scouts did carry a sense of respect for the lifestyle of those they were now hunting.

"The Indians typically travel as they need to for food, maple syrup, salt, clothing and household goods. They would then go to trade and share stories while the squaws would seek corn, beans and squash which were the main supplements of their meals. Most tribes preferred to live away from neighboring tribes. Most lived in those longhouses I talked about."

"What is a longhouse?" asked Andrew.

The scout again drew in the dirt as he answered. "The long-house was a rectangle shaped dwelling made of wood, bark, and woven branches. Most were between fourteen to sixteen feet long and seven to thirteen feet wide with dirt floors. There was a hole in the center of the roof to allow the release of smoke from the fire inside. The longhouse served as a home for extended families of various generations, all related to the matriarchal line. There could be as many as twenty different families within the longhouse. They lived as a clan and the clan was typically named after a bird or an animal. They would then decorate their household items and even their longhouse with that animal or bird. When a young man married, he moved to the longhouse of his wife. When a young woman married, her husband moved into her longhouse. No intermarriage was allowed."

Andrew sat puzzled. "We've called them savages, but their customs are much like our own."

"There are some differences. In their culture the women manage the farming and food and they also select which men will serve in the tribal council."

"Well, that is certainly different than our customs. Women have no power and do not participate in the decision making, although I am quite certain my mother could hold her own when making important decisions," laughed Andrew.

The scout laughed, and then continued. "The Iroquois tribes consider their entire population to be one large longhouse. Each tribe is to protect a part of the longhouse. The Seneca protect the Western Door. The Mohawks were keepers of the Eastern Door. The Onondaga were the Keepers of the Central Council Fire and Wampum. The Oneida and Cayuga protect either side of the Central Fire and Wampum."

Andrew thought about the logic of how the tribes worked together. He knew his father was working now on the plans for a new government and was seeking a plan which would have branches of government, all watching out for the other. That made sense. Just how was it that there was so little respect for these Indian tribes? Andrew turned to look at the scouts. "How have you learned so much about these tribes?"

The scout looked down at the fire and paused before answering. "We had been allowed at one time to live among the tribes. That was before this war began. We would listen to the stories they told about their history and the stories of their beliefs. They do not have a written language so when they are presented with treaties in writing the words have no meaning for them." Andrew thought back to when he was young and his father told them about his first document he studied which got him interested in law. It was a trade agreement with the local Indians for the property which became New Jersey. Basically the Indians had given up the rights to their land for meaningless trade items. Abra had shared the document with Aaron and Thomas when they were young and they, too, felt that there had been an injustice in the trade. Andrew, being much younger, had tried to understand the importance of what they were saying.

As Andrew got older he quickly realized that the treaties which left the Indians with little worthwhile trade items was troubling. When the tribes retaliated against the Americans, the government's plan was to harshly repay them by destroying their land. Of course, Andrew then thought of the horrific stories of how the white families had been massacred and soldiers tortured by the Indians. That was not acceptable. Andrew shook his head as he wanted to push the thoughts in his head away as he was torn in how to feel about the Indians. After having listened to the scouts tell their stories, he could see that they, too, were torn between their knowledge of the Indian culture and the necessity to stop them from barbaric attacks.

"Couldn't peace be maintained with the tribes," asked Andrew.

"Sadly, our war became their war. The British had asked the tribes to side with them because they needed easier passage of supplies. Then they were encouraged by Loyalist sympathizers to raid the colonial settlements as a way to punish those who were not following the British rule. The British offered them protection and lifetime support once the war was won. It was not long before the tribes began bringing chaos to the white settlements. In retaliation, General Washington knew he had to break this alliance between the Indians and the British and that's when this Sullivan Campaign was launched. We are heading up to meet up at Tioga Point with troops from Easton, Pennsylvania and then we are to meet General James Clinton's army coming from the Mohawk Valley. We should have about 5100 troops with horses, supply wagons, and cannons. We are ordered to destroy all major Iroquois villages. Most of the Iroquois villages are in the Finger Lakes Region. We also have orders to travel north to Catharine Valley and Montour Falls along Seneca Lake, then move to Geneva to Canandaigue, Honeoye and Hemlock Lakes. We will then head south of Conesus Lake and on to the Genesee River near Geneseo." The scout pointed out the route in his dirt drawn map. "Our orders are to destroy Indian homes and crops. Another group is moving east to Albany passing through Auburn and Skaneateles to do the same. When we are done, we should have accomplished what Washington wants, and this will put a major crimp in the British support."

Andrew's memories of his conversation with the scout came to an abrupt end as he thought about that campaign. It seemed surreal that he had been part of the Sullivan Campaign not even two years before. He remembered how the Indians tried to escape the advancing army to Fort Niagara and the protection of the British, however they met with a very bad winter and did not have the supplies needed to protect them. The British did not follow through in protecting them and providing for them. Stories were circulated throughout the troops about how the "people of the Finger Lakes" deserted the area when they realized they would not have the support of the British as the American troops advanced and destroyed their village.

For Andrew, much had happened since then including his incarceration on the hell ship and now his abandonment of his family and all business of war. The war had changed him. He shook his head in disbelief as he remembered how naïve he was about the politics of war and how bitter he had become. His distrust and anger so soured him that he could no longer think of the government or his father with any degree of forgiveness for their parts in not rescuing him and the others on the prison ships. He deeply breathed in the fresh air as if this would renew him and erase this misery he felt internally. No. The heavy sadness of his life was still there, despite his appreciation of the beauty surrounding him. Even the peacefulness of the area was dogged with the memory of the campaign he had served in and the destruction he helped wreck upon the Indian villages. Would he ever feel whole again?

Andrew pushed forward, always mindful of any sound heard near or far.

Andrew finally reached the Finger Lakes area of New York. Because of his slow progress, it was already the start of September in 1781 and he was already beginning to regret his move so late in the season. He would have little time to seek shelter and store food for the winter. He took his time in traveling and did not overtax his still recovering body. He was amazed that there was virtually no army traffic as he traveled north. When he would see signs of movement, he relied on his past experiences on the whaleboats to move onto paths following the rivers rather than using the main roads. He knew how to set his campfires in order to draw the least amount of attention to himself. Much of the area was forested and untouched. Occasionally he would come upon a clearing and he would remember the earth scorching they had done to rid the land of the Indians and wonder if this location was one where he had played a hand in its destruction. These thoughts did not help Andrew find the peacefulness he was seeking.

Andrew thought about the conversations he had with the other men as they traveled into this area during the Sullivan Campaign. The Iroquois Indians used this land for their hunting grounds. The Indians had not used the land for planting because the soil was too rich in lime. This knowledge would help Andrew as he selected a place to set up a cabin, but knew he needed to first find some place to winter since he had so few supplies. He spent two weeks traveling along Montour Falls, and along the east side of Seneca Lake. Here he found a small makeshift village of white men. There could not have been more than five homes scattered in the area, and each was spread out from the other. Andrew cautiously entered the rugged little town. His first thought was to find a blacksmith shop, but there was none in the small village. One of the folks pointed him in the direction of a blacksmith.

"Can't figure why that man would set up shop here. Instead he traipsed out toward the lake where no one else even lives. If you are intent in finding him, follow this path," he said pointing to a rough road which had been used by various travelers. Andrew thanked the man and set out to find the blacksmith. He finally reached the blacksmith's settlement before nightfall.

"What can I do for you, young man?" asked the blacksmith when he saw Andrew approaching on his horse.

Andrew did not really want to talk, but knew he had to converse in order to get what he needed. "I am looking for a place to settle. I need to find work so I can have provisions for the winter."

The blacksmith looked at Andrew skeptically. He had seen far too many young men fleeing the war to find solitude in the area. Each one had a story, but most did not share as to retell the nightmare opened the wounds of despair again. This young man certainly had the look of someone who had seen much, experienced much, and needed to escape much. Yet, there was something about this young man that made the blacksmith feel a sense of kinship. The blacksmith had come to these parts early on when some of the earlier explorers and trappers were traveling through the area. The area suited him and he remained, using the craft he had learned in shoeing horses and making metal work. The more he worked, the better craftsman he became, although in these parts it was mostly utilitarian needs for survival in this mostly unsettled area. He had taken an Indian arrow to his shoulder and upper leg which fortunately had not damaged any vital arteries.

The arrowhead was still within his leg and only bothered him when he walked too much or traveled too far. Thus, he had remained in this area, providing his services to the occasional traveler and to those who had settled in the area.

Prior to the Sullivan Campaign, the blacksmith had not invested in building as it would certainly have been destroyed, or even caused the Seneca Indians of the area to target him. Since the campaign he had not only built his barn, but he built a modest house nearby, and had even put in a garden with corn which seemed to thrive in the lime-rich soil. Surrounding his homestead were the pines and hardwoods which stood as home to the animals which he hunted. He also gathered nuts from the hickory and chestnut trees, and tapped the maple trees to make syrup. He had learned how to survive in the area.

The blacksmith also knew that with the removal of the Six Nation Iroquois in the area, the land would be highly desirable, especially to soldiers after this war would come to an end. Establishing his business before the end of the war would guarantee him success. He could certainly use someone who could help him expand this settlement. Perhaps this lanky young man would want to make his place here. He studied Andrew. "You got a name, young man?"

Andrew quietly answered, "Andrew, sir."

"Whereabouts are you from, Andrew?"

Andrew had to think about how he wanted to respond. Andrew's old instincts which had been ingrained in him

since the start of the war took over. He never wanted anyone to connect him to his family. Since he had spent nearly
a year in Wallabout Bay, he answered, "Most recently from
New York."

"Young man, are you with or against General Washington?"

Andrew felt a sense of panic. What if this man was a
Loyalist? This territory was still part of New York. Many of the
Loyalists had settled in New York. The blacksmith looked at
Andrew and realized this young man had a secret and sharing
it was not within his ability at the moment.

"Never mind, Mr. Andrew. As long as your politics are not
about harming me, then I guess we can strike a bargain that I
will not ask you any personal questions. If you are interested
in settling in the area, I am looking for some help. You don't
look like life has treated you too well lately. Have you any
experience in farming, or any trade?"

Andrew, with downcast eyes, began to answer, "My father,
uh, my family had a very small farm, and I did a lot of work on
it especially once the war started. I can manage a boat, and I
can fish and hunt, and I can handle most farm chores."

The blacksmith looked Andrew over and felt that this young
man needed time more than anything else, and perhaps he
could offer this to him as he got himself stronger. "How about
if you work here with me, doing what I need done to build up
my piece of land. I cannot pay you, but I can give you shelter
and food so long as you are willing to help me."

Andrew nodded in agreement. "Good," said the blacksmith. "You can tie your horse by the barn, and you can make your bed inside the barn. Go ahead and settle yourself. It is close to evening so I will see what food I can put together."

"Thank you, sir. Uh, can I ask your name?"

"Just call me Moses," said the blacksmith.

Chapter 16
Finding Trust

September, 1781

Andrew slept soundly that first night in the black-smith's barn. Moses had brought him a tin of hot stew and some bread and butter. Andrew hungrily ate it and quietly thanked his host who sat nearby as Andrew ate. Andrew kept his eyes cast downward, and did not offer any conversation, and Moses allowed him the space he needed. "In time," he thought. "In time he will come around."

In the morning Andrew rose and went to the trough to wash up. He dunked his head into the cold water and rubbed his face with his rough hands. As he pulled his head out of the water he looked around to ascertain whether anyone else was in the area. He saw no one, but he could hear Moses talking to the chickens as he threw seed to them. Andrew shook off the water from his hands and wiped them on his trousers. He walked toward the area where he heard Moses' voice.

Moses looked at Andrew and smiled. "You got some good sleep. Must have needed it, Andrew. Let's get some morning chow in you and we can talk about what work you can do." Andrew nodded and followed Moses as he walked toward the cabin which was built a safe distance from the smithy. Andrew remembered hearing stories of a smithy catching on fire and taking with it all the outbuildings and even the homes of the blacksmiths. Obviously Moses knew what he was doing when he laid out his building on his property. Moses went on to talk about himself and how he and his wife, Nancy, came to this area. There were many Dutch who settled in various areas of the New York territory. Moses looked to start out on his own, away from the other settlements, with hopes that he could take his learned trade of smithing and settle in an area where he could be successful. Moses laughed when he described the folly of that decision as there were not a lot of settlers who followed afterward as most were terrified of the Indians. "Now that the area has been safeguarded against the tribes, I suspect more settlers will follow out here. I also imagine that once this war is over there will be land grants given and many will take advantage of the opportunity to move away from the memories of war." When he said this he immediately noticed that Andrew's already ashen face whitened as he lowered his face. Moses decided not to further engage in this topic. Instead he asked Andrew to follow him toward the house.

As they approached the modest cabin he saw a short woman emerge with a large bonnet covering her head. She wore a large apron which she was using to wipe her hands. A small child hid behind her, holding onto her skirt. Andrew cast his eyes downward and stopped walking, ashamed to be in the presence of a woman after the harsh life he had recently lived. Moses stopped and turned when he realized Andrew had stopped following him. "It's ok, Andrew."

"No, sir. I will remain here, please. I, uh, I am not fit to be in the presence of a lady."

Moses stood, looking at this pained young man, then looked toward his wife and shook his head. By this time several children had stepped out to the front of the cabin and as they were about to charge toward this stranger, their mother gently restrained them by putting her hands on their shoulders. "Not now, young 'uns. Mr. Andrew is not ready to be surrounded by folks just yet." She motioned them toward the house, and the children reluctantly obeyed, looking back at the curious young man. Moses nodded toward his wife, and she, too, returned to the cabin.

Moses looked at Andrew. "I will get some food and I will bring it out to you at the smithy. You missed the morning meal, so I'll bring out the mid-day meal." Andrew nodded and turned and began to walk away. Moses thought to himself that whatever this young man witnessed or lived through was certainly hellish if he could not enjoy the beauty of this area and the hospitality of people who truly wanted to know him.

A Patriot's Price

When Andrew entered the smithy he walked around look-ing at all the equipment that Moses had compiled. It was a modest set up, but Moses had amassed the necessary tools to do the work that would be needed for the local folks, his own family, and any travelers moving through the area. The forge was a modest size, and the sledge and anvil were set up nearby, as well as the bellows and tongs, and a tub of water which was used to cool down the heated metal. On the wall Andrew saw the tools hanging which Moses would use. There were shears, files, chisels, saws, and grinders. Andrew had never spent much time in a smithy, other than to occasionally go with his father to get the horses shod, or to secure some item needed on the farm or for his mother. Once the war started Andrew had rarely entered the town as a safety precaution. He was always on alert that a stray Loyalist would recognize him and notify the British who were often moving through Elizabethtown. Andrew shook the memory off and continued looking at the items in the smithy. On another wall Andrew saw items that Moses had already made and had at the ready in case of a visi-tor arriving. There were horseshoes, which would need to be altered once a horse was sized. There were many of the items women needed in the kitchen including cast iron kettles, fry pans, fire pokers and kettle hooks. There was also chain, and various items farmers might need. Andrew was looking over the chain and his mind quickly jumped back to the Jersey, and his hands dropped the chain link, just as Moses entered the smithy with a plate of food. He noticed the reaction Andrew had when he touched the chain. When Andrew heard Moses he spun around and his face was putrid in color as if life had drained from it.

"Sit down, Andrew. Sit there on the bench and put your head between your knees. My God. You look like you saw a ghost." Andrew obeyed and worked to slow his breathing. Moses kept a distance and allowed Andrew the time he needed to reach composure. Once Andrew calmed himself, he looked up at Moses and noticed the concern on Moses' face.

"I am sorry, Moses."

"No need to apologize, young man. Whatever you are going through I pray that God will help you heal."

"God has no love for me," said Andrew. Andrew's voice became stern. "He abandoned me when I needed him the most."

Moses was started by this, but having lived as long as he had, he knew there were times when a man was faced with more than he could bear and he would sometimes question his own faith. He could only imagine what Andrew had faced to put him in such despair. "Why don't you eat this food, and then I will show you the work I need you to do out in the fields." Andrew nodded and took the wooden plate without looking into Moses' face. As Andrew ate, Moses proceeded to organize some of the supplies in the smithy. Andrew secretly watched him as he moved around the shop, putting tools in order, and shoveling some wayward coal back into the bin, and looking over his stock of pig iron. When Andrew finished eating, he returned the plate to the small table. Moses motioned Andrew to follow him out to the fields.

"What I need you to do is to help me with the crops. What do you know of fall harvests?"

Andrew quietly answered, "I know the end of the sweet corn comes in by mid-October. Also potatoes and tomatoes."

"We've got those and we also have some okra, blueberries and raspberries to gather. Those are in the gardens closest to the house, but my wife and younger children will handle those. My wife will be putting up preserves for the winter, and canning, pickling and smoking. I will need you to help with the other vegetables. In a few weeks we will be working on the next harvest of lima beans, cabbage and pumpkins. The last harvest will be the broccoli, cauliflower, and peppers. That keeps us pretty busy right up to the second week of December. Most of our crops we keep, although if the Lord is good to us, and we have more than we need, we look to trade with neighbors. I try to have a wide variety of vegetables because you can never trust that some pest, or the weather conditions won't attack one and if you put all your efforts into that, you'll be facing starvation in the winter. I'll be needing you to help harvest, and help set the outdoor fires for my wife as she handles the canning and preserving. My oldest boys can help you as well." Andrew looked up alarmed. "Don't worry, I will keep them from overwhelming you!" Moses laughed. "In the winter months we do some hunting, and that's when I spend a lot of time working in the smithy. It gets too hot in the summer months. If I have a productive winter we load up the wagon and go off to sell my wares, and pick up more iron supplies. I'd imagine it was the same for your family if you farmed."

Andrew nodded and his mind raced back to his mother making preserves and canning, and during the winter months working on sewing. For a moment Andrew felt a rush of heat coming over him, not caused by the warm autumn air, but by the emotion of missing his mother and the normalcy of home. Moses observed this, but said nothing.

Andrew followed Moses as his host pointed out the different crops and had stories to share about one year's harvest versus another, and of his oldest boys learning how to control the plow. Andrew wished that his father had been this involved with him on the farm. By the time Andrew was old enough to start working seriously on the farm, his father had left for Philadelphia and his older brothers, Aaron and Thomas, had left for officer training. Andrew had been left behind to be the man of the household with little opportunity to enjoy a father and son relationship like Moses described with his sons. Anger was beginning to rise again in Andrew's heart and he had to force himself to stop thinking of his father and only concentrate on the present.

After the horrible winter that hit the area in the winter of 1779-1780, Moses was relieved to have a milder winter this past year. Moses and other farmers were predicting they would not fare as well this year. They would have to stockpile as much food, firewood, and supplies as possible to prepare for the upcoming winter. Work would be continuous over the next two months and there would be a lot to do. Moses also wanted to build another small outbuilding which would be multi-purpose and guarantee enough shelter for the farm animals and their supplies. He wanted his equipment under roof to safeguard it against the harsh winter weather of the area, if indeed it would be a repeat bad year.

Andrew listened intently and vowed he would do everything in his power to help Moses who had been so kind to him. Andrew congratulated himself that since his escape in May, he was already getting much stronger, and with the hard work and good food and shelter, Andrew was beginning to feel a sense of confidence that he could weather anything that would happen.

That same day Andrew began working in the fields. The task of harvesting corn was difficult. Moses and his two older sons started on one end of the field, and Andrew, who preferred to work alone, started on the other. Each stalk had to be cut down by hand, then the corn was put into baskets to be gathered later, and the stalk and leaves were stacked into shocks to dry. The shocks would provide excellent food for the horses, cattle and even the sheep. At the end of the day Andrew looked at the field where he had worked and there was a row of what looked like teepees of corn shocks. As the light of day began fading, Moses rode the wagon over to where Andrew was working and he and his sons emptied the baskets of corn into the wagon. The boys and Moses then rode on the wagon seat and Andrew chose to sit in the back of the wagon as they headed back to the barn. Andrew felt bone tired, but he felt he had accomplished something good. The sense of well-being was nearly foreign to him as he had not felt this way since living at home. By the time they returned, they washed up and Moses' wife had dinner ready. Andrew hungrily devoured his food, which Moses brought to him in the barn, and then immediately retired to sleep. His night was not filled with the typical nightmares, but was blessedly free of dreams.

The corn harvest continued for several weeks as they harvested the acre plot of corn. There was more than enough for the family, feed for animals, and some for trade for other items they needed. Andrew worked alone and silently, and he did not allow his mind to drift to anything other than the task at hand. Every day he challenged himself to accomplish more than the day before. When Moses, his sons, and Andrew finished the corn, the plot looked magnificent with the drying shocks. Andrew stood in amazement at the sight. His typically stoic face morphed into a slight smile as he looked at what had been accomplished. It was the first time Andrew smiled since his escape. As he pondered this, the memory of Lefton's sacrifice and his neglect in helping him to escape, the hatred of the Jersey, the anger at his father and Washington and those who left them to rot on the prison ship pounded back to his memory, and the slight smile quickly faded to the worn misery of his memories. Andrew returned to the barn that night and the nightmares again returned. Andrew was unable to control when the demons returned.

Each day the harvested crop was taken back to the barn and Nancy would be seen waiting for the wagon to return. While the men were out in the field, Moses' wife and younger children would shuck the corn harvested the day before. Some of the corn was moved into the corncrib for further drying. Moses explained that they preferred the corn crop because it was easily preserved. Wheat did not grow well in this area, so Moses had only a small plot of wheat. He explained that he would have to trade some of his surplus crops or metalwork to secure the wheat needed for bread.

It was obvious to Andrew that Nancy had told the children to stay away from Andrew as they were careful not to approach him, however he knew they would watch him with great curiosity. Once he caught the eye of one of the young daughters, and she smiled and waved at Andrew. Andrew at first began to raise his hand to return a wave, thinking of his youngest sister Abigail, but quickly turned away and returned to his work.

Work on the farm was continuous. Moses was in constant motion, as was Nancy. Some days Andrew could smell the simmering pot of raspberries or apples as she worked to can them for the upcoming months. Her fireplace was much like the Clark fireplace. It had a brick oven next to the hearth where Nancy would make breads, cakes, tarts and pies. She could skillfully keep the fire going in the fireplace as well as keeping the oven regulated. This was a difficult task as she had to heat the walls of the oven hot enough to complete the baking process, and since the oven had no flue the fire could easily go out. Nancy knew how much to keep the door of the oven open to allow the smoke to escape while not blowing out the fire. She would then test the heat in the oven to determine whether it was hot enough, or if she needed to add to the fire. She would stick her arm into the oven and see if she could count to five. If she couldn't, the oven was too hot. If she could count higher than fifteen, the oven was not hot enough and she would need to add more fuel. Nancy's skill was exceptional as the breads, cakes and other products rarely were too crisp on the bottom. Nancy was proud of her kitchen, as well as her kitchen tools which she expertly used. She was most proud of her peel, which was a shovel like tool. Most women had a peel made of wood, however Moses had made hers of sheet iron. Nancy would skillfully put the breads and other dishes into the oven using the peel and then remove them with the peel.

Nancy's efficiency was not lost on the children. Even the young children were given jobs to do, however their mother would be standing over them talking to them and encouraging them as they perfected their work. One of the jobs the children handled was taking the canned or salted foods down into the root cellar. Root vegetables, fruits, cheese and dairy products, cider, beer, and foods that were canned or preserved were taken to the root cellar which was underground. Moses and Andrew also pulled barrels of salted meat into the root cellar all under Nancy's direction. Andrew secretly liked to look in her direction as she so much reminded him of his own mother, but when the emotional feelings would begin to overtake him, Andrew would quickly admonish himself and force himself to forget. Nancy not only cared for the children, tended the smaller garden near the house, canned and preserved food, cooked meals for her family, but she also spun yarn and wove cloth. Her hands were never still.

Andrew, Moses, and the two older boys, William and Joshua, worked from early morning before the sun rose, until late in the evening after the sun had set. William was about fifteen and Joshua was about fourteen. Andrew thought that Joshua was about his age when he had to take over handling the work alone on the Clark farm. William and Joshua were lucky their father worked with them, by their side, constantly talking with them about every topic imaginable.

The day started with a breakfast of either cornmeal mush, porridge with raisins or cranberries, bread and butter, or bread and milk. Moses continually invited Andrew to dine indoors with the family, however Andrew always refused. Finally it was Nancy who challenged Andrew to sit at their table. One day upon returning from the fields, Andrew was washing at the trough and Nancy startled him as she approached.

"Young man. You have been with us for several months. Packing up a meal to take out to the barn, then waiting for the dishes to return to be cleaned is cumbersome for me and I will no longer tolerate it. I want you to sit at our table. Neither Moses nor I will challenge you to talk or interact, and we will admonish the children if they bother you. For my sake, I ask that you grant me this small favor."

Andrew was startled by her directness, but in her he saw his mother and could see her doing the same thing. While Andrew would not raise his eyes in her direction, he slowly nodded his head. That day he slowly walked into the cabin. "Mam. Could I oblige you to allow me to sit in a chair by the fire rather than at the table?"

Nancy was pained at the struggle Andrew had in speaking to her. She wanted to embrace him, to drive away the torments in this young man's heart. She knew there would be no pushing him into sitting at the table with the family. Reluctantly she agreed. The children respectfully allowed him to have his space, however Andrew found himself learning to appreciate the interconnectedness of this family.

Once breakfast was done, the men left for the fields and Nancy began her long day of work in and around the house. A noon time meal was taken out to the fields, typically by Henry, the next oldest boy who Andrew estimated to be about eight years old. The dinner basket was filled with bread and butter and dried meat. There were also pickles which Andrew found he liked. Nancy would also put some apples into the basket, or occasionally a slice of leftover pie. The food was always devoured and the men would quickly return to their work. Andrew always took his share and moved to sit alone. Moses and his sons never pushed him to join them. Henry would return home with the empty basket.

Upon returning to the house, the men would wash up and would enter the small house for supper. The children stood quietly as their father would say a prayer before the meal. Andrew did not follow with the expected response of "amen." Instead he stood quietly. The children, who were boisterous throughout the day, were quiet and respectful at the table. Nancy's expectations were much like many other mothers that children not interfere with the adult talk at the table. They were to "talk not, sing not, hum not, and wriggle not." She expected good behavior, and that is what she received. Abigail, who was about six year old, was constantly watching Andrew and whenever he would catch her glance she would smile. Elizabeth, who was around four, and the youngest, Daniel, attempted to behave at the table, but were quickly distracted by any movement, or by something someone would say which would set them off in a fit of giggles. Nancy was quick to remind them to remain quiet at the table, however Moses would often encourage their laughing. Although Andrew watched the table interaction, it reminded him too much of home, so he tried to block out everything that did not directly affect him or his work.

Nancy would typically have a stew or soup prepared, a small vegetable salad with vinegar, and more bread and butter, and a piece of cheese. Her stews included pork, corn, cabbage, and other vegetables that the family had stored. A weak beer or cider was enjoyed, or just water. Some nights, for a treat, she would make pumpkin cornmeal pancakes, which the children enthusiastically ate in hopes of getting more. Sometimes Nancy would make coleslaw, something which Andrew had never eaten before, but found he enjoyed. Nancy explained it was a Dutch recipe, as were the pretzels she made. She also made sweetcakes which were fried in fat. Moses and the children enjoyed these treats, and Nancy smiled with pleasure that she was able to satisfy her hungry crew. She took special delight in watching Andrew try the new dishes.

William and Joshua took every chance they could to set traps in the woods in hopes of catching something worth eating and storing the fur or hide for other purposes. Some evenings the boys did target practice and they would ask their father if Andrew would like to join them, but Moses reminded the boys that they were not to bother Andrew.

On Sundays there was typically not a set plan for work which needed to be done, so Moses would sit by the fire and read from the Bible and the children would all sit at the table and Nancy would have them copy passages from the Bible. On one particular Sunday Andrew rose to leave his chair near the hearth as soon as he finished eating. Nancy was talking to Moses about teaching the children to read and write as Andrew quietly made his way toward the door. "They need to have some basic reading and writing," said Nancy. "Andrew, do you know how to read and write?" All six children stopped what they were doing and turned to look at Andrew to hear his response.

Andrew looked bewildered, then quietly answered, "Yes. My mother demanded that we learn how to read and write. She did much the same as you and we used the Bible as our textbook."

"There," said Nancy, smiling. "You see. Andrew knows how to read and write, and you need to do the same." The children kept their eyes fixed on Andrew as they had witnessed so few vocal interactions from him. Nancy smiled at Andrew. "Andrew, would you care to read some of your favorite Bible passages to the children?" The children's gaze moved from their mother to Andrew as they awaited his response.

Panic overtook Andrew and he was visibly shaken. "Sorry, mam. I need to get back to the barn to tend to the animals. I have some things I need to tend to." Andrew grabbed his coat and quickly left the house to return to the barn. Once back in the barn he was torn as to how he felt. He liked Nancy and the children. He knew Nancy was only trying to include him in the family circle, but he just couldn't read from the Bible. Andrew sat in the barn and tried to collect himself, questioning why his reactions continued to be so bizarre. He knew the family must think him odd, but he could not force himself to rid himself of the demons which constantly tormented him. Only when he was intently working could he erase the memories which overshadowed his thoughts. Remembering his mother and siblings and the life he had known before the war only made the night terrors worse as visions of the Jersey, his hatred for the British, his anger with Washington, and his total resentment of his father came crushing back into his dreams. Would he ever be able to rid himself of these torments?

Moses worked late in the evening, and with the help of Andrew they were able to build a small outbuilding which Moses planned to use for storage. Once the building was complete, Moses asked Andrew to help him take some supplies to store into the new building. Moses stopped outside the building to call to one of his sons who was nearby, and asked Andrew to carry the supplies into the building. Andrew entered the building and what he found was a lantern hung in a corner of the area, which he had not noticed before. He walked over to investigate and he found a narrow rope bed, a feather tick mattress, and several blankets stacked on it. Andrew looked in disbelief. By this time Moses had stepped in and stood beside him. "This building is closer to the house, and is much more weather proof than the barn. I am hoping that you will be able to feel our gratitude for your help here on the farm. Nancy and I are happy you chanced to come our way."

Andrew was dumbstruck. When he could focus he turned to Moses and said, "Thank you, Moses. And please tell Mrs. Nancy I said thank you."

Moses replied, "You can tell her yourself, Andrew." At that moment Nancy stepped beside her husband.

"Andrew. I want you to feel comfortable around us. I understand the children are overwhelming, but I hope that you will accept my kindness as sincere."

"Thank you, mam," stammered Andrew. His face and his heart heated and the emotion was almost more than he could bear.

"That's ok, Andrew. I just want you to be able to say good morning to me, or look in my direction without being afraid."

Andrew merely nodded, unable to use his voice. The lump in his throat nearly choked him. Moses laughed and said, "Andrew. You've been with us these past months and without your help we would never have been able to get as much done as we have. Please accept our hospitality in the spirit it is given."

"But when did you do this?" asked Andrew.

Moses said, "If you haven't noticed, I've kept you pretty busy with the harvest. While you were out in the field several days the boys and I returned here to work on putting up the interior walls. Actually, the boys enjoyed constructing the interior walls for the room, and the bed was one that we inherited from Nancy's parents. Nancy hung the rugs on the walls to keep out any drafts, and I put together the small coal stove so you can keep warm in the winter months. A man who works all day should at least have a comfortable place to hang his hat."

Moses smiled at Andrew, and Andrew lowered his head as he responded. "Thank you so much."

"Oh, yes," said Nancy. "The drawing hanging on the wall is from Elizabeth." Andrew's eyes looked at the small piece of paper which had a crooked house under a lopsided sun, and a stick figure of a girl with a long dress. Nancy added, "That is supposed to be Elizabeth waving to you in your new house." Andrew nodded, while he continued to stare at the childish drawing.

Moses and his wife left, but before she left, Nancy gently placed her hand on Andrew's shoulder, and tapped it lightly. "You enjoy your space here, Andrew," she said quietly, and turned to leave. Andrew watched her leave, and once again he was overtaken with emotion and dropped to the bed and collapsed into tears. How he missed his mother and his younger siblings, but he knew he could never return home again. The truth of this overwhelmed him and he pulled the blanket into his arms and buried his face into it and sobbed.

Chapter 17
A Winter of Learning

December, 1781

A winter storm blew in on December 1, 1781, and Moses and his family scrambled to protect anything that needed protection. Fortunately, with Andrew's help, they had harvested most of the crops. Moses stated repeatedly that Andrew's coming to the family was a blessing. Andrew felt kindly about the compliment, yet he was still unable to totally break free of the burdens in his heart and mind. He knew that the harder he worked, the further away he kept his demons.

The house's fireplace was constantly in use for cooking, and heating the small home. Andrew helped William and Joshua run rope between the house and the storage building and the barn. Andrew remembered a few winters where his father and older brothers did this in order to not get lost in the storm when they left the safety of the house to feed the animals. When the winds were capable of blowing a man off his feet and the snow was so thick you couldn't see in front of yourself, the rope was a good idea. "Everything points to another winter like the one we had two years ago," said Moses. Andrew thought back to his time on the Jersey and the freezing cold conditions on the ship. He shook off the memory as he could not allow himself to fall into that pit of despair again.

With the crops harvested Moses settled into the winter routine. The barn, house, and outbuildings were reinforced against the upcoming winter weather. Moses explained to Andrew that their winter would be spent making bullets, candles, shoes, and handle other household and farm necessities which had been put off during the farming season. He also wanted to work in the smithy every chance he could in order to have a stockpile of goods which could be taken for trade in the spring. Andrew looked forward to learning more about working in the smithy.

The winter storm did not let up, and Andrew found he was often using the rope as a guide to get him to the house. Nancy was tense as the winter storm was keeping Moses and the boys from hunting and she feared they would not have enough meat to last them for the winter. Andrew vowed to himself that as soon as the storm let up he would set out to hunt whatever he could to bring food to the table. Still, there was no release from the storm, and the drifts were so tall that the rope was buried within the drift causing Andrew to have to stay in the outbuilding on several occasions. Nancy had thoughtfully given him some food supplies in case this would happen, but

Andrew was surprised that when he could not get to the house to join the family for meals he felt disappointed. This was unexpected as Andrew had preferred to remain solitary and had resisted in any socializing or interaction with Nancy and the younger children. Even working in the fields he preferred to work alone. Now that he was isolated, he longed to be with Moses' family. A soft chuckle escaped Andrew's throat, which surprised him even further. Andrew felt chilled and he picked up his saddlebag to get out the additional blanket he had stored there. He spilled the contents of the saddlebag out onto the bed, and realized there was still something inside. He reached in and pulled out the Bible the old Dutchman had given him before Andrew left for New Jersey. Andrew sat on the bed and looked at the book, not daring to open it. He did not know what his emotions would be if he did open the pages. Instead, he put the Bible carefully on a crate in the room and sat on his bed just looking at it remembering his hatred for God for the abandonment he felt on the Jersey.

The Jersey had robbed him of his innocence and his love for God. He even questioned his belief in God as there could not be a higher being who would allow such mistreatment of humans as that he witnessed and was part of on the Jersey. As hard as Andrew tried to ignore them, the memories forced themselves back to the forefront of his mind. The screams of the tormented men on the Jersey, the mumblings of those who had lost their sensibilities, the moaning of those who sat among the filth and debris of the ship suffering from their sores and lesions, the swearing and cursing uttered by those overtaken by despair came crashing back into Andrew's brain. The feeble light had allowed him to see the shadows of the tormented souls as they fought their demons, and the lumps of human form strewn about the floor, perhaps dead, or perhaps wishing for death. He recalled the wickedness of those trying to survive by robbing those unable to defend themselves for their meager clothing, food, or possible coins which could be used for bribery. How many times was he near the depths of despair and tempted to join in the debauchery below decks? He was lucky for the friendship of Lefton who protected him and guided him, yet even this relationship was abandoned at the end when Andrew escaped. Andrew hated himself for the role he played on the Jersey. He lost his values, his trust, and his humanness in the madness of that ship. His once tender heart was replaced by the feeling of hatred which he could no longer control. Moments allowed him a brief smile or chuckle in his new life, but it never lasted long as the tortured memories once again took over. Once they did and Andrew did not close his mind to them, his night was filled with the never ending cries and torments of the Jersey.

Andrew remembered how he tried to pray. When he was first captured he recited the prayers of his youth which gave him comfort, but as time went on the comfort disappeared. Andrew looked at the Bible sitting on the crate and dared to open it, but his eyes would not focus on the page. He wanted the comfort that prayer once gave him, but this hatred and burning in his heart would not allow him release from his tormented thoughts. Andrew lay upon his bed, closing his eyes, demanding his brain to quiet itself.

After a fitful night, Andrew was grateful that the winds howling outside had stopped and there even appeared to be a hint of brightness in the sky. Andrew peered outside and saw Moses trudging through the snow drifts toward the outbuilding. Andrew quickly bundled himself so he could join Moses in the smithy. It would be a welcome change.

In the smithy, Moses quickly set about firing up the stoves and the stone built forge. Moses had built a stone forge as it could hold heat better than the brick forges found in other smithies. Andrew had learned enough to help get the supplies out and the necessary tools. Moses loved this work and immediately started talking, in hopes that one day Andrew might want to join him in a real conversation. For now, it was enough that there was companionship in the smithy.

"Ironstone is plentiful but you have to find enough to smelt the iron out of the ore. We do that through heating the ore until this smelly gas is released. You have to be careful to draft out the building enough to rid it of the gas, otherwise it would become dangerous for breathing, and can even cause explosions. No need to worry about venting today, right Andrew?" He looked at Andrew, but only received a nod in agreement.

Moses went on. "This spongy bloom of iron comes out mixed in with slag. We add some flux to it to separate the iron from the slag. You can use crushed seashells or limestone to do this." Andrew stood by and watched and learned. Moses was very adept at his work and moved flawlessly in his craft. Once he got the bloom of iron, he moved it from the furnace and hammered it on the anvil to rid it of any additional cinders or slag. "Once we do this, it becomes wrought iron. Some people call it 'worked' iron. A lot of smithies use wrought iron in the south to make grill work, gates and ornamental pieces. Up here we need it for more practical purposes. I make tools for farmers like sickles and scythes and plough shares, ax heads, saws, hammers, shovels, pitchforks, hoes, as well as nails, screws, bolts and hooks. There is always a need for door hinges, fireplace tools, pots and pans for inside the house as well. One of the main things I make are horseshoes and chains which are greatly needed."

Andrew's back shivered at the thought of the chains which were used when he was first incarcerated. He had to push the memory out of his mind and concentrate on what Moses was showing him in order not to be pulled back into the pit of hateful memories.

Although Moses was caught up in his dialogue, Andrew's reaction to chains did not escape him. He began to realize that this young man must have been mistreated as either an indentured servant or in the war. He wondered if Andrew would ever be able to tell him the whole story. Moses went on to keep Andrew's attention off the chains.

"When I knew I wanted to become a blacksmith, I knew I also had to become a farrier because that will be one of the jobs I would be asked to do most often. I had to learn how to shape the horseshoes to the exact fit for the horse's hoof, punch holes into the shoes for the nails used to attach them to the horse's hoof, rasp the hoof, then burn and nail the horseshoe to the hoof. The heat causes the horseshoe to attach to the hoof even before you start nailing it in place. There is a trick to this if you want to get the job done correctly without the horse retaliating against a novice farrier. You know, I am hoping we win this war because we are not allowed to compete with the British. Our folks who smelt iron are forced to export the iron to England, then import it back in the form of useable goods. Of course, we get taxed exporting and again in importing. We have plenty of smelters who can do this work and keep that income for themselves. When I need iron I often get it from the smelters in ingots and bars and trade for it, or pay for it through the sales I make from the products I make." Moses continued talking as he worked in the smithy, organizing his supplies for the projects he wanted to complete.

"With the war going on I make a lot of bullets made of lead in molds both for the farmers nearby and for soldiers. I personally don't make the cannon balls which are made out of iron as they take up too much product. I'd rather stick with what I can manufacture and sell to locals."

Throughout Moses' talk, Andrew watched him work. His arms were huge and strong, which was necessary in hammering out the iron. Moses was most proud of his anvil which was perfection. It was mounted on a firm block of wood and the face of it was completely smooth. At one end was fashioned a bickern which Moses used to round out hollowed pieces. Andrew recognized his own shortcomings and his diminished strength. He had certainly begun to fill out his frame with Nancy's good cooking, yet he doubted he was strong enough to do the kind of manual labor required to do smithy work. However, he thought that he could certainly help with some of the smaller tasks if Moses would teach him. Moses caught Andrew staring at his anvil and quickly said, "Andrew. Do you know what these holes are used for in the anvil?" Andrew shook his head. "They are for the tangs of the tools I use to bend or shape the metal. This hardy is like a chisel to cut the iron. When I hammer the metal over the hardy it forces the hot metal into this v shape which allows me to split the metal." Moses demonstrated the process to Andrew who stood by watching intently. Moses moved the bellows to get the fire blazing, and used tongs to hold the rod iron in the flames. Once the metal turned an orange-red color, Moses moved it to the anvil and began to hammer it with a flattening hammer. It was important to keep the metal solid, so Moses adeptly moved the iron into a tub of water to solidify it, then repeat the process of heating it, then hammering it. It was a continuous process, repeated until the metal took on the shape Moses intended. The piece he was working on eventually turned into a ladle with would certainly be sought after for kitchens and for outdoor troughs. Andrew watched in amazement at the choreography of movement to create the utensil.

"Why don't I teach you how to make some of the smaller items which we need for trade? I can then concentrate on some of the larger items. The boys are also learning how to make bullets and some household items, but I can teach you to make some of the tools. How does this sound?"

Andrew actually smiled, and Moses quickly swept through the smithy pulling out materials needed to get Andrew started. Andrew was very attentive and by the end of the day he had already made several ladles, each one being easier to form than the last. Moses was patient with Andrew and complimented Andrew through each step. The first attempt was rather rough in form, and Moses showed Andrew how to reshape it into a smoother version. Andrew was a quick study. Later in the day the two oldest boys came into the smithy and Moses motioned to them to not interrupt Andrew. The boys pulled out their supplies and began making bullets with the forms their father had set up for them to use. The boys talked to each other and stayed on task, while Andrew concentrated on his new project, and Moses swelled with pride as the smithy was actively producing products. When Andrew or Moses needed the fire tended, the boys would work the bellows to supply enough air to the fire to keep the workflow moving, or clean out the ash pit as needed. Moses had built the bellows to rest upon posts so that the bellows remained in place. The air was directed into a tue iron which was secured into the stonework of the forge. The air would then release into the fire to keep it flowing. Andrew was amazed at the efficiency of the smithy and the forethought that Moses had in building it. By the end of the day, Andrew felt satisfied that he had done a good day's work, and while he was not exactly happy, he had kept the demons at bay throughout the day. That night he enjoyed his evening meal, then fell into a much needed restful sleep.

As December drew to a close, Nancy and the children were in the final preparations for Christmas. Nancy had baked special pies and treats for the family, and the children created decorations they hung in the cabin. The family traveled to a church service and planned to visit with nearby family and friends for the afternoon. Although they invited Andrew to join them, he declined the invitation. Andrew remained in his solitary room and listened as the wagon which had been outfitted with some bells pulled away from the cabin.

Andrew looked out on the rarely quiet homestead. He spotted a deer grazing in Nancy's herb garden. Andrew retrieved his rifle and slowly walked into firing range. Just as he was about to fire, the buck looked up and looked intently in Andrew's direction. Without a moment's hesitation, Andrew fired. The buck leaped for an instant, then stumbled and fell to the ground. Andrew approached it and found he had killed the deer. He took out his knife and cut slits into the Achilles tendons of the two hind legs. He dragged the buck to a nearby tree and hung the deer upside down. He remembered helping his brothers butcher deer over the years on the Clark farm. He first cut off the genitals, then slit the underbelly from the genitals to the ribs. He pulled out the internal organs being careful to save the liver, kidneys, and heart. Andrew carefully washed out the inside of the animal and propped the opening with a stick allowing the cold air to get inside the animal. He knew that the meat would need to hang for at least a day before it could be butchered. Andrew hauled the deer to hang in the barn to keep it away from possible predators while keeping the meat cold in the December temperatures.

Andrew had just finished cleaning himself when he heard the bells on the wagon approaching the farm. He waited until the wagon pulled up, then held the horses in check as Nancy and the children descended. The children surrounded Andrew and talked excitedly about their adventures during their visit. Little Elizabeth handed Andrew a package." I saved these for you, Andrew. Merry Christmas," she said as she pushed the package into his hands. Nancy shooed them into the cabin.

"I'm sorry, Andrew. They do not get to visit too often, especially during the winter months."

Andrew looked at the package and was, for a moment, overtaken with emotion. He gathered himself and looked at

Nancy. "Not a problem, Mam. I'm glad they enjoyed their visit, and I hope you did too. By the way, there is fresh venison in the barn that we can butcher tomorrow. Merry Christmas." Andrew turned and quickly walked back toward the outbuilding leaving Nancy and Moses to watch him depart.

"Well, I'll be!" said Moses. "That was the most I heard that young man talk since he arrived here!"

Nancy smiled. "Surround him with positive memories and he will eventually surrender the hauntings of his past and join us in the land of the living." Moses looked at his wife and smiled. She certainly knew human nature and for some reason had taken a shine to this young man and he knew Nancy had made it her mission to break Andrew free of his demons. He wrapped his arm around his wife and the two entered into the house.

Back in his room Andrew opened the package and looked at the slices of cake. He carefully ate one, then wrapped the remaining pieces back into the paper and put it on the crate. He noticed the Bible sitting there where he had left it. Suddenly it occurred to him that he had said, Merry Christmas. It was the first time he had made reference to anything about God. In the quiet of the room he could hear the faint singing of Christmas hymns drifting from the house. He remembered his family singing from the Watts hymnals the various Christmas carols and his mind drifted to memories of his mother and siblings. He reached over and opened the King James Bible and leafed through until he found the passage he was seeking. Luke 2:1-16.

He read the words he had heard every year of his childhood of the birth of Christ.

Luke 2:1-16

1 And it came to pass in those days, that there went out a decree from Caesar Augustus, that all the world should be taxed.

2 (And this taxing was first made when Cyrenius was governor of Syria.)

3 And all went to be taxed, every one into his own city.

4 And Joseph also went up from Galilee, out of the city of Nazareth, into Judea, unto the city of David, which is called Bethlehem; (because he was of the house and lineage of David;)

5 To be taxed with Mary his espoused wife, being great with child.

6 And so it was, that, while they were there, the days were accomplished that she should be delivered.

7 And she brought forth her firstborn son, and wrapped him in swaddling clothes, and laid him in a manger; because there was no room for them in the inn.

8 And there were in the same country shepherds abiding in the field, keeping watch over their flock by night.

9 And lo, the angel of the Lord came upon them, and the glory of the Lord shone round about them; and they were sore afraid.

10 And the angel said unto them, Fear not: for, behold, I bring you good tidings of great joy, which shall be to all people.

11 For unto you is born this day in the city of David a Savior which is Christ the Lord.

12 And this shall be a sign unto you; Aye shall find the babe wrapped in swaddling clothes, lying in a manger.

13 And suddenly there was with the angel a multitude of heavenly host praising God, and saying,

14 Glory to God in the highest and on earth peace, good will toward men.

15 And it came to pass, as the angels were gone away from them into heaven, the shepherds said to one another, Let us now go even unto Bethlehem, and see this thing which is come to pass, which the Lord hath made known unto us.

16 And they came with haste, and found Mary, and Joseph, and the babe lying in a manger.

Andrew sat and stared at the words and waited for the hatred to once again swell in his heart. He waited, but instead he felt neither anger nor peace. He began to wonder why the anger had left him about God. He had lost his belief in God while on the Jersey. He had prayed with all his might and all his strength, but remained forgotten. Many on the hell ship had blasphemed God, but Andrew always fell short of doing this, although toward the end of his tenure on the ship his hatred and anger weighed heavy in his heart. He had escaped in May, and the hatred had remained hard and firm. Since escaping the Jersey the anger was kept alive within him. For these past seven months the hatred nearly devoured him. Yet today the hatred was gone. Was it the meager gift of cake from little Elizabeth a peace offering from God? Was God trying to force him to see that a mere child, like Elizabeth, or even the baby Jesus, could bring peace to those overwhelmed with despair? Andrew sat for nearly an hour, not knowing what he felt or what he believed. When he thought of Washington and those who lived in New York who knew the prison ships were filled with human cargo, sitting in constant misery, the anger and hatred returned. When he thought of his father, again the anger returned. But when he turned his attention again to the open page of the Bible laying before him, only a sense of hollowness was present. Perhaps his internal healing was beginning. He did not understand it. Perhaps it was only his own sentimentality of his childhood memories which brought the calm in his heart.

Chapter 18
A Fellow Victim

February, 1782

The early months of 1782 were brutally cold, however Andrew enjoyed the opportunity to work in the smithy and was proud of contributions he made to the stock Moses would be able to put up for sale and trade in the spring. The winter days were spent working in the smithy, hunting for fresh meat, or chopping wood for the cabin and his room. While Andrew did not have a large body frame, he finally had "meat on his bones," as Moses liked to tease him. In his spare time Andrew enjoyed twisting out more ornamental handles for some of the household tools. He found that he had a knack for doing this and thought that perhaps some of the women would find these wares desirable. Life was so hard on the women and perhaps they would find pleasure in using tools which had a pleasing appearance. Moses agreed and let Andrew explore his craft, secretly enjoying that Andrew had found something that gave him peace.

Andrew still remained quiet, but he did communicate when necessary with Moses and his sons. Despite Nancy's encouragement, Andrew had not been able to present himself comfortably in front of Nancy or the smaller children as he still felt the contamination of his past. It saddened him when he thought of it as he knew his life would be very lonely if he could never get over this feeling. Other men his age would be settling down. Of course, with the war still raging, men his age were thinking of other things besides setting down.

In preparation for the upcoming spring, Moses, Andrew and the two oldest boys worked out their planting schedule. This year, with Andrew's help, they would plant a larger and earlier crop, weather permitting. By mid-April they would plant beets, broccoli, Brussel sprouts, cabbage, carrots, cauliflower, kohlrabi, leeks, mustard, onions, parsley, peas, radish, spinach, turnips and rutabagas. Before planting, Moses and Andrew would load the wagon and try to sell the wares they had produced during the winter months. They would also take orders for items not stocked with the promise they would return during the summer months once new acreage was plowed and summer crops were planted. Nancy made her list of items she needed Moses to secure in trade. Among the items on her list were fabrics for clothing and household items which Moses could not make.

There was a break in the weather at the end of February which allowed Moses and Andrew to leave on their sales route, however they had to return after only two weeks as the weather caused travel to be difficult. After a week home, they left again for their southern route, retuning early April. Moses sold nearly all of his stock, and had orders which he would make for delivery later in the summer. There was no down time as the early crops had to be planted mid-April. Andrew once again put in full days of work and fell asleep at night, rarely having the haunting nightmares which disturbed his sleep for so many months. Occasionally the nightmares did return which were typically triggered when someone would talk of the war, which was still not over. Several episodes occurred while they were on the sales route, and Moses woke to the sounds of Andrew screaming in the night. Andrew would awaken and Moses would pretend to be asleep so Andrew would not feel the embarrassment of his night terrors. Moses would pray that God would release Andrew of these memories. It saddened him to think of what this young man endured to cause such mental anguish.

Andrew was still bitter and angry with both government and his father, however his feelings about God were ambivalent. He had not opened the Bible given him by the Dutchman since Christmas, and he could not identify his feelings as to his belief in God or in the faith he carried from childhood.

During the spring planting Andrew allowed himself to have short conversations with Moses and the two oldest boys when they were out in the fields. Instead of working alone, he began to work with them. The boys were beginning to become more interested in the war and when they approached the topic with Andrew his body tensed and he immediately became withdrawn. Moses would quickly change the subject realizing the heart of Andrew's burdens were because of the war. He later warned the boys not to approach that topic with Andrew.

As spring advanced and warmer weather enveloped those on Moses' farm, it seemed Andrew, too, warmed. It was little Elizabeth's persistence in trying to engage Andrew in conversation that finally drew Andrew into short conversations with her and the other children. He tried to remain distant, but he did not quickly retreat when approached. Nancy, too, recognized this and she would monitor the children's aggressiveness toward Andrew, allowing him to talk and interact as he felt comfortable.

It was in early June that a wagon filled with family and belongings approached Moses' farm. Andrew cautiously remained near the barn. He watched as the driver pulled the reins to stop near where Moses had walked out to meet them. The younger children all scrambled behind their father to see who was visiting.

"I was told this was the place where I could get my horses and oxen shod," said the man.

"You have come to the right place. Where are you heading to?" asked Moses. "It will take me some time to get this done."

"We left Connecticut in hopes of finding some land to settle on away from all the war business. Most of my farm was taken over by the Redcoats and if I stayed we would certainly have what little belongings and supplies we owned taken by either the British or the Continental Army. I should have cut my losses earlier and moved before we lost so much."

"You are welcome to use our barn and I am certain my wife will make your family comfortable while we take care of your horses."

The man smiled, and turned to talk to the children in the back of the wagon. Three little children, much the same ages as Moses' youngest children waited for their father to lift them from the wagon, and they were immediately surrounded by Moses' children. It did not take long for them to run off to play together. Sad, thought Andrew, that the innocence of children is spoiled by war. These children are pure hearted and not stained by the hatred that war breeds.

Also leaving the back of the wagon was a young woman who kept her head covered with a shawl. She walked behind the wife and stood outside the cabin, not entering. Andrew thought it odd, but his attention was pulled to the work at hand.

Moses signaled for William and Joshua to help with the oxen and unharness the horses so they could begin their work. Andrew quickly started the fires in the smithy and pulled the various tools off the wall so they could begin their work. The stranger came into the smithy and looked around. "My name is Smith. I come up from Sandy Hook, and I am heading past the New York territory so long as I don't come across any Injuns. Nice place you have here."

Moses and Smith talked at length about when Moses came here to settle in, and about building his smithy with hopes that after the war more veterans would move to the area. The two talked comfortably, and Andrew listened, but was careful not to draw attention to himself. Smith was content in talking about the various tools, and the smithy they had in Connecticut and pointed out differences in some of the equipment. Moses was in his element and conversation came easily as did his work. Moses had a ready supply of horseshoes, and some for the oxen. Not all oxen were shoed, but those that were needed two shoes for each hoof as they have a cloven hoof. Shoeing an ox was not an easy task. The ox could not balance itself on three legs when being shod. Instead the ox had to be lifted with a sling in order to shoe it. The sling had to be secured to a wooden frame in order to hold the beast in place. This process would take more time. It would take about thirty minutes to shoe the horse once the shoes were made to fit, but the oxen would take much longer and require more man power. There were two oxen and four horses, so Andrew knew they would be in the smithy for a good part of the day. Andrew was surprised Mr. Smith hadn't had the beasts shod before they traveled, but his explanation made sense. "Seems

Barb Baltrinic

all the supplies back in Connecticut were put toward the army, or taken by the Redcoats. I didn't think the oxen would need shod, but putting in so many miles I realized they needed protection if I planned on taking them cross country." Mr. Smith shook his head. "I'm just glad we found you when we did."

As the men worked in the smithy, conversation eventually changed to the Sullivan Expedition, which immediately made Andrew's heart skip a beat. He forced himself to remain calm and keep his head turned to his work. Smith said, "Yes, it was in '79 that Washington ordered Generals John Sullivan and James Clinton to destroy over forty Iroquois villages in this area. About a quarter of the Continental Army was involved in this mission. We heard tell that many of the Injuns starved or froze to death after the loss of their villages and homes. That's how the young woman in our wagon came to be with us. A trapper had found a mother and her daughter seeking food. They were near death when he came upon them. He took claim to them and had taken the woman as his squaw. When he reached a trading post it was obvious he had been drinking and he was looking to sell the young girl. The girl was outside the trading post, bone thin, and looked to be maybe sixteen. My wife listened as this trapper tried to negotiate a price from the other men in the store for the girl. No one was willing to meet his price either out of prejudice for her color, or for fear that she was as coldhearted as those we heard about slaughtering the white settlers and soldiers. You could take

314

one look at the girl and realize she was not a danger, but I wanted no part in offering refuge for her. We got our supplies and loaded the wagon and my wife stood watching the woman and daughter cowering outside the shop. The Indian squaw looked at my wife with pleading eyes. My wife took it to mean she wanted us to take charge of the girl. I had no intention of getting involved and even less interest in listening to what that man had to say. I told my wife we needed to move on. That's when all the commotion started."

Moses stopped for a moment, as did the boys and Andrew as they listened for the ending of the story. "The man came out of the store and he grabbed the young girl and ripped her dress from her and was shouting to anyone who would listen how she was 'fresh' and would make a good squaw. She stood naked with her dress fallen around her knees. That's when the mother took a knife she either had hidden or found, and went running at the man, half crazed. She stabbed him in the back, and the man fell to the ground. The earth seemed to stand still for a moment and suddenly a shot rang out and the Indian woman clasped her chest and reached out to her daughter and said, 'Juniata,' then fell to the ground. The girl stood shaking, half naked, and howling into the air. She tried to run toward her mother, but tripped over her fallen clothing and fell to the ground. My wife quickly intervened and wrapped her shawl around her, picked up the torn garment, and led her away from the crowd which was moving toward the trader and the

Indian squaw. I never saw my wife take action like that, but she was like a mother bear and she was blind to color and prejudice. She guided the girl to our wagon which was hitched a bit further from the trading post. She slipped the dress over the girl's head and tightly wrapped the shawl around her, as well as a blanket. She put the girl in the wagon on the bench between where the two of us would sit."

"My word," said Moses in disbelief. "And you agreed to take her?"

"I didn't want to. My wife just gave me a look that would have made the Sunday Bible preacher blush. I said nothing, but got up into the wagon and pulled up the reins and we started off. The children were stone quiet in the back, not knowing exactly what just happened, but mighty curious about this young Indian girl. I kept waiting for someone to come after our wagon to collect the girl, but no one came."

"The girl kept sobbing throughout our drive until we stopped for the night. My wife took complete charge of the situation. She settled our children for the night, and had the girl surrender her dress for one of my wife's. Sarah, that's my wife, sewed the torn dress for the girl and sat by her, stroking her hair as she fell asleep. I kept my distance, not knowing what to say to my wife and not wanting to start our own war."

"So what is your plan?" asked Moses, still in disbelief.

"Sarah and I talked and we really don't have a plan. The girl is kind of in shock. She has been traveling with us the past four weeks. The children are still mostly curious about her. The younger ones are trying to teach her our language. I think her name is Juniata which means standing rock. At least that's what we think she is telling us. She doesn't talk much, and cries a lot."

Andrew remained transfixed, listening to the story of this Indian girl, realizing he had helped this cycle of events to occur. He had served on the Sullivan mission. He had been part of the plan of famine and displacement of the tribes. He remembered being torn over the actions. On one hand, the stories of the warriors and even the Indian woman who had brutalized the settlers and the soldiers made the soldiers want to seek revenge. But, there was also the village of Indians who were friendly to the colonists, and lived in a civilized manner, yet they were ordered to treat them in the same manner. Now there was this girl who somehow survived, then had to withstand being treated like a slave, humiliated in front of strangers, then witness her mother kill their tormenter and then watch her die. How much could this girl tolerate? The Smith family certainly sounded like good people, but where would they rid themselves of this girl and what would be her fate. The prejudice was strong against Indians as they had fought against the colonists, and their practices were brutal and barbaric. This girl's mother dared to attack a white man and quickly met her punishment without benefit of being able to represent herself, although she probably would not have been able to do so anyway with the language barrier.

Moses and Smith went on to talk about the war, and Andrew became more and more agitated. The news was that the war was still going on although it sounded like much of the fighting had moved to the southern states. Moses looked up from his work and saw that Andrew's face was ashen. "Andrew, we are about done here. Why don't you go back to your room and call it a night. Mr. Smith and his family will be bunking down here for the night." Andrew kept his head lowered and nodded to Moses. He quickly left the smithy.

Back in his room Andrew sat and thought about the Sullivan mission. It was why he decided to come to this area to escape and heal. He had chosen it because he wanted to look at the beauty of the area and push the memory of what was done here out of his mind. Now the memories were shoved before his face and he could see clearly his part in the tragedy of this young woman and her mother. Andrew lay on his bed and his mind debated back and forth whether Sullivan's mission had been the right thing to do. The inhumanity of it was appalling yet they had to stop the barbaric treatment of the Indians on the settlers. His mind flashed back to his father telling them about his first lessons in law in reading the treaty which gave what was Indian property over to the New Jersey proprietors. The Lenape Indians were repaid with trinkets. They were not considered equals. When the Indians dared to join the British in fighting the Patriots, they once again became the enemy and actions against them, like what Andrew participated in with Sullivan, was the price they paid for the audacity of fighting those who had stolen from them. It was hours before Andrew fell asleep after having debated the pros and cons of the army's treatment of the Indians, yet he never reconciled a right or wrong answer. That night, the nightmares returned strong and hard and Andrew woke himself screaming in agony. He sat upright in his bed and listened to the quiet of the night. He hoped no one had heard him cry out from his night terrors.

That's when he heard her. He lit his candle and crept out of his room and looked around to the storage area. He saw her cowering on a bed of straw in a corner. His candle cast a little light on her face which peeked out of the blanket she held tightly around her. She appeared to be shaking in fright and began shaking her head, "no." Andrew stood there, stunned, embarrassed, and confused. He took one step toward her as to put her fears at ease, however it had the opposite effect and the girl pulled herself even closer to the walls, visibly shaking.

Andrew put his hands up in the air and backed away, holding the candle closer to his face so she could see that he was also shaking his head "no." He backed away until she was out of sight, then he turned and went back to his room. Her sat on his bed and imagined what this young girl thought was about to happen to her. For an instant, Andrew was fearful she would come in and attack him during the night. That feeling passed, and he sat remembering how he felt his first night on the Jersey. That night was the first of many nights that were living nightmares. He, never knew when he would be attacked, never knew when he would be released, never knew when he would see family or feel love again. She must be feeling these same things.

The night was long, but Andrew did not sleep for fear the nightmares of the Jersey would return, and fearful that the girl in the next room was having her version of the same fears.

Chapter 19
Climbing Out of the Abyss
April, 1782

In the morning Andrew quickly left the out building without looking in on the Indian girl. He wasn't even certain if she was still in there, but he did not want to cause her any more alarm. He walked to the trough and washed his face. Joshua came out and told him that his father and Mr. Smith had gone to a nearby town to talk about land that could be farmed for the season.

"Did you see the Indian girl, Andrew?" Andrew nodded. "She didn't talk at all last night. The Smith family set up in the barn to sleep last night, but they put the Indian girl in the out building in a corner. They didn't want to disturb you so they didn't wake you. We didn't see her this morning, so we stayed away. The Smith children wanted to go in and wake her, but Mrs. Smith said not to bother her. Do you think we should wake her for a meal?"

Just then, the Indian girl appeared in the doorway. For the first time Andrew could see her face. Her long hair had been pulled together along the side of her face. It surprised him that it was not black, but was instead a dark brown. A small leather band tied the end together so it did not blow about her in the breeze. Her face was not so dark as other Indians Andrew had seen, and her eyes were almond shaped and had a yellow-brown hue. Andrew guessed that she was not fully Indian, but was part white. He wondered if either of her parents, or even one of her grandparents were white. Her dress was obviously something given to her by Mrs. Smith, and it had been fitted for her small frame.

"Juniata!" screamed the Smith children as they spotted her coming from the out building. The children surrounded her and led her toward the cabin. Juniata allowed them to pull her forward, yet her gaze fell on Andrew, studying him just as he had been studying her. Andrew reddened and lowered his head and allowed Joshua to coax him toward the cabin to get food. He was aware that she had distrust of men, and probably with good cause considering what he had heard from Mr. Smith the night before.

Nancy and Mrs. Smith came out of the cabin and carried out a basket filled with fruits, breads, jams and wrapped meats for the young folks to enjoy. Both Andrew and Juniata waited until the children had taken food from the basket. Little Elizabeth gathered items for Andrew and presented them to him. Andrew nodded his thanks to her and turned to go back toward the barn. The children called to him to sit with them and enjoy the spring weather. "We are having a picnic, Andrew," said young Elizabeth. "Won't you sit with us?"

"Just for a few minutes," said Andrew and he followed Elizabeth to where she indicated and sat down. The air was not yet warm, but the sunshine felt good upon his skin. He ate slowly and watched the children interacting, and occasionally allowed his eyes to watch Juniata. Elizabeth took charge of the small group and offered up that they sing songs they knew. The Smith children giggled and agreed, and soon the children were singing various church hymns in an absurd sounding choir. Nancy and Mrs. Smith had taken seats on the cabin porch and laughed as the children sang their songs, eventually switching from hymns to songs they had learned from other children. The Smith children taught the song to their new friends, and it was repeated over and over again with giggles from all the children.

O what can the matter be
And what can the matter be
O what can the matter be
Johnny bides long at the fair

He'll buy me a two penny whistle
He'll buy me a three penny fair
He'll buy me a bunch o' blue ribbons
To tie up my bonny brown hair

O saw ye him coming
And saw ye him coming
O saw ye him coming
Home from the Newcastle fair

Andrew would have slipped away and returned to work in the barn or smithy, but Elizabeth held firmly to his hand. While Andrew did not participate, he found himself enjoying the children's singing. He occasionally looked at Juniata and saw that the stress in her face had lessened in watching the young children singing and hearing laughter.

It was not long before the Smith children pulled at Juniata and expressed their desire for her to sing. Juniata obviously did not know what they were saying, but she understood their request. The other children quickly moved to sit in front of her and all eyes were on her. Juniata bowed her head, either in hoping they would leave, or resolving herself to pick a meaningful song. She finally lifted her face and a song, which none of her audience could understand, came pure and simple from her throat. As she sang she made hand motions which Andrew watched and tried to interpret. Her hands started low, and her face was lowered. As the song progressed, she stood and then her face moved up as did her arms, and as her hands were outstretched, her face turned toward the sun. She sang the whole song, and upon its completion, she quietly sat down.

The children sat still for a moment, then gave a thunderous applause and repeated, "Again! Again!" Juniata realized the children wanted her to repeat the song, and she dutifully complied. As she did, the children did the hand motions with her, and when she finished, they again burst into applause. Juniata had to repeat the performance another three times before Mrs. Smith admonished the children that they should be helping with chores. Andrew's eyes never left Juniata's face, and he could see that there was a disturbed debate in her pleasure of the children's response to her song, and her own longing for her home. Andrew was immediately filled with guilt at having played a part in her disturbance. He quickly got up and went to the smithy. Andrew wasted no time in building the fire and pulling together supplies and tools from the wall. William and Joshua joined him and the three fell into their typical routine. Soon the air was filled with sounds of the hammers on anvils and the metal clinking as it took shape. For Andrew it was a much needed escape from his thoughts of his part in Juniata's loss.

By the time Moses and Mr. Smith returned, Andrew and the boys had finished various items including new horseshoe forms to replace those used on Mr. Smith's animals, and items Mr. Smith indicated he needed, as well as putting together some of the smaller products Moses needed for the orders he had taken in the early sales trip in March and early April.

"Andrew, nice job! I was hoping that you and the boys would get started on some of this work. Since you've got the fires going, let's go ahead and get a few of the bigger items finished for the orders."

"Where's Mr. Smith?" asked William.

"Back at the house talking with his wife. We learned that Mr. Cooper had to leave with his family to take care of his father-in-law. They will be living there for this season until they can close business and settle that estate. Mr. Cooper was hoping to find someone to farm out his property in his absence, and it was lucky that Mr. Smith came along when he did."

"How far is the Cooper place?" asked Andrew.

"Not so far off. Maybe an hour or so by wagon."

"What are they going to do about Juniata?" asked Joshua.

"I am thinking they will take her with them. The children are quite fond of her and she seems to be quite helpful to Mrs. Smith. The language barrier is a bit of a problem, but the children are convinced they can teach her. She has already learned some words in English, and I suppose the children have learned equally the same in Seneca.

"When are they going to leave for the Cooper place," asked William.

"I suspect they want to go soon as Mr. Cooper has already packed up a wagon load to take with him to the new place. Mrs. Cooper and the children have already moved in with her parents. He was mostly holding up trying to figure out what to do about his own farm. Several of the neighbors were going to pitch in, but now that Mr. Smith came into the picture, it will be easier to make the transition. Mr. Smith will probably go up there tomorrow to finalize all the plans, then he and his family will leave here to move onto the Cooper farm. Their wagon is already packed, so it is just a matter of making the move. I told him they are welcome to stay here until they are set to move.

Andrew strangely felt a sense of relief that the Smiths would be staying at least a few more days. One again Andrew's mind drifted to the Sullivan expedition, and he remembered the work they did. One of the jobs was to cut the heads off pack horses to keep the Indians from using them. The carcasses were left to rot in a heap. For Andrew this was unconscionable as farm animals and horses were valued so much. He also had a difficult time burning down farms and destroying the crops. He knew the amount of work put into laying out a farm and harvesting, and the heartache of destruction when nature interplayed, let alone man coming along and destroying it. Were they right to do what they did? He couldn't make up his mind. Such thought were mental and emotional torture.

William and Joshua left the smithy to clean up for dinner while Moses and Andrew finished off the work they were doing.

"Moses? Can I ask you something?"

Moses was startled because Andrew never started a conversation. Moses put down his hammer and gave Andrew his full attention.

"Do you think we were right to do what we did with Sullivan?"

"We? Were you part of that, Andrew?" It was the first time Andrew had divulged information about his past.

Andrew realized he was about to share information he had never vocalized to anyone other than his brother. "Yes. I had been injured in one battle, went home to heal, and then left to rejoin my brigade. We were part of the burning campaign. Our unit did not encounter many males, but we did see women and children and the elderly scrambling to escape from the carnage we created on their villages."

"Andrew, the Indians had joined up with the British and they were a part of our early defeat. Some of the barbaric treatment they perpetuated on the settlers and the soldiers is unspeakable, although I do not doubt that our soldiers had done much of the same to them. Perhaps it was their revenge on how they were cheated out of lands and they finally had an opportunity to pay back for the mistreatment they had received over the past hundred years as we took their lands and pushed them out of what they felt was theirs. We forced them to sign unfair treaties, we cheated them with payment of baubles and trinkets. War makes strange enemies and makes soldiers do things they would not normally do. Look at us.

We were called rebels, a filthy name given only to the lowest life forms, yet we were British citizens. Our only crime was fighting against the treatment our King put on us, burdening us to be nothing more than non-voting slaves, not equals. We became enemies with our brothers in Great Britain. War did that. We may have lived peacefully with some of the tribes, however once they joined forces with our enemy, they, too, were our enemy and the punishments we enacted were rightfully done in the name of war. Our leaders, Congress and George Washington, made decisions which had to be made to protect all of us from the penalties we will surely face if this war is lost. We may not agree with every decision made, but war changes all the rules."

Andrew nearly gulped when Moses mentioned Congress and Washington. He respected Moses, and Moses' words struck a chord that Andrew needed to hear. Moses said he understood that both Congress and Washington had to make decisions that not all agreed were right. However in war, such decisions had to be made. Andrew's brain was in a whirlwind. The old hurts and pains and hatred again welled within him. Moses could see Andrew's composure slipping away. Somehow he had said something which had stirred the very heart and soul of this young man, however Moses had no idea what it was.

"Andrew. Why don't you go back to your room and I will close up here. Come to the house for dinner." Andrew dropped his tools, nodded, and left the smithy. Moses looked after him and thought that the demons this young man had been harboring in his heart had come to the surface and it was best for Andrew to sort through the emotions alone without anyone watching his inner turmoil.

Andrew returned to his room and the words Moses said rang in his head. He had hated for so long. It was a year since his escape, but his hatred had started long before his escape. Suddenly he was forced to look at what he had believed to be his truths and realize that he was only focused on how he was treated and how he was affected. Was he any better than the people of New York who ignored the truth about what was happening on the prison ships in their harbor? Was he any better than Washington when he was an active participant in destruction of home and belongings of the Indians? Were the Americans right in their decision? After all, the Indians had sided with the Tories and the British. Didn't they deserve what happened to them? But, now that he has seen Juniata and her heartache and grief, did she deserve the treatment that Sullivan and his men, including Andrew, dealt them?

He had been angry, no, hateful with God for so long, yet at some point he had just stopped hating. The fulfillment he once had in having God in his heart was missing. His heart was empty. Andrew paused and thought to himself. Had he actually stopped feeling that God had abandoned him? Andrew began to think clearly for the first time in over a year. It was as if a veil was being lifted before his eyes. As if walking out of a fog and into a clear and burning light, Andrew could see himself in a whole new perspective. Did God intervene for him by having Lefton partner with him on the hell ship and taker him under his wing to protect him from the certain death he would have faced had he tried to survive on his own? Lefton had stood by his side while Andrew worked to save Thomas. Lefton, had sacrificed his own food to help Thomas to survive his torture. Lefton had encouraged Andrew when he began to sink into despair. Lefton had sacrificed his own safety to cause a distraction when he realized Andrew was planning to either escape, or die trying. Lefton was much like God, sacrificing and giving his life to save the souls of another. Had God put Lefton into his life in order to intervene and let Andrew survive? If so, why did God allow Lefton to die? The thought startled Andrew as he had never fully admitted it to himself, but he knew in his heart it was Lefton's hand which poked out of the shallow grave when the old Dutchman took Andrew to the burial ground. The sleeve of the coat Lefton wore was unique and Andrew knew when he saw it that Lefton had not survived. He had died so Andrew could live. Isn't that what Jesus did?

Andrew sat still while his thoughts whirled in his brain. He had hated God, yet it had to be God's hand that played a role in saving not only Andrew, but Thomas as well. Andrew took the Bible which sat unopened on the crate near his bed.

He searched the pages to find the words he remembered from his youth. He finally located Ephesians, 4:31-32 and read the words: "*Let all bitterness, and wrath, and anger, and clamour, and evil speaking, be put away from you, with all malice. And be ye kind to one to another, tenderhearted, forgiving one another, even as God for Christ's sake hath forgiven you.*" The passage was one that his mother had made them memorize when the Clark children would argue with one another. It had far more meaning now. The words pierced Andrew's heart.

Andrew fell to his knees, and for the first time in over a year he prayed. His eyes were filled with tears and his voiced choked with passion. He thanked God for His intervention. He thanked God for guiding him to those who helped him survive: Lefton; the old Dutchman who nursed him to heal after his escape; the fisherman who took him safely to the New Jersey shore; Tobe who kept his secret and brought him food; Thomas, who quietly listened to the sorrows of his brother and promised to keep his secret; and to Moses who led him out of his dark abyss of despair and slavery of his soul. Andrew prayed all the prayers he could remember from his childhood. He prayed for his brother Thomas that he would regain his health; he prayed for Aaron, who was still in the war; he prayed for his younger siblings who had lost their childhood to this war and only knew the secrecy they had to live in order to survive and keep their mother safe. He prayed for Tobe and Pete and Rose who helped his mother and his family throughout the war, helping to protect them and helping them survive. He prayed for his mother, the strongest woman he knew as she held the family together and stood by the decisions which had to be made to help them survive. He began to pray for his father, and he stopped short. Could he forgive his father?

Andrew was filled with exhaustion. He lay on his bed and closed his eyes and thought about his father. Could he forgive his father? The debate dulled his brain, and Andrew fell deeply and soundly in sleep.

Joshua wanted to go to the out building to gather Andrew for the evening meal, but Moses stopped him, telling him to leave Andrew alone as he had a lot of thinking to do and should be allowed his privacy. Moses looked toward the out building and hoped that Andrew was able to search his soul and find the peace which he needed to heal his soul.

Chapter 20
Resurrection

June, 1782

The following week was filled with much reflection for Andrew. He had found God and had once again welcomed Him back into his heart. The weight on his heart seemed to lighten with this newfound forgiveness. Moses could tell that Andrew had gone through some kind of transformation, but also knew there was more that Andrew had to sort before he was truly healed.

One evening Andrew and Moses were working in the smithy and Andrew approached the subject which was weighing heavy on his mind. "Moses, did you know that many men were held captive on prison ships in Wallabout Bay?"

Moses kept working, but knew that Andrew was reaching out. "Prison ships for what?"

"Men who were part of the militia, or part of the privateers were captured by the British and put onto prison ships. The conditions were not very good."

"I never heard of this. Of course, we don't live near the bay area, so I was unaware of it. Were you there, Andrew?" Moses asked, and he stopped his work and looked at Andrew.

Andrew was careful not to look at Moses, but continued working, keeping his eyes on his work. "Yes. I was captured after I had left the Army after the Sullivan expedition. I had worked as a privateer in the whaleboats and we had captured many of the skiffs with supplies being transported by the British to Staten Island, or shores of New York. It was a good business so long as you were not caught. I was not so lucky."

"How long were you held prisoner?" asked Moses, who had now put down his tools so he could listen intently to Andrew.

"I was on the ship for nearly a year. They must have done an officer exchange shortly before I was captured, so I was given a duty to remove the dead from the ship. For this, I was given more durable clothing and an extra half ration of food, which is probably why I lasted as long as I did on the ship." Andrew forced himself to only say the facts and not allow his mind to picture the reality of that tenure. "It was filthy business. At first there were only five to eight bodies removed for burial each day, but as time passed the numbers increased. The filth, disease, corruption on the ship was indescribable. Men acted like animals to steal food, clothing, and rob the dead in hopes of surviving an additional day. Only those who were officers had salvation as they could be used in the officer exchange. Those, however, who were merely militia or privateers were not needed by Washington. I was told that our lives had little value for him because he needed officers to lead the army and those who were in the militia were not dedicated to the Army and the cause as most only worked for a month at a time."

Andrew paused as he tried to collect himself. This confession of his soul he hoped would lessen the hatred he still carried in his heart. "I hated Washington because he did not see fit to stop the torment of those of us on the ship. I hated Congress because they did not fight for our release. The Jersey was said to have been the most brutal of all the prison ships. No one from New York came to our rescue. In fact, there were those who made money from the dirty enterprise by taking contracts to provide food to the prisoners, but then pocketing the money and feeding those of us on the hell ship the foulest of food. Many became ill from the contaminated food and water. Many died of it. Many died of the conditions on the ship. Many died of madness being locked below decks with the horrors of those who lost all sense of humanity. The stench, the rot, the blasphemy against God, country and mankind all pushed us to the limits of endurance. Our captors tormented us with tales of our losing the war and that we would be hung for being rebels. There were days many of us begged for such release."

Moses did not interrupt. He let Andrew talk, knowing that at times the vision of his nightmares overtook his control. After one bout where Andrew outwardly sobbed, he regained his composure and went on. "Moses, am I wrong in the hatred I felt toward Washington and those who lived and worked in New York that had to know what was being done to us on the ship?"

Moses carefully weighed his words. "My God, Andrew. I had no idea what you endured. All I can say is that war is indeed filthy business. It pushes men to act out of their character. It is an excuse some use to misuse their power and purposefully ignore the rights of humanity in their dealing with others. I can understand your hatred, but I will say that in war, the leaders must think of what is best for the greater good. Officers were needed. We have so few compared to the British. I think Washington has always had the best interests of his army at heart and all decisions were for winning the war, for to not win it meant that every man would be punished or even enslaved if the British won the war. It is cruel that you were caught on the wrong side of the war and not valued as a contributing member of the cause. Too often, in war, decisions are made by men who must ignore the small number of those in need in order to gain what is best for the majority. I don't know if my words make sense to you, but when you were subjected to such horrors, you needed to hang your blame on those who you felt most likely would rescue you. Unfortunately, neither Washington nor Congress could do that. As for those in that area of New York, don't forget, they were mostly Loyalists who felt the Patriots were wrong to fight against their king. In war people take sides, and in doing so, they must stand with a blind eye to the atrocities their side enacts on others."

Andrew pondered Moses' words. He knew he was right. It was the first time he had talked about his experience and his hatred. He also knew that Juniata had hatred in her heart for those who had caused her nightmares. Andrew was part of that process. He was part of those that had enacted atrocities on the Indian villages, many of which were only inhabited by women, children and the elderly.

Andrew spent the rest of the day thinking about what Moses had said, and weighing in his mind how he could justify what he did to the Indians, and how Washington, Congress, and his father seemingly turned their backs on the plights of those who were martyred on the prison ships. That evening in his room, Andrew thought again about Moses' words. Andrew had been enslaved with the hatred he held in his heart and his mind. The intensity of his hatred was subsiding, but it was not completely diminished. "Time," he thought. "It will take time before I can move from this weight."

Before he fell asleep, Andrew could hear the soft weeping of Juniata who was also dealing with her own demons.

In the morning Mr. Smith and his family were organizing their wagon to make the move to the Cooper farm. Andrew carefully watched Juniata from a distance and knew that she had been going through the same thing he had. She, too, was angry with her God, the inhumanity of the soldiers, and of man's prejudice. Andrew knew it would be no easy task for her to heal and come out of her abyss, but he knew that the kindness of the Smith family, and certainly the friendship of Moses' family, would eventually help her escape her demons. Andrew knew he was a part of what caused her demons, and for that he would need to find forgiveness from Juniata and from himself.

As the family was packing the wagon, Andrew approached Juanita and gave her a small cross that he had fashioned out of some twigs and twine. She looked at it, not really knowing what it meant. Andrew motioned first to the sky as if embracing it. He then scooped the sky above him as if to pull it into his heart, then placed the cross on his chest in that spot. Juniata watched his motions, which were similar to the motions she had made in her song. "Hope," said Andrew. "Hope."

Juniata looked at him, and gave a small smile, "ope," she repeated.

Andrew nodded. He then pointed to himself and said, "Andrew. Andrew."

She looked at him questioningly. Andrew pointed at her and said, "Juniata." He then pointed at himself and said, "Andrew."

Juniata repeated,"Ndew." Andrew nodded.

Mrs. Smith called to Juniata, and Juniata turned to go to the wagon. She then turned back and looked at Andrew. "Goobye," she said. She had obviously learned "goodbye" from the Smith family and had used the word properly. Andrew smiled and knew that with the help of the Smith children, Juniata would begin learning the language and perhaps this would help her talk about her nightmares so she could begin to release them, just as Andrew was beginning to do.

Andrew smiled and made a small waving motion toward the Smith wagon. Juniata climbed into the wagon and the Smiths pulled out with Moses, Nancy and the children all waving and saying their goodbyes and making promises to visit soon. Andrew watched as the wagon disappeared down the road, then turned and went back to the barn. Moses, William and Joshua would be going out to the field to prepare the next plot for planting, and Andrew would join them. He helped to gather the supplies and tools needed, and loaded the plow onto the wagon, and they all left together with a basket of food that Nancy had prepared. Moses and the boys talked about the Smiths, and about the Cooper farm, and the work they had to get done in preparation for the next planting. Andrew quickly became lost in his own thoughts.

Moses took the first shift of plowing leaving the boys and Andrew to break up the sod after the plow had moved through. Andrew used this time to think about Washington and the New Yorkers who had not intervened for those on the prison ships. He was surprised that the burning hatred was now an emptiness or hollowness within him. Perhaps this was the first step toward healing.

Andrew remained with Moses' family throughout the planting and harvesting season. The family would periodically visit the Smiths, but Andrew remained behind. The Smiths were quite busy with the farm work, and since the Smith children were still young, much of the work was on Mr. Smith's shoulders. It was at the end of the harvest season that the Smith family came to visit Moses and his family. Andrew heard their wagon approaching, and was surprised when he quickly scanned the wagon to see if Juniata was with them. She was. After all the greetings, Juniata began to pull out of the wagon some pies and preserves they brought to share with the family. Andrew quickly stepped beside her to help unload the wagon.

"Hello," said Juniata.

"Hello to you," said Andrew. "How have you been?" he asked, not knowing if she would completely understand what he asked.

"I fine," said Juniata. Since he last saw her she still carried the saddened face. He recognized the heaviness in her spirit as he, too, had carried these burdens for so long they nearly destroyed him. He wondered if her living with the Smiths had helped her to ease some of her sorrows as well as her hatred for those who had forced her into this state.

Juniata and Andrew carried the last of the food into Nancy's kitchen, and all around them the children were talking excitedly with one another. It was then that Andrew noticed Mrs. Smith was heavy with child. Nancy had moved her to a chair near the table as she finished preparing the meal they would all share. The Dutch oven, one of two which Moses had made for Nancy, held a stew which was sitting on the coals in the fire. Another was filled with bread. Nancy was directing the children in helping to ready the house for the additional guests. The combination bench and table was pulled from the wall, revealing a large table which would allow them to sit at the table together. Benches were pulled up to the table and chairs that had been stored in the barn were brought in. Andrew waited for Nancy to give him his orders to help.

"Andrew, if you and Juniata would work together to make the beaten biscuits I would appreciate it." Andrew left to get a flat board and a mallet. He carefully cleaned the mallet which he would use to beat the biscuits. Juniata pulled ingredients together to mix the batter. She was not used to Nancy's kitchen, but she found what she needed easily enough on Nancy's well organized shelves. She mixed the flour, water, salt, molasses and lard and began mixing the dough. By the time Andrew set up the flat board, and added more wood to heat the oven, she had the mixture ready for beating. Juniata was set to start beating the dough, but Andrew quickly took over the job. It would take about twenty minutes of whacking the dough to make it smooth and glossy with blisters appearing in the dough. This would make them light and fluffy. Once the dough was ready, Juniata put two inch balls of dough on a flat sheet to be placed in the oven. She pricked each ball with a fork before sliding the tray into the oven opening.

When Juniata turned from the oven opening, Andrew saw flour traces on her face. He reached over to wipe it off. At first she pulled away, then realized he was just wiping off flour. Her almond eyes looked at Andrew, and a small smile appeared. Just then Elizabeth walked behind the two and said, "Andrew. Do you like Juniata?" Andrew was startled and his face reddened. Mrs. Smith and Nancy both stopped talking and turned to look at Andrew and Juniata. Andrew quickly turned and went outdoors to join the men while Juniata remained in the kitchen. Andrew moved to the smithy, which had become his recluse, and began to work on making more of the trade items Moses would need for his next trip. This would occupy his time for a couple of hours and keep little Elizabeth and her siblings from following him and asking him uncomfortable questions.

Andrew had never had any sort of relations with women. He had been left to handle the farm when his father left for Congress, and shortly afterward he had joined the privateers. Between his time with the privateers and as a private in the Army, he had no opportunity to talk with girls. After his experience on the Jersey, he felt he was not worthy to even approach a woman. But for some reason, he felt comfortable with Juniata. Perhaps in her he saw parts of himself. She was an outcast. She was also at odds with the white world, and she could not speak English. She was also a victim of injustice and the sadness and hollowness of her experience caused her to withdraw and distrust everyone. He, too, had felt this way. His feeling of attraction to Juniata would not be acceptable to nearly everyone, as she was part Indian and with the long history of hatred toward the Indians, she was not acceptable in any society. Even though Mrs. Smith was kind and accepting of her, there was no doubt in Andrew's mind that even she would not accept a relationship between Juniata and a white man. For the first time in months, Andrew began to feel the old feelings of anger when he thought of the inequities. "We preach peace and equality. We preach of God's love. Yet why couldn't we get beyond the prejudices carried from generation to generation? When will we stop placing barriers and hatred in every discourse? Had war created this, or was this just the nature of man?" Andrew thought. His mind raced with the debate, and was startled when called to dinner.

Andrew slowly returned to the cabin, and when he entered to get his food he could not help but notice that Nancy and Mrs. Smith were carefully looking at him and at Juniata to determine if there was any truth in Elizabeth's suspicions. Andrew kept his head down and made certain not to look in Juniata's direction.

The family joined together with a prayer before the meal. Andrew had not said the prayers out loud in the past, but he no longer blocked his mind with anger. He had begun his journey back into a relationship with God, and he had prayed his own prayers of thankfulness. He carefully sneaked a look at Juniata as the families' heads were bowed in prayer and noticed she was not praying, but she was also shyly looking at Andrew. When the prayer came to a close, Andrew took his meal and excused himself to eat out in the smithy. Nancy was about to object, but she stopped herself as she could see Andrew was again struggling.

There were sounds of singing and laughter coming from the house as Andrew worked in the smithy cleaning up materials and putting things in order. He heard something in the doorway. He turned around and saw Juniata standing in the doorway holding a plate of pie. She looked down to avoid the gaze of his eyes, and said, "I bring you dis. I make." Andrew stood there transfixed. He was amazed that she had already learned enough English to be able to communicate. He was also taken aback by the softness of her face. The glow of the lantern and firelight in the smithy gave her face a soft and innocent glow.

Juniata became nervous when he just stood staring, and she looked for a place to put the plate down. Andrew shook himself out of his rudeness and quickly said, "No, wait, Juniata. Thank you." He quickly reached out and took the plate, but in doing so his hand slid over hers and he went to grasp the plate. For a second time stood still as their hands touched ever so briefly. Andrew felt a flurry within himself that he had never experienced before. Juniata kept her head bowed, and Andrew saw her eyes darting about as she tried to decide what to do or where to move. She dropped her hand from the plate, which Andrew now held, and turned to walk away.

Andrew quickly ran out to face her as she was walking away. "Juniata. Thank you," he said, still holding the plate of pie. She nodded. Slowly she looked up into Andrew's face, then she lifted her hands up into the night sky, grasped the air, pulled it to her heart and said, "Ope."

Andrew smiled and nodded. "Yes, Hope," he said as he touched his own heart. "I hope you are able to find happiness."

"Appness," repeated Juniata, but her eyes showed she did not understand.

"Happiness," repeated Andrew, and he smiled and moved his hand to his face to show his smile.

Juniata moved her hand to her face and softly smiled as well. "Appness," she repeated. She then moved to walk back to the cabin leaving Andrew to watch her. Andrew returned to the smithy and sat on a stool looking at the pie Juniata had given him. He slowly ate it, enjoying the flavor of the fruit. She had obviously been learning a lot from Mrs. Smith and perhaps she was beginning to find trust and some form of happiness in her life. Andrew finished his work in the smithy, listening to the singing and laughter drifting into the night air, and smiling to himself, for the first time, truly feeling a sense of happiness.

Chapter 21
A New Life

July, 1782

Early the next morning Andrew was awakened by the sound of a woman screaming. He jumped from bed and rushed immediately from the out building. He ran toward the cabin only to be met by the Smith children and Moses' children as they stood outside in the morning air. Mr. Smith and Moses were splitting wood and William and Joshua were carrying water toward the cabin. Little Elizabeth ran toward Andrew. "Isn't it exciting? Mrs. Smith is having a baby. Mother and Juniata are helping her, but we were told to go outside so we wouldn't be in the way." Andrew's thoughts went back to his own mother who he remembered giving birth to his younger siblings and he was charged with getting the other children out of the way and keeping them occupied while his grandmother helped with the birthing.

Andrew walked over to Moses and asked what he could do. "Andrew, you may as well know that this could be an all-day affair."

Andrew nodded, "Yes sir. I can remember my own mother giving birth. The day seemed to go on forever. It was difficult keeping the little ones occupied while the women folk did what they needed to do."

"Nothing has changed then," laughed Moses. "How about after we stock up the wood, Mr. Smith stays indoors to help out with anything they need, but we get the children busy with the morning chores and with preparing corn for canning. That should keep them busy for the day, and they can do that away from the cabin so they are not worried about the commotion inside? William and Joshua, that's your task, and Andrew and I will go get some work done in the smithy." Andrew knew that the boys would rather be working in the smithy, but they also knew that keeping their younger siblings and the Smith children busy was an important task.

Andrew smiled at the efficiency of it. Even with company and the birthing of a new baby, life on the farm went on. Andrew followed Moses into the smithy and Moses told him about the evening's events in the cabin. He laughed at the games the children played, and the singing. The children even performed for the adults who applauded and laughed. Andrew chuckled at some of the stories while he pulled out the supplies, tools, and got the fires started. Before they began the noisy work of hammering iron, Moses said, "Andrew. Nancy tells me that you and Juniata had a moment together in the kitchen."

Andrew's face reddened and he said, "It wasn't anything. She just had flour on her face and I went to wipe it off."

"Nancy has got a good eye for this sort of thing, and she told me she thought perhaps you might be developing feelings for Juniata."

Andrew felt a bit trapped, and didn't know where the conversation would lead. He also felt he could not lie to Moses who had been kind to him. "I don't really know what I feel," said Andrew.

"When I first met Nancy I couldn't take my eyes off her. She was having no part of me and she thought I was foolish and not serious about life. I was hurt, but made up my mind I was going to show her the stuff I was made of was not a foolish boy, but someone serious about life. That's when I apprenticed to be a blacksmith. I was away for two years before I returned to town. By that time some other man was trying to win Nancy's heart, but when I returned and she learned I had a trade, she quickly sent that other man on his way. We married a year later and not long after that I moved us to an area which needed an assistant to a blacksmith. It was in a city, and the streets were busy and lots of people travelled through there. By then Nancy and I had already started our family and I didn't want to be an assistant, but I wanted my own smithy and I wanted to raise my family away from the danger of that city and the talk of war. I didn't want my family to be in an area where the army would be beating a path past our home and taking supplies without compensation as is often the case during a war. That's when we picked up and moved out here. I know that right now we are in the middle of nowhere, but I am fairly certain that once this war ends many veterans will move out this way. I still make a good living making items for trade, and I also have the farm. The boys are getting older and hopefully by the time they are of marrying age, there will be more families nearby. Funny, when I was a boy, I really never pictured myself worrying about a wife and children and my business. Now that is all I think about."

Andrew nodded, and continued listening. Moses went on. "Now, Juniata is part Indian, that much is plain, and I have to say, even though she may be part white, people still look at her as a savage. The reality of what the Indians did during this war and the stories you hear about the Indians out west make for heated conversations. Everyone knows, as well, that there are Indians who are none too pleased with the white man moving out west, once again taking over their lands. We may be ending a war with other white men, but the issue with the Indians is not over. Juniata will be viewed as Indian, regardless of her heritage. Mrs. Smith seemed to think that her grandfather was a white man. Seems her father had joined up to fight, but had been killed in the war. Her mother and she were living in one of the villages when Sullivan came in. They fled and that's when that trapper found them. He was a wretched creature and only saw Juniata as a way to make money, which is probably the only reason he did not attack her himself. That poor girl had to live through her father dying, her mother being abused, her nearly being sold, then her mother being killed right before her eyes. There are some that might think that since Juniata's mother killed a white man, that Juniata would be capable of doing the same thing. Mr. Smith was none too keen on having her living with them, but Mrs. Smith was insistent and Juniata has proven to be a great helper with the family."

"Is she their slave?" asked Andrew.

"Heavens, no! To hear Mrs. Smith talk, she looks at Juniata as a helpmate. If Juniata wants to leave one day, there will be no selling or bartering for her." Moses paused. "Why, were you thinking of buying her?" asked Moses.

"Buying? No! I don't know what I am thinking. I only know she is as troubled as I have been. My past has burdened my soul, haunted my dreams, and erased many of the good memories of my youth. I think Juniata has the same experiences. I would like to be able to help her heal those wounds."

"Be careful, Andrew. You may find support here, but there is no guarantee how people outside this farm would view a relationship with a half-breed. Would your family accept her?"

Andrew had never put much thought into this. He had not even thought about starting a life with Juniata, but he also knew that his family would not open their arms to a half-breed. His father was in Congress and they were the ones who gave the approval for Sullivan to invade the Indian villages. Andrew had participated in those attacks. He had been surrounded by other soldiers eager to give the Indians what was due to them because of the savage attacks made on both citizens and soldiers. His father always talked of protecting the common man, but would he consider Indians worth protecting? It was hard to say. His brothers were in the war and they had to worry about the attacks of Indians and the brutality of those attacks on Army men and on the families they would protect. His mother and younger siblings had been isolated from the realities of the prejudices outside their own home. He thought about how his mother felt about Rose and her boys and her disdain for slavery. She was very verbal about wanting to protect Rose and her boys and grant their freedom with the guarantee that they would not be captured and sold into real slavery. Would she, however, allow one of her daughters to marry a Negro? Heavens no. He couldn't see that ever happening. Nor would she want to see her son marry and Indian. She would be fearful of the retaliation they would receive from the non-accepting public. Would his family accept a decision regarding Juniata? No. "I do not believe my family would be accepting, nor do I think it realistic that people of the general public are ready to accept such relationships."

Moses nodded. He wasn't certain what Andrew had planned, but he felt it was his duty to at least bring these realities to the table for Andrew to consider.

The day drew on and Andrew and Moses finished the last of the summer orders which would be delivered before winter. Moses' business was growing already in the short year that Andrew had joined him. Once the war was over there would be plenty of work at the smithy, and William and Joshua would be able to provide all the help Moses would need. They were growing into strong and capable young men and Andrew knew that as time passed, he would need to think about moving on. His staying with Moses was meant to only be a seasonal decision, and he was to move on after winter, however he was now approaching a second winter and had not made any indication he was ready to leave. He knew that his coming to this farm truly gave Moses a chance to further develop his farm, and to further develop his blacksmithing, but with his own sons growing and learning both the farming and the smithy work, there would be a time when Andrew was no longer needed. Perhaps now was the time to start thinking of what he wanted to do.

Mrs. Smith had a difficult birth. The ordeal began with horrifying pains early in the morning, then the contractions became mild, but built in intensity as the day drew on. It was nearly dinner time when the newest son made his appearance. Juniata assisted Nancy and helped Mrs. Smith finally deliver the baby. Mr. Smith came out of the cabin to announce to everyone that he had a new son, and the children all danced about and begged to see the new baby. Moses and Andrew congratulated Mr. Smith. Juniata came out of the house to clean up and Andrew walked over to talk to her.

"So, a baby boy?" said Andrew.

"Boy," said Juniata. "Beetful baby boy," she said smiling. "Gives ope to evey one."

"Hope," repeated Andrew. He smiled knowing he had taught her that word.

"Appness," said Juniata.

"Yes, there is much happiness with a new baby. And lots of hope for a world that had gone mad." Juniata looked at him, not knowing completely what he said, but understanding enough that she smiled and nodded.

Juniata began making dinner while Nancy settled Mrs. Smith with the new baby. Once both were sleeping, she joined Juniata and the two put together a good meal. The children waited dutifully to see the new baby who slept next to Mrs. Smith in the pull down bed in the corner of the room. They had moved the bed closer to the fireplace to keep them warm, and moved the table to the other end of the cabin. The table was much more subdued than the night before, and the children quietly left the table after dinner. William and Joshua had them all do various chores to keep them busy, then they sat outdoors singing songs until the air became chilly.

Andrew entered the out building and he could see Juniata was already in her space. He looked at her briefly, then moved to his room. He opened his Bible and began to read, something he was doing more regularly now in an effort to mend the peace between him and God. He had much to be thankful for in his life, and he knew he was still fighting his demons, but they were kept at arm's length most of the time.

He heard movement outside his room, and Juniata then stood in his doorway. "You read?" she asked. Andrew nodded, and quickly moved a crate for her to sit on. He placed the Bible another crate with the lantern illuminating the page. He invited Juniata to look at the pages. She shook her head not knowing what the markings on the page meant. He decided to open to a Proverbs, Chapter 3, and verse 5. He pointed to each word and said the words, then he tried to act out each word. *"Trust in the Lord with all thine heart; and lean not unto thine own understanding."* He was certain she did not fully understand the passage, but she pointed to each word and repeated it with him.

Juniata looked at the words on the page and Andrew could tell she wanted to know what they said. Juniata recognized that everyone read from these books and afterward they looked far more peaceful. Perhaps this book would become her salvation. Andrew was patient and slow with saying the words and enunciating each word so she could imitate it. As the night drew on, Juniata stood to return to her corner of the out building. She then turned abruptly and touched her heart and said, "'Hope." Andrew smiled. It was the first time she had been able to pronounce the word completely. She moved away and Andrew's heart was also filled with hope.

The Smith family stayed for nearly a week, allowing Mrs. Smith time to recuperate before being jostled on their journey back to the Cooper farm. Mr. Smith had just received word that Mr. Cooper wanted to sell the farm as Mr. Cooper was going to take over his father-in-law's farm and the family would live there permanently. Mr. Smith and Moses had gone into town to make arrangements for the transaction, and Andrew felt a strange sense of jubilation that Juniata would remain with the Smith family nearby for the time being. When the Smith family left, Andrew vowed that he would seek a way to earn some money so he could build some savings for himself.

Andrew approached Moses and asked if he would begin making some ornamental pieces out of the iron rod which he might be able to sell, then repay Moses for the supplies, and save the profit so he could afford to move on. At first, Moses was taken back, but Andrew explained that he recognized William and Joshua were already becoming very adept at working in the smithy and managing the farm duties, and there would be little use of Andrew. It was time for Andrew to begin earning an income so he could one day start out on his own. Moses understood Andrew's desire to move on, and highly suspected it had to do with Juniata. Moses knew that Andrew would not be able to live locally once people from the war began settling in the area as the levels of prejudices against Indians would be intolerable.

Andrew had been working at making some ornamental pieces in the past, but knew that there was not as much need for these compared to the practice items made in the smithy. However, he also knew that adding extra touches to some of the items would be more appealing to the women folk, especially in their household tools. His first foray into making ornamental pieces was creating a twisted metal work handle for one of Nancy's Dutch ovens. Her Dutch ovens were her pride in her kitchen, and with the novelty of the especially created handle she took additional pleasure. Andrew found he was good at this kind of work. He hammered out numerous pieces from some of the scrap pieces of iron. It did not take much to put some kind of ornamentation to the spoons, pot handles, trivets and andirons. In their winter load of wares, Andrew took along many of the ornamental pieces. Both he and Moses were surprised at how quickly they were purchased. Upon their return Andrew had many additional orders to complete. He quickly paid Moses for the iron he had used, and continued to help Moses with all the regular items made for trade. Andrew would often work late into the night on his ornamental pieces, and would proudly display them for Moses in the morning. Nancy, who typically avoided the smithy because of the noise and smell could come by each morning to look at Andrew's handiwork. Andrew made numerous pieces which he gifted to Nancy, and she would proudly add them to her kitchen tools.

Visits with the Smiths were typically every few months, however Andrew would remain at the farm working in the smithy when the family would leave. Only when the Smiths visited Moses' farm would Andrew spend time with Juniata. Mrs. Smith continued teaching Juniata to speak English and to read and Andrew was amazed at how quickly she learned. He would also enjoy sharing with her what he created of the scraps of iron.

News came that the war was finally ended in April, of 1783, although news of this took longer to reach those in this area. Andrew knew it would be time to announce his plans. He asked Moses if he could travel with them on their next visit to the Smith farm, and Moses suspected big changes were soon to follow.

It was in the fall of '83 when Moses announced they would be going to the Smith farm as Mr. Smith needed help repairing one of his wagons. Andrew took with him gifts of ornamental handles for Mrs. Smith's cooking pots, and some very fancy trivets he had created. He then asked to speak to Mr. Smith.

"I think you know I like Juniata. I know that with the war finally over, more veterans will be moving into the area, and I know that many of them will not react kindly to Juniata because of her Indian background. I, too, have nightmares from my past, from the war, that I do not care to relive my nightmares through the stories that the veterans may bring with them as they move to this area. I want a place of my own, more secluded, where I can start my own life and work to finally erase the memories of my past, and begin creating new ones. I want to ask Juniata to join me. Do you have objections?"

Mr. Smith had already discussed the likelihood that Andrew would want to be with Juniata, but had not thought they would leave the area. He knew that what Andrew said was right. They would be better off away from the prejudice and hatred that would follow those who had fought in the war. "You know we don't own Juniata. What she decides is her decision. I know Mrs. Smith will miss her help, but she always knew this would be temporary. When would you plan to leave?"

"I believe I want to leave in the early spring next year. That will give me time to make some more money with my wares, and help Moses with his spring stock. I suspect we will see the first installment of veterans moving to the area next year."

"I suspect you are right. Have you talked to Juniata?"

"Not yet. I wanted to get your blessing first."

Mr. Smith agreed, and Andrew left in search of Juniata. He found her working on canning berries that had been picked and cleaned. One of the Smith children was helping her. When she saw Andrew approaching, the young girl took her leave.

Juniata looked up to see Andrew. "Hello, Andrew. I heard you came today."

"Yes. Juniata, I want to ask you a question." Andrew stammered for a moment, but thought it best just to ask outright.

"I would like to know if you would move with me away from here before the soldiers from the war begin moving here."

"Soldiers coming here?" asked Juniata. She looked startled.

"No, they are not soldiers any more. The war is over, but they will be coming this way to live. I do not want to be here when they begin arriving. I want to leave this area and move some place where fewer soldiers will want to settle."

"I move with you?" asked Juniata.

"Yes, if you want."

"I want," said Juniata. She smiled and for the first time she stepped forward, and awkwardly, the two embraced. As a minute passed, the tension in both Andrew and Juniata relaxed, and they stepped apart, embarrassed and looking down at the ground.

After a moment, Andrew looked at Juniata and spoke. "We will move in the spring. Is that fine with you?" Juniata nodded, and Andrew smiled. "Well, then. We will move in the spring. I will let you finish your work, and I will go help Mr. Smith with the wagon he needed repaired." Andrew awkwardly began to walk away, then drew back his shoulders as he walked toward the smithy. Juniata smiled, and watched as Andrew walked away.

The fall harvest and winter passed quickly as Andrew prepared for his eventual move out west. Moses allowed him more time to make more of his ornamental pieces to sell both in the winter and early spring sale. Andrew had carefully saved every penny he earned. Moses generously allowed Andrew to take orders during the winter sales which allowed him to make substantially more as he was allowed to make his own products, only repaying Moses for the iron rod used. In the spring sale Andrew traded many of his wares for products he would need to take with him. He also traded for two horses and a pack horse.

One evening Moses approached Andrew as they worked in the forge. "Andrew, why don't you make claim for some land as a veteran? You certainly earned it."

"Andrew's old anger once again rose within him. "I want nothing from this government," he snapped. Andrew took a moment to calm himself before he continued. "As hard as I've tried, I cannot forgive those who let us rot on the prison ships. I also do not want my family following me. I left without saying goodbye to my mother and younger siblings, and I would rather they believe I died on the Jersey than have them deal with my life choices. I cannot take Juniata to my family. I doubt they would accept her. It is best that I wash my hands clean of this business." Moses had worked alongside this young man for the past couple of years and knew that it has taken him this long to let go of some of his demons, and he still had some which may take forever to sever.

After the spring sale, Andrew returned and gathered his gear and supplies, packing his horses and packhorse with his belongings. He said his goodbyes to Moses and his family. Nancy wrapped preserves and food for him, and tearfully said goodbye. Little Elizabeth, who was now a great help to her mother, had the hardest time saying goodbye to Andrew, and he was surprised at how choked up he became when he said goodbye. As he rode away from the farm, Elizabeth ran following him. "Goodbye, Andrew. Goodbye. God bless you and Juanita." Andrew feared looking back as his was suddenly overcome with emotion.

The ride to the Smith farm allowed Andrew the time to contemplate this new beginning. Only for a moment did he wonder if he should leave alone, but that thought was quickly forgotten. When he arrived at the Smith farm he found Juniata was already packed. Mrs. Smith had also given her some clothing, blankets, and food for their journey. Andrew carefully packed everything, then helped Juniata onto the horse. They said their goodbyes and slowly rode away.

About a mile into their journey neither had said anything, both shyly looking at the other as they traveled. Andrew caught Juniata's eye and smiled. She said, "Hope."

"Yes," said Andrew. "Hope." That is what they took with them as they moved in the direction of the northern borders of New York territory. Andrew knew the area where they were heading had belonged to the Seneca Indians, however it was sparsely settled. He hoped that they would be able to settle there, do some farming, build a small smithy, and build their lives there, far away from the hate and distrust that both Andrew and Juniata longed to escape. It was "hope" that would help them build a new and fresh life together.

Afterword

This novel is a part of a planned series titled, "The Fighting Clarks." That title came from newspaper articles written during World War II which were about the Clark family of Cleveland and Bedford, Ohio, who had fought in various wars. My Great Grandfather, Hiram Booth Clark, fought in the Civil War. His sons, William, John, and Hiram, all fought in various wars. William, my great uncle, fought in the Spanish American War. My great uncle John, a marine, was among the first American soldiers who entered into China. William and John's youngest brother, Hiram, who was my grandfather, fought in both World War I as an army intelligence officer, and was called back to active duty in World War II where he trained army officers in Texas. He died in 1943. Hiram's son, my uncle Henry Clark, fought in World War II, fighting at Normandy. My Clark cousins served during the Vietnam War.

The family stories heard by all of my cousins as we grew up date back to Abraham Clark who our family says is our family ancestor. Abraham Clark signed the Declaration of

Independence. He was the subject of my first novel, *A Founder for All*. In researching for that novel I discovered that two of his sons, Thomas and Andrew, were imprisoned on the British Prison Ship, HMS Jersey, which was reputed to cause the mass number of American deaths. Our family stories lend us to believe our family line could be tied to either Thomas or Andrew. We have not found the paperwork to date to prove that lineage. I continue to search for this information.

In developing this novel's plot, I combined fact and fiction. The information about Thomas is mostly accurate, however the information for Andrew is mostly accurate up to his incarceration on the Jersey. The story I developed from that point on combines some family legends and historical facts about the New Jersey soldiers, militia, and privateers and, of course, the prison ship, Jersey.

It must be mentioned that the Department of Defense states that there were 4,435 who died in battle during the Revolutionary War. What most of America doesn't acknowledge is that there were an estimated 11,500 deaths of prisoners of war on the sixteen British prison ships. The bodies of the dead were buried in shallow graves on the shore, and for years after the war skeletal remains washed ashore in Brooklyn, NY. Remains were gathered and eventually buried in a crypt in 1808. Finally in 1867, spearheaded by poet Walt Whitman, a new Fort Greene Park was re-designed by Frederick Law Olmsted and Calvert Vaux. A new crypt was built and the remains of these patriots who perished on the prison ships were buried there; however by 1873 the remains were once again moved to another crypt beneath a small monument. Stanford White, an architect, was commissioned to build a larger monument through private fund raising. The design was made of granite, a single Doric column obelisk measuring 149 feet tall stands above the crypt which is at the top of a 100 foot wide staircase. An eight-ton bronze funeral urn designed by sculptor Adolf Weinman, sits atop the column. President-elect William Howard Taft made the dedication speech in 1908. The monument is called the Prison Ship Martyr's Memorial. By the 1970's the base of the monument was covered in graffiti, and one of the bronze eagles was stolen, so the remaining decorative eagles were removed, and the elevators which once took visitors to the top of the monument for great views of the city, was closed down. Donations are always sought to restore the monument to its former glory. It is so sad that people who disrespect the monument are unaware of the price these Patriots paid to help us gain the freedoms we presently enjoy. It is also sad that we do not dedicate even a paragraph in our history books to the torments and deaths of the prisoners of war during the Revolutionary War. Perhaps this novel can help correct those wrongs.

In the future I plan to continue The Fighting Clarks series and explore other American wars seen through the eyes of character based on my ancestors.

I thank my husband, Michael, and our sons, Mike and Mark, for their continued support in my writing. I have been blessed to have people who have supported my love for history, genealogy, and writing including my cousins Helen Pratt, Dennis and Thomas Clark, and niece, Christy Shula. I also thank those who assisted in the proofreading and editing of this novel: my husband, Michael Baltrinic; friend and respected reader, Sarah Hamlin; and colleague and historian, John Gurnish. I am also thankful for the cover artwork submitted by my former student, Dani Reedy. I also thank Dale Robert Pease, of walkingstick.com, a former student, and now writing colleague, for his work on the book layout and book cover editing.

About the Author

Barb Baltrinic is a Kent State University M.Ed. graduate; a 35 year classroom teacher in the Akron Public Schools, and presently a full-time liaison for The University of Akron. She is a National Board Certified Teacher; has spoken at many state and national conferences; 17 published articles in educational magazines; national, state and local education award winner. She is the wife of Michael Baltrinic, a former teacher, and mother to two grown sons, Mike and Mark.

This is Baltrinic's second novel, a sequel to A Founder for All. She has shared her novel at various book talks in Ohio and in New Jersey. Her website is **baltrinic.wix.com/bbaltrinic**.

Made in the USA
Middletown, DE
12 October 2016